BURNOUT

A KENZIE GILMORE THRILLER
BOOK 4

BIBA PEARCE

LIQUID MIND PUBLISHING

Liquid Mind Publishing
This is a work of fiction. All characters, names, places and events are the product of the author's imagination or used fictitiously.

KENZIE GILMORE CRIME THRILLER SERIES

The Kenzie Gilmore Crime Thriller Series

Afterburn

Dead Heat

Heatwave

Burnout

Deep Heat

Fever Pitch

Storm Surge (Coming Soon)

Do you like Audiobooks? Find the Kenzie Gilmore Crime Thriller series on Audible here:

1

REID STARED down at the twenty-foot python. Its body was so swollen and distended, you could just about make out the figure of a human form inside.

"It's double the size." The gator hunter, a beefy man who'd introduced himself as Selwyn Price, waved his single shot bolt-action rifle in the air. "As soon as I saw him, I knew there was a body inside. Could be a hog or a boar, but my money's on a human being." He pronounced it like bean.

The snake lay on the dry ground beside the waterway, its skin glistening in the harsh midday sun, stretched to breaking point around whatever it had eaten. It had died of natural causes, most likely an acute case of indigestion.

"We thought we'd better get you down here before we cut it open," Officer Dwayne Griffith said, sweating in his new Sweetwater PD uniform. "Just in case."

Beatrice, his wife, had helped Reid out of a sticky spot a few months back, so when her husband had approached him for a transfer, he couldn't say no. As soon as he met the tough old beat cop, however, he'd known it was a good decision. Sweetwater was on the up, thanks to their successes over the last year, and they were recruiting. Reid was slowly building a team he could rely on, losing the old legacy of laziness and corruption that had turned them into a backwater laughingstock.

Dwayne Griffiths was in his mid-fifties, experienced and tough as nails. There wasn't much he hadn't seen in his time, and he knew the streets of Miami like the back of his hand. A valuable asset to any department.

"Okay, let's do it." Reid nodded to the gator man who put down his rifle and picked up a lethal, foot-long hunting knife. "If it's human, I'm calling forensics, and we'll need to get this reptile to the morgue."

Selwyn inserted the knife, a foot below the head, where the bulge started and sliced downwards along the snake's belly, careful not to nick whatever or whomever was inside.

"Easy." Reid stood on the other side, his eyes fixed on the reptile.

"I knew it!" The gator hunter straightened up. "That's human legs in there."

A putrid stench oozed out of the snake carcass, and they all took a step backward. "Yeah, that's a body alright," Reid agreed grimly. Two partially decomposed feet with narrow ankles covered in a slimy substance were clearly visible.

"Holy Mary," murmured Dwayne.

"Get on the phone," ordered Reid. "Call the local CSI unit and get them out here."

The beat cop gave a shocked nod and turned away to make the call. Reid bet that in all his years on the Force, he'd never seen anything like this. The Glades were as dangerous as the streets of Miami, but the predators weren't always human.

"ETA forty minutes," he told Reid, pocketing his phone. In reality, it could be longer. The dirt road into the Glades was narrow and dusty, and they were pretty far in. The swamp stretched for miles around them in all directions, the surface of the water hidden by an endless sea of sawgrass and cattails.

Above them, the careless blue sky seemed inordinately high up, while the white-hot sun beat down, relentless in its intensity. It was

Miami's dry season, and they hadn't had rain in weeks. After the notorious heatwave last summer, which had resulted in monstrous thunderstorms and a mini deluge, come October it had dried up, and now they were entering a brand-new year under drought conditions. The vegetation was dry and brittle, and the environmental services were talking about organizing a controlled burn ahead of schedule to prevent wildfires.

"Okay." Reid swiped at his brow. "Officer Griffith, I'm putting you in charge. Make sure whoever is in there gets to the morgue safely."

"You don't want me to slice her open all the way?" the gator hunter asked hopefully.

"No." Reid turned to him. "I want to preserve him or her as much as possible."

No doubt Price would be telling his buddies at the swamp bar how he'd cut open a twenty-foot reptile to reveal a human body. It was a once in a lifetime story.

"You don't expect foul play, do you, boss?" Griffith loosened his collar, his dark skin glistening with perspiration.

"I don't know," Reid replied. "But until I do, I'd rather be cautious. At the very least, we need to know how he or she died."

"Squeezed to death," the hunter supplied with a shrug, as if that was obvious. "That beast's a constrictor. Strangles the life out of its prey before it eats it."

"Most likely," agreed Reid, "but we'll let the medical examiner determine that."

He jiggled his car keys in his pocket. "I've got to get back. I'll see you at the station, Griffith."

The beat cop gave a firm nod. "Sure thing, boss. I got this."

"It's female," the medical examiner declared. Reid wasn't sure if she meant the snake or the person inside. The snake lay dissected on the steel table, sliced open like a science project.

It was a Burmese python, according to the gator hunter. An invasive species and a threat to local wildlife. So much so, state initiatives had been introduced to eliminate them. According to Selwyn, you could earn $8.46 an hour and $50 per snake measuring up to four feet and an extra $25 for every foot over that. Not bad, if, like the gator hunter, you were out working in the Glades, anyway.

"About five foot two, Hispanic origin, roughly forty-five years of age."

Reid grunted in acknowledgement. That cleared that up.

"She is partially digested, so it's hard to make out her features," the ME continued, bending over the body.

He grimaced. "Any indication of how long she's been dead?"

"I'd say minimum forty-eight hours, judging by the state of her. Stomach acids are incredibly powerful," she added, as if to back up her statement. "Especially in these types of creatures."

Predators. Hunters. Animals that ate anything and everything.

Two days. "What about fingerprints?"

"Gone, I'm afraid. Completely corroded. I'll take a DNA swab."

Her DNA might be in the system. Fingerprints would have been useful, though. "What about the cause of death?" he asked.

"Give me a minute."

The ME, assisted by a lab helper, lifted the woman's body out of its slimy cocoon, while a second lab assistant pulled the carcass out from under her. It landed with a thud on the floor, before it was dragged to the side of the room, out of the way. Reid was glad he was watching from a viewing gallery through a pane of thick glass, rather than standing next to the body. The stench must be overpowering. He marveled at the ME's fortitude—even her assistants were wrinkling their noses—but then, she would be used to such things.

She inspected the victim's body in its entirety, starting at the head and working her way down the torso and finally to the legs. Reid watched as the fluorescent light in the autopsy lab illuminated the partially digested body. He could make out dark hair, a slender frame to which fragments of clothing were still attached, and running shoes, fully intact. They might be able to get some forensic evidence from those.

"Her ribs are broken." The ME pushed in the middle of her torso. "And there is bruising around her midsection consistent with constriction. I'd say she died from cardiac arrest."

Reid raised his eyebrows. "A heart attack?"

"Yes, it happens when the body is deprived of oxygen." She glanced up. "If it's any consolation, she would have been unconscious in minutes."

That did help. A little.

It was as the gator hunter had said. No foul play.

"Okay, thanks." He turned to go.

"One moment." The ME frowned and reached behind the woman's leg. She glanced at her assistants. "Help me turn her over."

They rolled the woman onto her stomach. Her limbs were as stiff and unyielding as a plastic doll's. Reid sucked in a breath. It always shook him up, seeing a once-healthy person so rigid and inflexible. Perhaps because it drove home the indignity of death, or maybe the movements were so unnatural that his brain struggled to process them.

She pulled the spotlight closer. Reid waited, unable to see what she was looking at. One of her assistants was blocking his view.

"Anything?" he asked, after a long pause.

She grunted, then straightened up. "There's a small circular wound in her upper right thigh. It's raw and inflamed."

"Like a snake bite?" he asked, even though he knew reticulated pythons lacked venom.

"More like a knife or bullet wound," she corrected, pulling in a giant magnifying glass on a stand beside the table. "Scrap that. *Definitely* a bullet wound."

"She was shot?" Reid leaned his forehead against the glass. Now that was a surprise. "Before she was eaten?"

The ME probed the wound with a pair of surgical tweezers. "Looks that way." She removed a small, silver chunk of lead. "There's your bullet," she said with a grin, dropping it into a petri dish.

Reid stared at it, frowning. "Is that what killed her?" Maybe it had hit an artery or something.

"I doubt it." She touched the skin around the wound with her gloved finger. "She didn't bleed out. A shot like that wouldn't have killed her, not right away, but it would have slowed her down."

"Slowed her down enough for the snake to grab her?"

"It is possible. Predators like snakes and alligators rarely go for prey that is already dead. A live victim would be far more appetizing. The most likely scenario is the victim was dragging herself through the swamp, trying to get to safety when it attacked. She'd have been too weak to fend it off. It would have squeezed out whatever life was left in her."

Before eating her.

Jesus.

Reid raked a hand through his hair. "Okay, thanks." It amounted to the same thing, though. The bullet would have killed her if she hadn't found help, and out there, remote as it was, help would have been a long time coming. Chances were, she'd have been out there all night by herself with no shelter, no protection, wounded and bleeding.

He left the morgue deep in thought. This was no accident. Whoever fired that gun was responsible for that woman's death. Snake or no snake, they were looking for a killer.

2

KENZIE SHOWED the austere prison officer her press ID card and driver's license and waited to be escorted through to the meeting area. Maria Lopez, the notorious head of the Morales cartel, was being held in the Miami-Dade County Women's Correctional Center, serving out her 30-year sentence. Last year she'd been found guilty of four counts of engaging in a criminal enterprise, drug trafficking, money laundering and conspiracy to commit murder.

Her saving grace had been that she'd only taken over from her husband two years prior, so she hadn't had time to amass any more counts, otherwise Kenzie was sure she'd have gotten life.

There was no private interview room, no soundproof chamber, no recording devices. Kenzie had to join the other desperate relatives during visiting hours to conduct her interview. Maria got no special privileges, not to the general observer, anyway. She appeared just like everyone else.

Inside the prison, however, was another matter. The cartel queen was revered. So much so, she had her own cell, a television, and a cushy job in the prison kitchen.

The guards tiptoed around her, reluctant to make an enemy of one of Mexico's biggest cartel bosses. She still had a lot of influence, even though the Miami branch of the cartel had imploded. Last year's sting operation had seen several of her inner circle gunned down in a DEA-orchestrated bust.

Maria still had an ace up her sleeve. The Californian leg of the cartel was flourishing, and part of the deal the DEA had made with her was that she would hand over the names of those involved, in exchange for Kenzie writing her memoirs.

"When you publish the book," she'd told Kenzie, "I will give you the list."

Maria was using her incarceration to document her rise to power, and how she'd gone from a poor kid living on the streets of Mexico City to running one of the biggest drug cartels in America's history. It was an inspirational story by anyone's standards, and if she'd been running a legit business instead of a criminal enterprise, she might have graced the cover of Fortune Magazine. Such was life.

A buzzer sounded and Kenzie walked through an interlocking door into a wide, drafty meeting area filled with two-seater tables and metal chairs bolted to the floor. The message was clear. Nobody could be trusted. Not here.

Fluorescent lights served as a stark reminder that they were in an artificial environment where smiles were forced, tensions ran high, and many meetings ended in tears or arguments. Even the windows, too high to see out of, had thick wrought-iron bars across them, filtering out the sunlight.

She took a seat at a table, her notepad and pencil in front of her. They wouldn't let her bring in a cell phone or recorder, so she was old-schooling it. Not that she minded. There was something comforting and familiar about holding a pencil in her hand and scribbling notes on lined paper. In this place of desolation, it gave her a sense of control. It might just be over words on a page, but it was something.

A steel door on the opposite side of the room clicked open and a line of prisoners shuffled in, bound by ankle restraints, but their hands were free. Kenzie supposed the logic was that even if they got out of the meeting room, they couldn't move fast enough to escape.

Maria was first out of the gate. Slim and upright, she drew the eye. In her forties, she was an attractive woman with long dark hair, an elegant neck, and a haughty tilt to her head. Kenzie thought she appeared taller than her five-foot four frame, but that had everything to do with her commanding presence, rather than her stature.

Orange looked surprisingly good on her. It made her black hair appear more lustrous and her skin bronzer. Was that mascara she was wearing?

Maria sank into the chair opposite Kenzie with a broad grin showing her neat, white teeth. "Kenzie Gilmore. How lovely to see you again."

Kenzie plastered a smile on her face. "Likewise, Maria." Last time they'd talked, Maria was holding a gun to her head.

This assignment had her tied in knots. Sure, it would do wonders for her career—a book on the notorious female crime boss—but one wrong step and the DEA wouldn't get the names they needed to bring down the California branch of the network, and she'd make an enemy of a woman who had more clout inside prison than most politicians had outside it.

A shiver passed over her. "How have you been?"

Maria shrugged. "You know..."

Kenzie didn't, but she could imagine. Life inside the penitentiary couldn't be fun.

The unusually retro digital clock above the door flipped over to the next minute, making the passing of time audible to everyone in the room. They had just under one hour. "Shall we get started?"

Maria gave a brief nod.

Kenzie had thought long and hard about how she was going to structure Maria Lopez's memoirs. "Let's begin with some background material, your upbringing, your life before you met Federico." It would frame the early chapters of the book.

Maria's eyes became hazy as she looked through Kenzie into the past. "It's not a pretty story, but I want to tell it." Her shoulders hunching as she caved in toward her middle. A protective gesture, perhaps. A subconscious defense mechanism to prevent the past from breaking through the wall she'd built around herself.

"Let's start with your parents," Kenzie probed.

"I don't remember my father. He left when I was a baby." She spoke like it didn't matter, like he was a man who'd come around to visit once and never returned. A forgotten guest. "My mother raised me while working at a factory as a seamstress." Her eyes hardened. "We were very poor. Sometimes we didn't have enough money to put food on the table."

Kenzie bit her lip but kept writing. She didn't look up. Maria wouldn't want her sympathy. "That's when she would go whoring."

That got her attention. "Excuse me?"

Another enigmatic smile, dark eyes flashing. "I used to hide in my room while she entertained men downstairs. They didn't stay long, and it paid well." A scoff. "Better than factory work, anyway."

Kenzie stared at her. "I'm sorry, I didn't know."

"How would you?" She inhaled and Kenzie got the impression she wished she were dragging on a cigarette. She could almost imagine the smoke curling up towards the ceiling with the exhale.

Kenzie glanced back down at her pad.

"I was eight when José moved in." She shuddered. A small, involuntary movement, but noticeable to one trained to look for clues in body language.

"Who was José?" Kenzie asked.

"Her pimp." Maria shook her head as if trying to shake off the memory, but of course, that was impossible. Kenzie knew that better than most. After her mother's disappearance, she'd tried to put on a brave face, to pretend she wasn't hurting, but it was all a facade. Inside, she'd been screaming for answers. Answers that never came.

"At first, he occupied most of her time. I didn't like it, but at least she was happy, or pretended to be. José didn't like her seeing clients, so the parade of nameless men stopped. I was glad about that."

Kenzie sensed there was a 'but' coming.

"I was twelve when he first noticed me."

Kenzie went cold.

Maria didn't flinch. "He used to come into my room at night and make me do things. Horrible things." The words tumbled out of her, raw and edgy, even though her expression was blank.

Kenzie felt the bile rising in her throat. Twelve years old. What kind of sick man abused a twelve-year-old girl?

"Did you tell anyone?" she breathed.

Maria snorted. "I tried. Mother called me a tattletale and a liar. *He* backed her up. I just wanted attention. I was jealous of their relationship. The usual shit."

Kenzie's skin crawled. Unfortunately, this story was far too common.

"What did you do?"

"I endured it for two years, then I threw acid in his face and ran away."

Kenzie balked.

Holy crap.

Maria squared her shoulders. The worst was over and she was back in control. "It was the day before my fourteenth birthday. I stole a bottle of bleach from beneath the kitchen sink and hid it under my bed. When he came to me, I threw it at him and ran out of the house. I never went back."

Kenzie stopped writing. "You left at fourteen?"

Maria gave a firm nod.

"Where did you go?"

"The park. I slept on a bench that night. The next day I turned fourteen."

Kenzie's heart went out to her. "I'm so sorry, Maria." Losing her own mother had been hard, but not like this. Maria had been in an impossible situation and had resorted to drastic measures to escape the abuse.

"Don't be. Shit happens. It's how you deal with it that's important."

She wasn't wrong there.

"How long did you sleep rough?" Kenzie asked.

"Not long. I found a squat and stayed there. I stole from shops and pickpocketed to stay alive. Those druggies and wastrels became my friends." Her eyes lifted to meet Kenzie's. "That's where I met Federico."

The retro wall clock thumped, and a male voice called, "Finish up, folks."

Shit. This was just getting interesting. "Federico was homeless, too?"

"No, he was supplying the kids staying there with cheap drugs. A runner for a low-level drug dealer connected to the Morales cartel. I got his attention." She smiled, the first genuine smile in the last hour. "I was mature for a fifteen-year-old and looked a lot older than I was."

"Is that how you got together?"

"Time's up, people." The guard's voice grated through the cool air.

Maria stood up in a smooth, effortless motion, as if their weighty discussion had never taken place.

Sighing, Kenzie put down her pencil. "I'll come back next week."

Maria dropped her voice. "You know the deal. None of what I tell you in here gets out before the book. No leaks. If anything appears in the press before the publication, your policeman friend won't get the names."

Kenzie stood up so she could meet her eye. "I'm aware of the terms of our agreement."

Maria nodded, then turned away and walked with as much dignity as a person in chains could muster, through the door, and back to the cells.

3

REID WAITED until everyone had squeezed into the incident room at Sweetwater Police Department. This was a full department meeting. He needed everybody present if they were going to find out who the mysterious woman inside the python was.

By now, the news had flown around the department. This was the most unusual case any of them had ever dealt with. A body in a snake. A murdered woman with a bullet in her leg to prove it.

"I remember back in '92 we pulled a guy out of a gator," Detective Monroe was saying. He'd been a cop a long time. "The guy'd been in there for days and there wasn't much left to identify him." At nearly sixty, Monroe was the oldest member of the squad. Reid hadn't been sure about him at the beginning, but the seasoned detective had proved himself, and as a result, Reid had promoted him to the station supervisor. He hadn't let him down yet.

Hamilton, a young rookie fresh out of the academy, wrinkled his nose. "Had he been shot too?"

"Nah, eaten alive. He was a weekender who thought he'd have a go at catching himself some gators. Biggest mistake he ever made."

"Last one too," murmured Diaz, who'd been listening in.

Reid cleared his throat, and they settled down. Detective

"Willie" Vargas, his second in command, strode to the front, followed by Diaz, who'd just been awarded her detective badge. Well deserved, in his opinion.

"As you know, we found our mystery woman inside a twenty-foot snake," he began, knowing that would get everyone's attention. "Vargas has run her DNA through the various databases, but there's no match. Unfortunately, her fingers are too dissolved to get any prints off, so we're shooting in the dark here."

"What about her clothes?" asked Hamilton.

It was a good question. Reid nodded at Diaz who said, "Her clothing was unremarkable. We couldn't find any labels or insignia on the items. Same with her shoes, which were intact. They were cheap running shoes, faded and discolored. There was dirt on the soles, but that could have been from the Glades. We're waiting for forensics to get back to us with a more definite analysis."

"We need to find out who this woman was," Reid said. "Let's look into missing persons in the greater Miami area. Someone must be worried about her. If that doesn't work, we'll expand it to a state level, and then beyond."

Nods all around.

Reid's phone buzzed in his pocket. He ended the meeting, then reached for it and smiled when he saw the caller ID.

Kenzie.

"Hey, how'd it go?" She'd had her first meeting with the felon, Maria Lopez, today.

"Good, I think." Kenzie didn't sound her usual upbeat self.

He frowned. "You think?"

"Yeah. She opened up about her childhood, which was interesting, and a little disturbing."

Reid walked to the window to get away from those who were lingering in the incident room, talking about the case. "In what way?"

"Abuse. She ran away from home at fourteen. Reid, she was living on the street."

There was a short pause.

"Most career criminals start life in a similar way," he said gently. "It's never a good story."

"No, I guess not." She was in an introspective mood. He'd known her for long enough to realize she'd been thinking hard about Maria's background.

"It doesn't excuse what she did," he added.

"I know." A sigh. "I suppose I just feel sorry for her, that's all."

"Did she give any indication of when she'll cough up the names?"

"Not until the book is published. She was adamant about that."

It was to be expected. He'd hoped she might relent and help them out sooner. The DEA agent in charge of the sting, Agent Wilson, was waiting with bated breath to reel in the Morales cartel members, most of whom had already gone to ground. Reid didn't know who the major players were, but they were probably across the border in Mexico now, regrouping.

"You okay?"

"Fine. Shall I stop by later? It's Friday. We could order a pizza or something."

They hadn't seen each other recently. His team had been busy putting a case together for Governor Talbot's trial, of which the fallout had been stupendous. The trial had dragged on and on, which meant the media frenzy had too.

"Let's do that." He smiled into the phone. "It's been a while."

"It has." A slight pause. "Did you hear the news? The appeal you asked for went out an hour ago."

"I didn't, but thanks for that. Hopefully, we'll get an ID on our snake woman."

"So, I'll see you at eight?"

"Great." A red convertible pulled into the police parking lot. A fiery redhead in a short skirt and dark glasses climbed out. He watched as she walked towards the department entrance, balancing a tray of takeout coffees in a flat, white box. "See you then."

There was an outburst of laughter from the squad room. Shannon had arrived. Vargas's new girlfriend was something of a live wire. Everybody loved her, and on the few occasions they'd been out as a team and she'd joined them, she'd been the life of the party. He was still amazed she and Vargas had got together, not being at all alike. The conscientious, dedicated, and reserved detective seemed the furthest thing from a girl like Shannon's type, but then what did he know? Clearly, opposites attract.

Walking into the squad room, he smiled. "Shannon, great to see you again."

Vargas colored. "She came by to drop off coffee and donuts for the team." His boss had spoken to him about Shannon swinging by the police department unannounced before. Visitors were supposed to check in at the front desk, but since they were a small department, they only had one duty sergeant on at any given time and once you'd walked through the security screener, you were practically in the squad room already.

"Thank you, Shannon." Hamilton dived into the box of donuts followed by most of the young officers.

"Won't you have a donut, Lieutenant?" Shannon smiled at him, holding out the box.

"No, I'm good." Before the briefing, he'd been looking at the autopsy report and the memory of the woman's partially digested body was still fresh in his mind. Coffee was what he needed and the stronger, the better. He reached for one, nodding his thanks.

"What's this I hear about a body in a snake?" she asked.

Vargas spluttered on his donut. "How did you hear about that?"

"It was all over the radio on the way here. You were mentioned by name." She grinned at Reid. "Anyone with any information is to contact Lieutenant Reid Garrett at the Sweetwater Police Department."

He knew that. He'd issued the press release.

Vargas relaxed. "You sent out an appeal?"

"Yeah, I gave Kenzie a ring at the *Herald*. She took it from there. I forgot to mention it in the briefing."

"Kenzie?" Shannon tilted her head to one side like a bird.

"She's my contact at the paper." Reid didn't meet Vargas' gaze. His second in command knew she was a lot more than that. She was his confidant, his sounding board, his friend, and briefly, his girl-friend. Too briefly, truth be told, but it was best not to dwell on that.

"Ah." The glint in her eye told him she suspected there was something more. Well, he'd let her wonder, even though he was sure Vargas would fill her in later. "So, do you have any leads?" Her eyebrows rose in delicate arches.

"Not yet." Reid took the coffee back to his desk. He had work to do, and he didn't want his team getting distracted for too long.

Vargas got the hint and steered Shannon out of the squad room. "Thanks for coming by. I'm sorry you can't stay, but you know the rules." He grimaced ruefully. Reid couldn't hear her retort since they'd moved outside into the sunlight.

"Detective Diaz," he called, sitting down.

Diaz smiled at him, her cheeks flushed. It took a while to get used to a new title. He ought to know. He'd only been a lieutenant for a couple of months, although it didn't sound so strange when he said it anymore.

"Yes, boss?"

"Follow up with forensics on the dirt on those running shoes. If it's not from around here, we need to know."

"On it." She went back to her computer. Diaz was a good cop, dedicated and thorough. Even before she'd made detective, he'd admired her drive and ambition, and he was pleased she was part of his team. He needed to know that he could count on each and every one of them when the time came. They were a young crew, apart from Monroe, who was close to retirement, and Dwayne. Next came Reid, who was in his late thirties, and even that was young for a lieutenant.

There was a chance the soil had come from another part of the state. It might shed some light on where the mystery victim had been before she'd ended up running for her life in the Everglades, pursued by a hungry python.

He shuddered. It was a terrible way to go.

"I can't find anything in missing persons," Vargas confirmed. "I've gone through every report submitted in the greater Miami area in the last seventy-two hours. Nothing."

"Somebody must be missing her." He frowned.

Vargas shrugged. "If they are, they haven't reported it."

Reid scratched his head. Who the hell was this woman and what had she been doing running through the most isolated part of the Glades with a bullet in her leg?

One way or another, he was going to find out.

4

KENZIE GOT TO WORK EARLY. She scanned in using her work ID card, which hung on a lanyard around her neck, and smiled at the security guard who manned the entrance.

"Morning, Doug."

"Morning, Miss Gilmore. You're in bright and early this morning."

She rolled her eyes. "Avoiding the traffic."

A knowing nod. Driving from where she lived on Bay Harbor Island to the *Herald's* offices downtown took the better part of an hour if she wasn't careful about her drive times.

Kenzie took the elevator to the fifth floor. The Miami Herald occupied the top three floors of the six-story downtown building; the crime beat, along with the Editor-in-Chief's office, and most of the editorial team were on the fifth.

The double doors hissed open, and Kenzie stepped out into the deserted open plan office. Rows of workstations stood empty, their computer screens dark. The only sign of human occupation was the used coffee cups on the desks and the AC humming in the background. She glanced up at the office clock. Six thirty AM.

The doors opened again, and a cleaning crew member walked in pushing a cart loaded with buckets, wipes, and detergents.

"Hola Rosa," said Kenzie. The woman didn't speak much English, but they smiled and greeted each other whenever they were both in the office at the same time. Kenzie worked odd hours, which meant she was often there when the cleaning crew came in.

Rosa didn't turn around or make eye contact. That was strange. Usually, she was so friendly. Kenzie thought she heard a soft sniveling sound.

"Rosa? Is everything alright?"

The slender shoulders trembled and then came a shuddering sob.

Kenzie put her laptop bag down on her desk and walked over to where Rosa was standing. "Rosa, what's wrong? Has something happened?"

The maid's face was shiny with tears. It was clear she'd been bawling her eyes out long before Kenzie arrived.

"Tell me, what's wrong?" She put a hand on the woman's arm.

A sniff, then Rosa said something, but it was interspersed with so many sobs and hiccups that Kenzie couldn't make it out.

"What is it, Rosa?"

Rosa tried again, speaking slower. "My sister, Daniela. I am scared for her."

"Scared? As in worried about her?"

"Si."

Kenzie put an arm around her. The woman was too distraught to carry on working. "Let's sit down for a minute." She led her to a vacant desk where Rosa sank into a chair. Kenzie rolled one over from another desk and sat opposite her. "Why are you worried about Daniela?"

"She is missing."

Kenzie frowned. "Missing? As in lost?"

A tearful nod.

"How do you know this?"

"She come from Cuba." Rosa rubbed her eyes, making them even redder. "But she is not here. It has been more than one week. He promised." Tears ran down her blotchy cheeks.

"Who promised?" asked Kenzie, concerned.

The woman shook her head. "The man I pay to bring her here."

Kenzie's eyes widened. "You paid someone to bring your sister to Miami?" From what she could remember, Rosa's sister lived in Havana with their parents.

"Si, but then he call and say he want more money." Fresh sobs. "I couldn't pay him." When she'd finished crying, she sniffed and added, "Now his phone not working. I can't speak to him."

Crap. That didn't sound good. A chill shot down Kenzie's spine.

This wasn't the first time she'd heard this story, but never involving someone she knew. Her heart went out to Rosa. "Okay, why don't you give me his number and I'll try?" He may have blocked Rosa to frighten her into paying. It was a common enough scam. Unscrupulous traffickers transported people across the border and then extorted an additional surprise fee from the relatives in exchange for their loved ones' release.

Rosa fumbled in her pocket for her phone, then pulled out a scrap of paper with a number scribbled on it. Her hand was shaking as she handed it to Kenzie.

"Who gave you this?" she asked.

Rosa's gaze dropped to her lap. "A woman I met. She told me he could help us."

It was possible the woman was involved in the scam.

Kenzie took out her phone and dialed the number. "Does he have a name?"

"Luca. His name is Luca."

The number went straight to voicemail. Rosa was right, his phone was switched off, or it was a burner and no longer operational. She was betting on the latter.

"Sorry." She took a picture of the piece of paper with her phone. "What is the woman's name who gave you this, Rosa? Do you know her well?"

Rosa shook her head. "She works at this, how do you say? Refugee charity?"

Kenzie nodded.

"Her name is Gabby. She's nice. She said this man would help us." The desolation was palpable.

"What was the charity called?" Kenzie asked. "Does it have a name?"

"Open Arms."

"Then that's where we should start," Kenzie stated.

The cleaner's eyes widened. "You going to talk to her?"

"Of course. We need to find out what has happened to your sister, and this is the only way to trace Luca." If that was his real name.

Hope flared in Rosa's eyes as she clutched her hand. "Thank you, Kenzie. Thank you."

Kenzie smiled. "I haven't done anything yet. Let me send Keith an email and then I'll drive to the charity and pay them a visit." A charity was a brick-and-mortar business. It would be hard to hide a trafficking side-hustle. If the woman was involved, Kenzie would find out pretty soon.

Open Arms was situated in Little Havana, six miles from the *Herald*'s offices. Kenzie parked her brand-new all-electric Chevrolet Bolt outside and studied the squat brick building. It was three stories tall, but the charity seemed to occupy only the ground floor. Above it was an accounting firm, and above that, residential apartments, by the looks of things.

She got out of the car. The dirty green awning stretched over the pavement like a drooping eyelid, and the front of the office looked just as sleepy. The door was worn and needed paint, and it creaked in complaint as she pulled it open.

The interior was divided into two sections: A front reception room with a large desk, a whole wall of mismatched filing cabinets, an overstuffed orange sofa that clashed with...well, everything, and a sputtering ceiling fan that would have been just as effective off. And a back area, partially hidden by two bamboo screens, containing a collection of desks and whirring computers. Peering into the dimness, she made out a shadowy figure bent over a keyboard, typing furiously.

"Hello?" she called out.

The shadow glanced up at the sound of her voice. "Be right with you."

Kenzie waited, her gaze wandering over the posters on the wall.

Do not neglect to show hospitality to
strangers, for thereby some have
entertained angels unawares.
Hebrews 13:2

Perhaps the charity didn't have anything to do with the people trafficking operation.

"How can I help you?" The shadow moved into the brightly lit front room. He spoke with a slight Spanish accent and was slim and neatly dressed in jeans and a black shirt. Kenzie was surprised to see a priest's collar around his neck.

"Hello, I'm looking for Gabby."

His eyes crinkled at the sides. "Gabby's not in yet. Can I give her a message?"

It was still early, not yet nine o'clock. "What time are you expecting her?"

He glanced at his watch. "Soon. She usually gets in around nine."

"In that case, I'll wait." She scrutinized the orange sofa that had been re-stuffed to an inch of its life. It was so bulbous it resembled a squidgy beanbag with a dent in the middle.

"Make yourself at home."

I hope I can get out of this thing once I've sat down. Immediately, the couch swallowed her up.

"Do you run the charity?" she asked.

He gave a proud nod. "I'm the founder, yes. My name is Father Diego Hernandez."

"Pleased to meet you. I'm Kenzie Gilmore. Are you originally from Cuba yourself?"

"No, born and bred in Miami." He stacked a pile of papers neatly on the desk. "All my life I've wanted to do something useful, so five years ago, I started Open Arms. It's affiliated with our church, St. Michael the Archangel."

"I see." Hence the Bible verses on the poster.

A camera mounted on the cornice above his head caught her eye. The charity might not look like much from the outside, but it hadn't scrimped on surveillance equipment. She didn't know the exact model but recognized that it was a high-end video security camera and the flashing light on the side told her it was recording right now and wasn't just for show.

He followed her gaze. "We help a lot of very desperate people, but there are others we can't help. Desperation makes people do crazy things. The camera is there to protect the volunteers."

It made sense. Besides, everyone had surveillance these days.

Fifteen minutes later, a voluptuous woman in her late twenties with curly black hair and clothing two sizes too small, sauntered in. "Father Diego, you'll never guess what happened this morning," she began, not noticing Kenzie enveloped in the orange sofa.

Father Diego nodded towards her. "You have a visitor, Gabby."

She swung around. "Oh, hello. Do I know you?"

Kenzie struggled to her feet, the smile back in place. Disarming, reassuring. "No, we've never met. I'm Kenzie, and I'm a friend of Rosa Martinez."

Gabby frowned in confusion. "Rosa Martinez?"

"Yes, would you mind if we had a word in private?"

Gabby glanced at her boss, then gave a nod. "Follow me."

She walked through the screens into the back office, her heels clacking on the vinyl floors. Kenzie followed, shooting the priest a grateful grin.

"Have a seat." Gabby gestured to a plastic chair on the other side of her cluttered desk. In the center, an enormous pile of paperwork stretched upwards like the Leaning Tower of Pisa. Kenzie sat, but could barely see her through the mound of paperwork.

"Busy?" she remarked.

"Always. It never ends. Each one of these is a refugee seeking asylum in the United States. We give them safety, security, food, and shelter."

"You house them too?" Kenzie asked, surprised.

"We try," she said. "There's a small center attached to the church, but there isn't always enough capacity. We work with a handful of housing charities to place them. Now, what can I help you with?"

Kenzie studied Gabby. She had a fresh, youthful face with expressive brown eyes. Easy to read. "I believe you gave my friend Rosa the number of a man called Luca. I'm trying to find him."

Gabby paled. "Luca?"

"Yes, I'm sure that was his name." Kenzie kept the smile in place. "He was helping her sister, Daniela get to America."

Gabby shook her head, her eyes darting to the front room. "No, I don't know that name. I'm sorry."

Kenzie was pretty sure she knew exactly who Luca was, but didn't want her boss to know. Father Diego wouldn't approve. She leaned forward and dropped her voice. "Gabby, Daniela is missing. If you know who Luca is, please tell me. Her life could be in danger."

Gabby's eyes widened. "I would if I could, but I don't know a Luca. We help refugees resettle in this country. We provide legal advice, temporary housing, food. But we don't bring them over ourselves."

"I'm aware of that," Kenzie said. "And it's a good thing you're doing. I'm sure it's sorely needed. But you gave Rosa Luca's number, didn't you?"

A hurried shake of the head. "I told you, I don't know any Luca."

Kenzie hid her frustration. Railroading her wasn't going to get anywhere. Gabby was shutting down. She wouldn't talk in front of the priest. "That's okay." She tried a different tack. "Rosa must have been mistaken. I'm sorry to have bothered you." Giving the volunteer a pointed look, she slid her business card over the desk. "If you do happen to hear from Daniela, please let me know."

Gabby stared at the card.

Kenzie got to her feet. "I'll see myself out."

"Thank you," she called to the priest as she left.

As the sunshine hit her, she shook off a sinister chill. Gabby was lying. That much was obvious. The bad feeling Kenzie had been carrying with her since she'd spoken to Rosa intensified. One thing she knew for sure was that she had to find Daniela before it was too late.

5

A HAWK SCREAMED in the deepening dusk as it circled overhead. Reid stood on his deck and took a deep breath, watching it float on the updraughts. What a day.

He still couldn't get the snake victim out of his mind. Every time he blinked, she was there, hovering just behind his eyelids. It happened with all his victims. They haunted him until he figured out who'd killed them and why. Only when the case was closed, could he sleep without seeing their faces.

What he needed was a distraction. Something to take his mind off the investigation, even if only for a few hours. Right on cue, Kenzie's voice carried across the still evening air from around the side of the house. "Reid? You out back?"

"Yeah," he replied, grinning. He didn't have a doorbell, and when he was out here, he couldn't hear the knocking. Kenzie knew to come around the side and up onto the deck, but most people just left—and that was how he liked it.

The water stretched for miles out in front of him. Indigo now, instead of blue, the shadows giving it an oily appearance. In the distance, beyond the sawgrass, the horizon bled orange.

Solitude. Nature. Clarity.

Everything he craved after a long day at the station, or when he wasn't on duty, to still the workings of his mind. Or amplify them— depending on how you looked at it.

"There you are." Kenzie pulled herself up onto the deck and ducked under the railing. She wore jeans and a white T-shirt, her hair pulled back in a no-nonsense ponytail. Standard work attire. Still, she looked great. Her smile was genuine and her face sun-kissed, thanks to the warm winter weather.

"Hi, good to see you." He meant it.

She grinned. "Likewise. I heard the appeal on the radio. We managed to get it out fairly quickly. Any luck with the callers?"

"Not as yet." Appeals like this always took a few days to gain momentum, and then people started calling in. They'd set up a dedicated hotline for anyone who knew of a missing Hispanic woman in her forties. "Although, to be honest, I don't hold out much hope." A rough description was all they could provide, considering the state of decomp.

Kenzie shrugged. "You never know. It's worth a shot."

That was true. All it took was one tip-off to change the direction of an investigation. He knew that firsthand.

"Beer?"

"Please."

He came back with the beverages, and they sat side by side on the swing chair, watching as the sky darkened and the night sounds emerged. A soft rustle, a splash of a tail, a muted cry from deep within the vegetation.

"Tell me about Maria," he said.

Kenzie took a swig. "I didn't realize she'd been abused as a child. By her mother's pimp, no less." She grimaced. "I can quite understand her leaving."

"How long was she on the streets?" Reid asked.

"Not long. She moved into a squat with a bunch of addicts and hookers. It must have been awful." She shuddered despite the balmy evening.

"Probably safer than her home situation," Reid replied.

Kenzie gave a sad nod. A creature broke the surface of the water, and they watched the ripples radiate outwards. "It does give you an insight into why she chose a life of crime, and why she took over her husband's organization. I think readers will relate to that."

He shot her a sideways look. "Are you saying you want your readership to sympathize with Maria Lopez? She was charged with conspiracy to commit murder. Even if she didn't pull the trigger, she was implicit in those crimes. People died because of her."

"I know." Kenzie didn't meet his gaze.

"She shouldn't be allowed to profit from her crimes. This book was a bad idea."

Kenzie bit her lip. "We'll have to agree to disagree on this one, Reid. Everyone has the right to tell their story, even the bad guys."

Reid let it go. Arguing with Kenzie when she had her mind set on something was never a good idea. "Agree to disagree, then."

Her lips broke into a smile. "Anyway, that's not why I'm here. There's something else I wanted to talk to you about. I thought you might be able to help."

His eyes narrowed. When Kenzie asked for his help, his internal alarm bells went off. Either she'd stumbled across something she couldn't solve herself, or she needed information on something that she couldn't get her hands on. "What is it?"

She elbowed him in the ribs. "Don't look at me like that. I came here because I wanted to see how you're doing, okay? This is an aside, something that happened at work today."

Leaning back, he relaxed his shoulders. That didn't sound so bad. "Okay, shoot. You know I'll help you if I can."

It was strange, their symbiotic relationship. When they'd first met, he'd vowed to have nothing to do with her. She was a reporter, and worse, she was *the* reporter. The one who'd blown the story about his undercover agent that had consequently gotten her killed.

Now they were friends, partners even. He used her resources and her uncanny ability to morph into someone else to acquire information, and in return he gave her exclusivity on the cases they worked together. He was her source.

It was unsanctioned, it was unusual, and sometimes it bordered on unethical, but it worked. They made a fantastic team. And they solved cases. He got to put the bad guys away, and she got the scoop. It was a win-win.

Reid fingered the edges of the label on his beer bottle. Until feelings had gotten in the way. Then everything had fallen apart. Since then, they'd decided their working relationship and their friendship were too important to jeopardize, so they'd reverted back to how it was before. Before *that* kiss... before he'd fallen for her.

Her eyes crinkled. "I know, thanks." She took a moment to compose her thoughts. "There's a woman at work, Rosa Martinez. Her sister's gone missing."

He perked up. "Missing?"

"Yeah, it doesn't sound good. Rosa paid some guy to traffic her into the States from Cuba, who then asked for more money to secure her release. Rosa couldn't pay up."

"Let me guess?" Reid scowled. "Now she can't get hold of him?"

Kenzie bit her lip. "It's bad, isn't it?"

Inhaling, Reid drew the silty swamp scent into his lungs. "These scenarios very seldom end well. Do you have any leads?"

It was unlike Kenzie to leave it there. She was one of the best investigators he knew, probing until there was nothing more to find. And, she had a gut instinct that he'd stake his career on.

"The woman who gave her the trafficker's number works for a charity in Little Havana. Open Arms, it's called. I paid them a visit this morning."

Hiding a smile behind his bottle, he asked, "Find anything?"

"Kind of. The woman, Gabby, wouldn't tell me who this guy Luca was or where to find him. In fact, she denied giving Rosa the number. I didn't want to push, so I gave her my card. I'm hoping she'll call when her boss isn't around, but so far, nothing." She shrugged. "I thought maybe you could talk to her."

"I can't bring her in for questioning," he said. "There are no grounds for it."

"No, but you could pay her a visit. It might shock her into telling us who this mysterious Luca is. What do you think?"

"Hmm...maybe. Are you sure she knows?"

"Yeah, one hundred percent. I saw it in her eyes."

That was enough for him.

"Okay, I'll see if I can find time tomorrow. Text me the address."

"Will do. Thanks, Reid." She squeezed his hand and smiled. It wasn't quite enough, but it would do.

"Do you have a description of the missing sister?" His mind leaped back to the woman from that morning.

"No, but I can get one." Kenzie gasped. "You don't think...?"

"I don't know. How old is she?"

"Early twenties..." Her eyes were huge.

Reid frowned. "We think the woman in the snake was older, but it's hard to tell. She was partially digested."

Kenzie wrinkled her nose.

"Still, it's worth checking. Can you bring Rosa down to the station tomorrow and get her to look at the body?"

"Seriously? She's traumatized enough. What if it's not her sister?"

"What if it is? We need to rule her out. Rosa might recognize her clothing or something. We've scanned missing person reports, and there's nothing definite. Several possibilities, but without distinct markings or jewelry, we can't make a positive ID." He raked a hand through his hair.

"Okay," Kenzie relented. "I'll bring her in tomorrow morning. It'll be early, as I'm due at the prison at eleven for another interview with Maria."

"Fine. Thanks, Kenzie."

"No problem." She stared out over the water. "Let's hope it's not Daniela. Rosa will be devastated."

Reid hoped not too. But if it wasn't, it meant they had two missing women on their hands.

6

"It's okay, I'm right here." Kenzie gripped Rosa's hand as they walked into the viewing room at the morgue. An attendant hovered beside the body. Reid remained outside the door to give them some privacy.

The woman's body lay on a steel gurney, a white sheet covering her from head to toe. Average height, curvy and feminine, it could be anyone.

Rosa took a shuddering breath. Kenzie could only imagine what was going through her mind right now.

"Ready?" she asked.

Rosa gave a reluctant nod.

The attendant peeled back the cloth to display the victim's head. Rosa gasped when she saw the disfigured features and quickly looked away.

Kenzie stared, transfixed. The only thing that was still intact was the dark hair. The features were eroded and misshapen, giving her face a grotesque appearance. She resembled a wax figurine that had been in the sun too long and started to melt.

"It's not her."

"Are you sure?" Kenzie turned and made eye contact with Reid through the door's glass panel. A small shake of her head was all he needed.

"I'm sure. I'd recognize Daniela, even like that." Rosa's voice caught in her throat. "Besides, Daniela has a bird tattooed on her shoulder blade." She gestured to the body. "No tattoo. It's not her."

Reid gave a stiff nod and walked away, while the attendant covered the woman's face. Kenzie escorted Rosa out of the building.

"I'm sorry to put you through that," Kenzie said, as the sunlight encased them in its comforting glow. "Especially at a time like this."

"It's okay," Rosa replied. They walked towards Kenzie's car. "It's better I know."

"She's out there," Kenzie said. "We'll find her. Lieutenant Garrett will find her. He's the best detective in Miami."

"I hope so," she murmured. "It's been four days now."

Gabby was the key. She hoped Reid would find time to visit the charity and speak with her. The charity worker was the only person who could tell them who Luca was.

Kenzie dropped Rosa at the *Herald's* offices and drove towards the women's penitentiary. It was situated out of town in an industrial area, with warehouse buildings on one side and a highway criss-crossing overhead. The sound of traffic was a constant backdrop.

She parked in the lot and went through security, handing in her phone, her purse, and her keys, taking only her notepad and a pencil with her. The routine was becoming familiar. This was how relatives must feel when they came to visit their incarcerated spouses. This was their reality. She couldn't imagine conducting a relationship in one hour a week.

Visiting hours were about to start and she'd booked an eleven AM to noon slot. The guards opened the door, and the visitors were let through into the meeting room. Cool air, steel furniture, and beige vinyl flooring. Come to think of it, everything was beige. The floor, the walls, the expressions on the guards' faces, the pallor of the prisoners.

The digital clock thumped eleven and seconds later, the security door to the prison cells swung open and in walked the inmates, Maria first in line again. How did she manage to look so glamorous, despite wearing that awful orange prison outfit?

Kenzie smiled as if she was greeting an old friend, hoping it would put Maria at ease, but the cartel boss merely nodded, her olive-shaped eyes roving over Kenzie, scrutinizing her hair, her casual attire, and her lack of makeup. Without a word, she sat down.

"How are you?" Kenzie asked.

"Okay. You know, you'd look a lot prettier if you put on some makeup and styled your hair. Beauty can be a useful weapon."

She did know, but when she was working, she preferred being natural. It was who she was. While investigating a case, if she was assuming a different persona, she would dress up, wear makeup, transform into someone else.

"Against whom?"

"It's a man's world out there, Kenzie. You know that as well as I do. Don't be afraid of your femininity. Use it to your advantage."

"I'll take it into consideration."

Maria left it at that. "How is that handsome detective friend of yours?"

"If you're referring to Lieutenant Garrett, he's fine."

A knowing smile. "That is who I'm referring to, yes. You know he's in love with you, don't you?"

Kenzie frowned. They were getting way off base here, but Maria was fickle sometimes. Kenzie was learning her ways. This was fore-play, warming her up before they got down to business. Besides, life in prison was boring. She'd interviewed inmates before. They liked to talk about life outside the prison bars. "That's nonsense, but even if he were, it's not relevant to our discussion."

"Do you always stick to the rules?" Maria asked.

Kenzie blinked, surprised at the question.

Amused, Maria gave a deep, throaty laugh. "I know you don't. You're a maverick, like me. I recognized that trait in you when we first met."

It was true, they did have a connection. Under different circum-stances, they might even be friends.

"Rules only get you so far," Maria was saying, on a roll. "Rules are made to stifle progress. To keep people in line. It's the rule breakers who make history."

"Like you?" Kenzie asked.

A smug shrug.

Kenzie took a deep breath. She had to get this discussion back on topic. Time was ticking by, and they only had an hour. "Today, I thought we could talk about Federico and how you met." She'd spent most of the evening, after she'd gotten back from Reid's, working on the opening chapters of the book. They were going well, but she still needed more information.

Maria's gaze softened. "Federico, yes. He was my savior back then, my knight in shining armor."

"You said he was a drug runner?"

"A delivery boy, but even back then he'd caught the attention of Ruben García Morales, the head of the cartel. Federico was reliable, dependable. He got the job done. Soon, Morales promoted him and gave him more responsibility."

"Did you know him then?" Kenzie wanted the human-interest angle. She wanted the love story.

"We met when he delivered gear to the house," Maria explained. "I caught his eye. He was so handsome back then with his dark hair and serious eyes. I loved his eyes..." She petered off, lost in the past.

Kenzie scribbled on her pad, letting Maria gather her thoughts.

"We got talking. Eventually, he asked me out. I was so excited." A small smile played at her lips. "I remember borrowing one of the older girl's dresses for the occasion, and before he arrived, I went to the local store and used all the makeup testers. I wanted to look my best."

Kenzie thought about Reid, and how after they'd kissed, she'd got butterflies every time she'd thought about him. But that was in the past now, and they were back to being friends. Much less disconcerting.

"Where did you go?"

"To a local diner. We had blueberry pancakes and a vanilla milk-shake. It was very romantic. I knew then that he was the one for me."

"Love at first sight?" Kenzie didn't believe in such things, but it made for good reading.

"You could say that." Maria was a closet romantic. Kenzie filed that detail away for later. Despite her hard exterior, her quick mind and ruthless streak, she longed for love, just like any other woman. And she'd found it with Federico, arguably the most ruthless cartel boss in American history.

"What happened next?"

"He asked me to move in with him after a few weeks of seeing each other. There was some shit going down at the place I was stay-ing. One of the women had gotten herself knocked up by a John. Her pimp didn't like that and beat her up. It was a good time to leave."

"Where did Federico live?" Kenzie asked.

"He had an apartment in Mexico City. It was small, but comfort-able. I got a job waiting tables, and then as a store assistant, while he worked his way up the ranks. We were happy."

The faraway look was tinged with longing.

Kenzie felt a stab of envy. She'd never had that with anyone. After her mother had disappeared, relationships had been difficult. She'd joined the police academy straight out of school and made a lot of male friends, but that's all they were. Her barriers were too high. She couldn't let anyone in.

Reid was the only person who'd come close, and even then, she'd done her best to lock him out again. She shook away the thought and focused on Maria. "When you say he worked his way up the ranks, do you know what jobs he did?"

The nostalgic look vanished. "Of course. Federico told me every-thing. There were no secrets between us."

"He must have really trusted you," Kenzie said, thinking out loud. As an enforcer for the cartel, those jobs would have gotten messy.

"He did," she snapped. "I supported him every step of the way.

Even when he took over from Morales himself, I was there by his side. By the time Federico died, I knew every aspect of the business."

Kenzie didn't doubt it.

"Did you help him run it while he was alive?"

"No one knew," she murmured, her eyes gleaming. "But he discussed every decision with me. We worked as a team."

It made sense. Kenzie was beginning to understand how Maria had taken over so smoothly after her husband had died, and how nobody other than his inner circle had realized.

She said as much and watched Maria's chest swell. "They thought they were dealing with Federico, not his wife. Imagine if they'd known...?"

There would have been anarchy in the ranks. Kenzie knew how these things worked. Any sign of weakness and the sharks began to circle.

"That's why I had to do it my way." She fixed her dark gaze on Kenzie. "That's why I chose you."

Maria had continued the farce for two years, and then announced her takeover to the world in the form of an article written by Kenzie and published in the Miami Herald. Her moment of glory had been marred by her subsequent arrest, but in a way, it had blown the news way out of proportion, and Maria had become a household name.

Now Kenzie was writing her memoirs. Her fame would grow, as would her wealth. The book deal was worth millions.

They discussed Federico's role in more detail, and Kenzie noted specific anecdotes that Maria recalled, all of which would make interesting reading. She was just finishing up when Maria said, "How is my good friend Alberto Torres doing?"

Kenzie stiffened. "Torres? He's dead. You shot him, remember?"

"How could I forget? He betrayed me. I'm in here because of him." A flash of annoyance crossed her face.

Kenzie didn't respond.

"I heard a little rumor that he was still alive. Is that true?"

Fuck.

How had she found out?

She kept her voice steady. "Not that I know of. Last I heard, he bled out on the floor of the Ritz-Carlton."

"Maybe you can ask your handsome detective?" Maria suggested, her eyes twinkling. She knew very well that Kenzie would do no such thing.

"I'm not privy to that kind of information," Kenzie said. "Reid wouldn't tell me even if I asked."

"Except you could find out..." She left the implication hanging.

"No, Maria. I can't." Kenzie shut her notepad and stood up. "I think we're done for the day."

"He's alive, isn't he?" Maria leaned forward. "I know it."

"If he is, nobody told me."

But she could tell Maria wasn't convinced. There was a strange, unsettling smile on her face as Kenzie left. A smile that sent chills down her spine.

7

"SHE KNOWS," Kenzie hissed down the phone.

Reid frowned. "Knows what?"

"About Torres. She knows he's alive."

Reid, who was lounging in his desk chair, bolted upright. "What? How?"

"A rumor, or that's what she said, anyway."

"Fuck."

"My thoughts exactly. Should we warn him? Tell the DEA?" Her words tumbled over each other.

Reid considered this. "That could be what she wants. She might have someone watching them, or us, in the hopes we'll lead her to him."

"Something must have triggered this," Kenzie speculated. "It can't be a shot in the dark."

"I think you're right." Reid tipped his chair back, gnawing on his lip. In the background, Vargas was talking on the phone and Diaz was standing behind Hamilton, guiding him through a query on the police national database. It was business as usual at the Sweetwater Police Department.

"Okay, I'll give Agent Wilson a call. I don't think we should panic yet. This could be a fishing expedition. We don't want Wilson to meet Torres and blow his cover."

"He'll know the risks. He's a seasoned DEA operative," Kenzie said down the line.

You'd think, but then Reid had seen even seasoned cops make rookie mistakes when under pressure. "Leave it with me," he said.

After they hung up, he stared out over the squad room, deep in thought. How had Maria sniffed out that Torres was still alive? There must be a leak.

To be fair, it was impossible to keep a secret like that for long. It was too big a secret and there were too many people involved. His team, the DEA officers who'd been involved in the bust, the hospital staff, the WITSEC personnel—they were all potential leaks. One accidental slip up, one drunken story at a bar and it could find its way back to Maria.

It was pointless trying to figure out who, but he had to let the DEA agent know, regardless. Torres would have to be warned. Worst case scenario, they'd have to relocate him again. Make him disappear once more. Reid grimaced in sympathy. The veteran undercover agent wouldn't be happy about that.

He sent Wilson a text message asking to meet. This wasn't the type of conversation to have over the phone.

The DEA agent replied:

Ronnie's Taverna. 8pm.

Ronnie's was a grungy dive bar downtown. It had live music several days a week and served a basic menu, mostly burgers and fries. The food was decent, and if you picked your night, you might get to see an up-and-coming rock or metal band. Reid had been once or twice in his youth, but not recently. He couldn't believe it was still going. But first, they had work to do.

"Vargas," he called. His deputy looked up. "Let's go and talk to that woman at the refugee charity and see if we can get her to tell us who this mysterious Luca is." He'd briefed Sergeant Vargas on Kenzie's preliminary investigation the day before.

Vargas nodded. "Are we thinking the snake woman could be an illegal immigrant?"

"It's a possibility. It would explain why nobody has claimed her and why she hasn't shown up on any database." He'd been thinking along those lines since Kenzie had approached him about Rosa's sister. The victim had been Hispanic, with cheap, unbranded clothing and no form of ID.

A short while later, they pulled up outside the charity. "It doesn't look like much," Vargas said.

Reid surveyed the building. The drooping awning was faded and threadbare, and the glass windows desperately needed cleaning. In fact, it was so dirty, he could barely see inside. Still, just because the building was run down, it didn't mean the charity was at fault. For all he knew, they did a stellar job at supporting refugees who needed help when they arrived in Miami.

They walked inside and approached the guy at the front desk. Reid eyed his dog collar but didn't comment. "I'm Lieutenant Garrett and this is Sergeant Vargas from Sweetwater PD," Reid introduced them. "Who are you?"

"My name is Father Diego."

"Father, we're looking for an employee of yours named Gabby. You wouldn't happen to know where she is, would you?"

"I'm sorry, detectives, but she's not here. She called in sick today."

"Got her home address?" Reid asked nicely. He didn't want to intimidate a priest.

"Why?" His forehead creased. "Is she in some sort of trouble?"

"No, we just need to speak to her."

He didn't look convinced. "Yes, I have her address. It's right here in the system."

He switched on an ancient desktop computer that took forever to boot up. Reid rolled his eyes at Vargas. They waited while the priest navigated to the right screen, then scrolled through a list of names. "Here we are. Gabby Rosenbaum. NW 1st Terrace, 2028. Does that help?"

"It sure does," Reid said. "Thank you."

. . .

2028 NW 1st Terrace was on a wide residential street characterized by run-down, single-story houses with fenced in yards. Clusters of date palms, cacti and other foliage clung to the perimeters, bending the fences, and creeping from one plot to another.

"That's the place," Vargas said, as he pulled over and parked. They got out of the car, squeaked open the rusty metal gate, and proceeded up the path to the front door. It was clear by the over-grown yard that Gabby didn't have a green thumb.

"You go around the back," he murmured to Vargas. He couldn't explain it, but something didn't feel right.

Vargas peeled off and disappeared down the side of the house. A dog barked next door. Reid knocked, then tried the door handle. Unsurprisingly, it was locked.

He stepped off the porch, around an acacia bush, and peered through the window. It was dark inside, the lights off, no sign of any movement. No cups of tea on the coffee table, no items of clothing lying around, no sign of life.

It didn't look like she was home.

His phone buzzed in his pocket. It was Vargas.

Back door open.

He joined his sergeant at the back of the house, which was even more dilapidated than the front. The clapboards were weathered and in need of painting, the screen was filthy and several sad-looking pot plants gasped for water on the porch.

Vargas held the door open. "Shall we?"

Reid drew his gun, gave a quick nod, and stepped inside.

"Hello?" he called, looking around a small kitchen. "This is the Sweetwater Police Department. Is anybody home?"

No answer.

He shook his head and proceeded further into the house, holding the weapon steady in front of him. It was dark, the shades down, the lights off. He felt around for a switch. Finding it, he flipped it on, and a naked light bulb sizzled awake.

A wooden table and four chairs stood in the center of the room, covered by a rose-patterned tablecloth. There were unwashed dishes in the sink and the smell of sour milk in the air.

"Looks empty," Vargas murmured, coming in behind him.

"Let's check it out, just in case." Reid gestured for Vargas to proceed down the hallway to the front of the house, while he turned into a bedroom. The floorboards creaked under the thin carpeting, but there was no movement from inside the room. No rush of air as the occupant darted for a window, no scramble for cover. Just a cool void of emptiness.

"Clear." He backed out of the room.

"Clear," came Vargas's voice, having checked the living room.

There was another door on the opposite side of the hallway. That must be a second bedroom. Reid opened it, twisting slowly, his body angled behind the frame in case of flying bullets. But there was nothing. He pushed it open, his weapon ready.

This room looked bigger than the last and messier. It must be Gabby's since it was filled with personal items, make-up, costume jewelry, and clothing scattered across the unmade bed. It looked like she'd pulled a bunch of stuff out of the closet in a hurry.

"The house is clear." Vargas came in behind him, holstering his weapon. "She's not here."

"I think she's on the run." Reid studied the bed. There was a rectangular indent, the size of a small bag or backpack. "Kenzie must have spooked her when she came asking questions."

"That means she's got something to hide." Vargas eyed the mess on the dressing table. A beaded necklace lay discarded on the surface, along with several mismatched earrings and a cluster of silver bracelets.

"Definitely," Reid agreed. "But is she running from us—or Luca? That's the question."

8

"KENZIE, GET IN HERE!"

It was Keith, her boss and Editor-in-Chief of the Miami Herald. He didn't bother with formalities, but she was used to his brusque ways after so many years at the paper.

"What's up?"

"Take a seat. We need to talk."

Uh-oh. That didn't sound good. She perched on the leather chair opposite his desk, which was piled high with newspapers, memos and an assortment of pens and pencils. Keith was old school. Even though he had a high-end laptop and tablet, he still preferred to print out the articles his feature writers sent him and scribble over them with a red pen. Consequently, his office always smelt of hot printer paper and ink. It was a smell she'd learned to love over the years, synonymous with frantic activity, impending deadlines and going to press.

"Raoul," he said, glaring at her like she'd done something wrong.

She heaved a sigh. Raoul was her researcher, an assistant she was supposed to make use of, but never had. She preferred to work alone.

"What about him?"

"Don't flash those baby blues at me, young lady. He's a valuable resource, and I expect you to use him."

"You know I don't trust anyone to do my research for me."

"I *want* you to use him," he continued, as if she hadn't spoken. "He's a good investigator. I interviewed him myself."

Kenzie took a metered breath. "Keith, honestly, I don't need..."

"I've assigned him to you, Kenzie. I expect you to hand over some of your research to him this morning." At her exasperated look, he added, "That means right now. He's been working on the political desk with Trev, but it's wasted on him. What he needs is to be working on the Maria Lopez case. I know you're writing her memoirs, but the deal was we get to print the precursors and follow-ups, and I want material to go with that."

He was right. The memoirs were taking up a lot of her time and Keith had agreed to let her run with it if she accompanied the book with corresponding write-ups for the paper. Her confidentiality agreement with Maria meant she couldn't give too much away, but she was able to build buzz about the book. *Lady Caine*, as the book had tentatively been titled, was the most anticipated read of the year, and Kenzie, the most sought-after writer. Ever since the story broke, she'd been inundated with offers of interviews and television appearances.

"Okay, I'll put him to work," she promised, more to get Keith off her back than because she wanted to hand over her research to the new addition to the crime beat team. Raoul had started several months ago, a graduate from a fancy tech college with skills that any hacker would be proud of—apparently. Office gossip was he could weasel his way in anywhere, through any firewall, without leaving a trace. She didn't believe the hype. If he was that good, he wouldn't be working here.

"I also want him to have access to your work calendar," her editor said. She gasped.

"What? That's private. I use it for all my appointments. I can't divulge my sources."

"He's bound by a confidentiality agreement." Keith formed a triangle with his fingers on the desk. "Someone has to know where you are at all times. Remember what happened before? This way, you'll be safer."

"I'm perfectly safe," she huffed.

"No, Kenzie. You were kidnapped last year. Not to mention how close you came to losing your life when you were driven off the road." He shook his head. "I'm afraid my mind is made up. From now on, you'll be more transparent in your movements, and Raoul will know where you are at all times."

"This is ridiculous," she fumed. "It's like being back at school."

"It's for your own safety," he persisted. "You can trust Raoul. He's discreet. I think you'll find he's a real asset."

Kenzie gritted her teeth. "Can I go now?"

"One more thing."

She glanced up, exasperated. "Yeah?"

"What the hell is wrong with Rosa? I couldn't make any sense of your email."

"Rosa's sister has gone missing," she said, getting to her feet. "She was trafficked into the country and now she's disappeared. I'm looking into it with Lieutenant Garrett."

"Is there something there?" Keith's eyebrows arched.

"Could be. I'm more concerned with getting Daniela back safely at this stage," she told him. "But if this is a trafficking organization, we could have a story."

He gave an interested nod. "Keep me posted. These types of human-interest stories are always good for the paper."

Not so much for the people involved, Kenzie thought, but she didn't say anything. Keith had lived and breathed the newspaper for so long, he was oblivious to anything else.

"Let Raoul help with that, too," he added, as Kenzie left the room.

"Okay." Kenzie sank into her desk chair. Her laptop was open in front of her, but the screen was dark as she'd been away so long.

Raoul stared at her expectantly, like an eager puppy waiting for her to toss him a ball.

Oh boy, she thought. Still, she'd promised Keith.

Alright, Raoul, let's see what you can do.

"As you know, I'm interviewing Maria Lopez," she began. He nodded, bright eyed and bushy tailed. "I could do with some background information. Whatever you can find. There isn't a lot online, but I need to fact check a few things she told me. Do you think you can handle that?"

"Sure." His smile stretched from ear to ear. "How in depth do you want me to go?"

"The deeper the better." He wouldn't find much. She'd done some intensive searching herself to prepare for the interviews, so she knew firsthand that discounting the last few months, Maria Lopez had an infinitesimal online footprint. The wife of the notorious Federico Lopez. Born in Mexico City, 1970. There was nothing about her upbringing, her marriage, or her role in her husband's criminal organization. Only her shocking revelation last summer and the subsequent media frenzy originating from that.

"I'm going out now," she told him, as an afterthought. "But I'll be back later. We can discuss anything you've found then."

She sure as hell wasn't going to tell him where she was going. This was a personal project, one she'd been working on in her spare time, but due to the pressure of the book, hadn't gotten around to completing yet. Except she couldn't put it off any longer.

"Okay." He jumped up and went back to his desk.

Nick Murray.

That was the man who'd helped her when her car had been forced off the road last year. She'd hit a telephone pole and rolled her little Honda, finally smashing into the barrier and narrowly missing plunging into the bay far below. The sound of screeching metal and breaking glass would be forever etched in her memory. In fact, just thinking about it made her shudder.

A passing driver had stopped and come to her aid. He'd hauled her out of the crumpled car, checked she was okay and lent her his jacket while they'd waited for the emergency services to arrive—not that she remembered much. There was the driving rain, the puddles forming on the asphalt around her, the pounding in her head and blurry vision, followed by the sound of sirens. His voice kept her calm. His assurances that she wasn't badly hurt. That the ambulance was on its way. At the very least, she owed him a thank you.

After looking up every veterinary clinic's website in Miami, she'd finally found one with his picture on it. South Kendall Animal Clinic. There were hundreds of reviews saying how wonderful Dr. Murray was and how Trixie the Persian had her appetite back, or how Sparky the labradoodle had recovered from his operation.

Without a word to Keith, she left the *Herald* and drove her Chevrolet twenty minutes southwest to South Kendall. The veterinary clinic was next to Palmetto Golf Course and had lovely views across the greens from the parking lot.

A board outside read, *Serving the dogs and cats of Miami.* Cute.

A friendly receptionist smiled as she entered, her gaze automatically dropping to Kenzie's feet, as if expecting to see a furry friend in tow.

"Hi," Kenzie smiled. "It's just me. Is Dr. Murray here?"

"Oh, no, I'm sorry. He's at the Everglades National Park this afternoon. Dr. Simpson is available if you'd like to make an appointment, although there's a bit of a wait."

Her shoulders sank. "No, thank you. When will Dr. Murray be back?"

"Not today, I'm afraid." She glanced at the computer screen. "He'll be in tomorrow morning. You can catch him then."

Kenzie hesitated, his jacket in her hand. "Would you mind giving this to him?" She placed it on the countertop. "He lent it to me some time ago, and I wanted to return it in person."

The receptionist glanced from Kenzie to the jacket and back again. "I see," she said knowingly.

"I had a car accident." Kenzie was quick to put her straight. "He very kindly helped me." Not that it was any of her business.

"Oh, I'm sorry. I didn't realize."

Clearly. Kenzie was getting annoyed.

A poster of Dr. Murray smiled warmly at her from the waiting room. She turned to survey the clientele and realized most of them were women in their thirties and forties carrying lap dogs or pedigree felines in cat carriers.

She was beginning to understand.

"Could I leave a note?" Kenzie asked.

"Of course." The receptionist thrust a piece of note paper across the counter toward her. Kenzie wrote: *Thank you for your help. Sorry it's taken so long to get this back to you. Kenzie Gilmore.*

She was tempted to leave her business card but figured that would be like asking him to call her, and she didn't want to do that. From the looks of things, he had more than enough female attention. Maybe she'd stop by another day—but only if she had time.

"Yeah, we know about him."

"Oh?" Reid was speaking to Detective Lawrence of the Border Patrol. He'd stopped by the office on his way to meet Wilson.

"We call him the ghost because nobody knows his real identity. Luca, that's all we ever hear. Border Patrol has picked up boatloads of Cubans, none of whom have met him. The crews get recruited by a guy in Havana. They're paid in cash. On this side, the ones who make it aren't talking. All we know is they're taken to a holding facility while money is extorted from concerned relatives. Once the relatives pay up, they're released, usually by a man in a balaclava. He never shows his face."

"What happens if they don't pay up?" Reid asked grimly.

Lawrence shrugged. "They end up in the swamp or wash up in the Keys. More often than not, we never find their bodies."

Shit.

"Sorry I can't help you, man. I hope you find the missing girl."

"Thanks."

Reid walked away feeling depressed. Lawrence hadn't asked for the details of the case. It was as if he knew it would be a fruitless endeavor.

The ghost.

Reid didn't believe in ghosts.

Ronnie's Taverna was filling up when Reid got there, just before eight. He took a seat at the bar and waited for Wilson to show up. They'd worked a sting operation together last year, and while he liked the guy, the DEA agent was a stickler for protocol. Federal operatives usually were. There were always boxes to check and rules to follow.

Reid wasn't anti-regulation, but he found the red tape frustrating and acknowledged that sometimes you had to follow your gut. There was no mention of a cop's instinct in the police manual, although in his opinion, there should be.

The band was setting up in the corner. Where was Wilson? If he didn't arrive before they kicked off, it would be impossible to hear each other talk. He reached for his beer and took a swig. It tasted good after his long day. The air was dry, almost electric, and the air-conditioning only made it worse.

As the musicians tuned their instruments, tables began to fill up. The ambient noise level ticked up several notches.

"Garrett," came a deep voice over his shoulder.

He turned. "Wilson, good to see you."

The two men shook hands. "What can I get you?" Reid asked.

Wilson nodded towards his beer. "One of those will be good, thanks." He took a seat beside Reid and looked around. "I haven't been here since my college days. Used to love metal nights."

Reid was surprised. Agent Wilson did not look like a metal head.

"What's up?" the DEA agent asked once his drink had arrived.

Reid leaned closer. To the rest of the bar, they looked like old friends catching up over a few beers. "We think Torres might be compromised."

The agent's face crunched into a frown. "What makes you say that?"

"Maria Lopez. She asked Kenzie Gilmore if he was still alive."

"Jesus H. Christ," the man exploded. "She came right out and said that?"

"Yes, sir. Took Kenzie by surprise, too. She covered best she could, but she thinks it was a fishing expedition. Maria's heard a rumor that the man who betrayed her to the feds is alive and is looking for confirmation."

"This is bad," Wilson muttered. "Real bad."

Reid knew as well as he did no one bore a grudge like the cartels. If Lopez knew Torres was alive, his days were numbered.

"It could be smoke and mirrors," Reid said, his voice low. "She might be throwing it out there to see where it leads. Perhaps she doesn't know, but she suspects. Rushing into a panic would only serve to confirm her suspicions."

Wilson stared into his beer, watching the bubbles rise to the surface. "How do you think she found out?"

"No idea. Could be anyone. How many people know he survived the shooting?"

"A handful. I know them all personally. They're good guys. I can't see them ratting him out."

"If it was a mistake, they might not want to admit it," Reid warned.

Wilson gave him a hard look. "I'd know if they were lying. These are my men. I trained most of them."

"Okay," Reid nodded. "I'll leave that with you. In the meantime, you might want to give Torres a head's up—just in case."

"Yeah, I will." He shook his head. "Fucking hell, this is all we need. Maria freakin' Lopez. I've never known one woman to cause so much trouble."

"Wait till her book comes out." Reid rolled his eyes.

"Her son is following in her footsteps," Wilson said.

"Oh, yeah?" This was the first Reid had heard, but then cartel business wasn't his remit anymore.

"He's in Cali now, but we suspect he's working with Romeo Herrera."

The name rang a bell. "Wasn't that Federico's right-hand man back in the day?"

"Yeah, good memory." He worked his jaw. "Well, we think Herrera is grooming Matteo Lopez to take control of the Miami part of the enterprise now that Maria's inside."

"It's like a vicious cycle," Reid muttered. "You cut off one head, and another one grows back."

Wilson's chin was set firmly, the tension visible in his neck. "That's something we both agree on."

10

Maria Lopez stared moodily across the table.

Kenzie sighed and put down her pencil. "Maria," she began, after the inmate had once again ignored her question. "Is something wrong? You're very distracted."

Maria crossed her arms in front of her body. "I'm not in the mood for this today."

That much was obvious.

"Why not? Did something happen?" Something must have put her in a bad mood.

There was a long pause.

It wasn't like Maria to hesitate. Usually, she came right out and said it like it was, or else she told Kenzie she wasn't prepared to discuss that particular topic. Either way, she was specific and decisive. This uncertain version of the infamous cartel boss was unusual, if not a little alarming.

"Maria?" Kenzie pushed, hoping she'd relent and open up to her. They'd spoken about sensitive subjects before and had—in Kenzie's mind—established a tentative sense of trust. Would it be enough for Maria to let her in now?

A sigh, faint but audible. "I'm getting death threats."

Kenzie's eyes widened. "Death threats? Has someone said something to you?" If this was the case, they had to alert the warden. Maria Lopez was essential to the arrest and apprehension of the Morales cartel, both in Miami and California. Her safety was paramount.

Maria rolled her eyes like this was a mere annoyance rather than a life-threatening situation. "I found this in my cell." She pulled a small fabric toy out of her pocket and laid it on the table.

Kenzie looked closer. No, it wasn't a toy, it was a head, a doll's head, but brightly colored and wearing makeup.

Kenzie stared at it. The design was vaguely familiar.

"It's a calaveras." Maria's voice was a whisper.

"What does it mean?" Kenzie asked, although she thought she knew. It reminded her of the painted skulls she'd seen in the Day of the Dead celebrations. Red floral patterns wrapped around the eye sockets, and the teeth were exposed in a macabre grin.

"It means death."

It was kind of creepy. Kenzie studied it from all angles. It looked homemade, put together in the prison by someone who knew how.

"Whoever put this in my cell is sending me a message." There was a flicker of annoyance in Maria's gaze. She hated being in this position. Trapped.

"Who do you think it could be?" Kenzie asked.

A shrug. "I don't know. Anyone with a grudge, but it's most likely a message from a member of the cartel. They know I've made a deal with the devil." The devil being the DEA. Kenzie, the messenger.

"How would they know?" Kenzie shook her head. "We never divulged the deal we made with you to anyone."

Maria scoffed. "Don't be naïve, Kenzie. Of course, they know. Why else would you be writing my memoirs? I'm a convicted felon."

"Other felons have written books," Kenzie argued.

"I've met some unscrupulous people in my time, and they're worried. Very fucking worried."

She was right. There were any number of ruthless people who would like to see Maria wiped off the face of the earth.

"What can we do about it?" Kenzie asked, always solution oriented.

"Ha!" A rough, coarse laugh. "Do about it? Do you know how things work in here? No, of course not. Let me tell you something, Kenzie Gilmore." The name was a sneer. "There is another set of rules inside a prison, and they have nothing to do with the guards. The inmates run the show here. There is nothing I can do other than watch my back. Watch it very fucking closely."

"How are you going to do that?" Kenzie squinted.

"That's for me to worry about." A snarly smile, but Kenzie got the impression Maria had a plan, or if not, she was working on one. Hence the distraction.

"Do you want to carry on with this, or should we continue another day?" Maria wasn't in the right mindset for sharing confidences. This was a side to Maria that Kenzie hadn't seen before. She was spooked but determined not to show it. This was the woman who'd taken over from her husband when he'd died unexpectedly two years ago. This was the person who'd fooled everyone. It was the woman she was writing about.

Adversary was no stranger to Maria Lopez. She'd faced worse before and come out on top. Kenzie had no doubt she would do it again.

Maria didn't reply.

"Let's leave it there," Kenzie said, making the decision for her.

Maria gave a curt nod, then got up and in one smooth movement, turned, and glided towards the door. A guard opened it, and the cartel boss disappeared back into the bowels of the prison.

Kenzie scribbled a few notes on her pad, then packed up.

"I'm sorry, Lil. I can't do this no more," came a tearful female voice from the table next to her. Kenzie looked across and saw a rake-thin woman with stringy hair and a nose ring wringing her hands.

The prisoner she was visiting, a sturdy female inmate, slammed her hand down on the steel surface, making Kenzie jump. "What are you saying?" It was a low growl.

The woman got up. "It's over. I don't love you no more. I've met someone else."

The growl turned into a roar as the inmate launched herself across the table at the woman, who stumbled backward and careened into Kenzie. If the tables and chairs weren't bolted to the floor, they would have gone flying.

"Whoa." Kenzie grabbed the woman's arm in an attempt to steady her. She was so skinny, she weighed next to nothing. Not like the oversized Amazonian bearing down on them. The inmate reached out and ripped her away. Kenzie fell on her backside. "Hey!"

The two wardens on guard sprang into action. They got the prisoner by the arms and wrestled her away from the screaming woman.

"You're crazy," the thin woman yelled in a high-pitched voice. "Why do you think I'm leaving you, you bully?"

The female inmate surged forward, trying to shake off the prison guards, but she was unsuccessful. Beaten, she yelled out in frustration as they led her away.

Kenzie exited the penitentiary and stood outside in the sunshine, letting the rays wash over her. The sudden violence had left her shaken. It felt good to be outside the prison walls in the fresh air with the boundless blue sky overhead. Things Maria and Lil, the 'bully', wouldn't experience for a long time.

She took a deep, steadying breath and walked over to her car. She'd parked at the far end of the prison parking lot, which was always crowded during visiting hours. Maria's words echoed in her mind.

The inmates run the show here.

She suppressed a shiver and then stopped.

"What the hell?"

All four tires on her brand-new car were flat. How? Had she driven over glass or something? She bent forward and inspected them closely, gasping as she did so. They'd been slashed. Each tire had a wide cut in the rubber.

Kenzie stood up, her heart hammering. This was no accident.

11

REID COAXED the airboat through the canal and out into the wider expanse of the swamp. The jet engine roared behind his head as he accelerated and surged over the surface of the water. The warm air made his eyes water. It was exhilarating.

When he'd bought the cabin nearly three years ago, he'd planned to sell off the airboats that had come with it. The previous owner had operated a tour company out of the property. He'd sold two but kept the third after giving it a whirl. You couldn't beat it for a sheer adrenalin rush, particularly at speed, soaring over the Glades.

The waterways were busy today, comparatively speaking. It was a beautiful Saturday morning, and the tourists were out in full force, as well as those who made a living from the swamp. The unseasonably dry weather made Florida a popular winter vacation spot. Still, the Everglades National Park was a big place, and it was easy to lose yourself amongst the sawgrass and cattails, or in the mangrove swamps where the splash of a silver tail was the only sign of life, other than the screeching birds overhead.

Reid knew the swamp well now. He knew where to go for peace and quiet, or where to drift for nature watching. He knew the open stretches of waterway where he could floor the airboat and feel it drift over the water beneath him, and he knew the location of every dead body that had been pulled out of here over the last two years. Three in the first year he was here, including Natalia Cruz, the celebrity heiress.

Right now, he wanted to take another look at the place where the python had been found. It was deep into the swamp, difficult to get to by road, which was why the emergency services had taken so long to get to her. Selwyn Price, the man who'd found her, had waited half a day for them to show up.

This was private land, owned by a nature reserve company, so hunting was allowed all year round, not just during the designated season. The airboat hummed over the sea of grass towards where they found the body.

There.

That was it, he was sure of it.

He took out his phone and checked the coordinates against those he'd taken at the crime scene. Virtually spot on.

Reid cut the engine and drifted for a while, surveying the bank. The water was shallow here, where it merged with the land, creating a marsh-like plain, an in-between zone about three feet deep. For a five-foot two woman, that would be above the knees. Hard to run in, more so if you were bleeding from a leg wound.

He glanced around at the exposed strip of land. The blood would have attracted all manner of predators, and with her energy sagging as she dragged herself through the swamp, she wouldn't have stood a chance. If the python hadn't got to her, a gator would have.

He bobbed around for a while, enjoying the sun on his back and the sound of the water lapping against the side of the boat, just think-ing. What the hell was she doing out here? There was literally nothing around. The nearest civilization was Homestead to the north, and the Florida Keys to the south, both too far to get to without a boat or a vehicle. If the mystery woman had gotten here in a vessel of some sort, where was it? Why hadn't it been discovered or reported missing? A boat wasn't hard to find, even if it was adrift.

Drifting made him think of the currents and the nearest way to the sea. Far to the south and east of him were the lagoons, lakes and sounds between the Glades and the Keys. Was it possible to get there via boat using the canals and waterways through the Glades? It wasn't unfeasible that she'd come in that way.

Had someone bought her here and left her to fend for herself in the swamp? He thought of Detective Lawrence's words.

They end up in the swamp or wash up in the Keys.

Is that what had happened here? Was his mystery woman a refugee, like Daniela? There were just too many questions. He swiped at his brow with the back of his hand. It came away wet. Damn, it was warm for this time of year.

Eager to feel the wind on his skin again, he started the motor and headed southeast towards the coast. Call it stubborn curiosity, but he wanted to see how long it would take to navigate the waterways of the Glades from the coast. The airboat flew over the sawgrass, flicking it against the hull. It took him almost two hours before he passed Flat Point and the windswept waters of Manatee Bay opened in front of him. He cut the engine and drifted a while, enjoying the tang of salt on the breeze.

It was possible that the traffickers used this route to smuggle people into the Glades, in order to escape detection by the Coast Guard. It was a longer route and less efficient than dropping them off along the coastline of the Florida Keys, but probably had a higher success rate.

He imagined the refugees would disembark somewhere south of Florida City in the Southern Glades. From there, they'd make their way to friends or relatives, or for those without anyone, the various charities set up to help them. Charities like Open Arms.

A large fishing vessel motored past, back from a deep-sea adventure. The tourists on board, overexcited from a successful morning, waved and raised their beer bottles to him. He didn't respond, distracted by his thoughts.

The wake from the motorboat slapped against the hull, bringing him to his senses. He glanced at the fuel gauge. That wouldn't be enough to make it back, but he had another gallon in reserve. Swamp survival 101: always come prepared. Being stranded out here wouldn't be fun, particularly as night drew in. The sun set around six-thirty this time of year, which meant longer hunting times for both the natural predators and their human hunters.

He restarted the engine and turned the boat around in a wide, lazy circle. Then he sped up, causing the vessel to leap forward like an athlete at the starting line. Within minutes, he'd overtaken the motorboat. This time he did wave as he flew past on a cushion of air, a wide smile on his face.

It was only when he got within range of a cell tower that his phone picked up reception. It beeped several times as his missed calls and messages registered. Scowling, he ignored them all and kept going. The sun had set, and it was getting dark.

He kept going until he pulled up beside the wooden walkway that ran from his deck down to the boat mooring. Finally, he was home. He cut the engine, his ears singing in the sudden silence. After tying the airboat to a post, he strode up the walkway and onto his deck. Damn, it was good to get home.

He stretched, feeling his back crack. A buzz in his pocket reminded him he had a ton of messages to read. Taking out his phone, he scrolled through them.

Kenzie had called a couple of hours earlier. Ignoring the others, he called her back.

She answered right away. "Reid, hi." He heard relief in her voice.

"Are you okay? I've been out of range all day."

"Yeah, I'm fine." She hesitated. "But something strange happened at the prison yesterday, and I'm not sure what to make of it."

"What happened?" He caught his breath. "Are you okay?"

"I'm fine, but Maria Lopez is receiving death threats."

He frowned. "I'm not surprised. She pissed off half of the Morales cartel. Those guys are in prison because of her, and the other half are probably shitting themselves."

"She's spooked," Kenzie said. "She found a calaveras in her cell."

"A death mask?" He'd seen them during the Mexican festivals in Miami.

"Yeah, I think someone's out to get her."

"Occupational hazard," he replied. "Although nobody knows she ratted on the cartel. They might suspect, but we've kept the details of the agreement very quiet."

"You know how these things get out," Kenzie said.

"Is there something else bothering you?" He got the feeling that wasn't it.

A sigh. "My tires got slashed yesterday."

Her words sank in.

"Where? Did you see who did it?"

"It was while I was at the penitentiary interviewing Maria," she said. "I found them like that when I got back to my car."

"Any other cars vandalized?"

A pause.

"No, just mine."

Which meant she was the target. A nasty feeling gnawed at his gut. "Did you report it? If you talk to prison security, they're bound to have CCTV cameras in the parking lot."

"That's the first thing I did," she replied.

"Sorry." Of course she would have. "I got ahead of myself. What did you find out?"

He had to get out of cop mode. Kenzie was a seasoned investigator; she knew what to do in these circumstances.

"Not much." He heard the disappointment in her voice. "My car was in a black spot, the camera didn't cover it, and the closest one picked up a man in a beanie hat. It would be hard, if not impossible, to identify him, even if we were sure he's the one who did it."

"He must have been, though. Why else would he be dressed like that in a prison parking lot?"

"True, but apart from a slim build, I couldn't pick up any features. It's hard to tell if it's a man or a woman."

"Let me have a look. Will you forward it to me?"

"Yeah, I have a copy on my phone."

"Kenzie." He paused.

"Yeah."

"This could be a warning. You need to be careful."

"I know," she whispered.

"Someone could be worried about what Maria is telling you. She may have secrets they don't want to get out."

"That's what I thought."

"Watch your six, okay?"

"I will."

"And if you want me to come over... if you'd feel safer with me there, then I will."

He heard her smile. "Thanks, Reid. I'll let you know."

His phone buzzed. She'd sent through the photograph.

"I mean it, Kenz. Call me if you notice anything out of the ordinary."

"I promise."

He hung up, feeling unsettled. He didn't like this. Didn't like it one bit. Those memoirs were a bad idea from the start. Sure, he wanted the names of the cartel members in California, but was it worth a life? Possibly two? Maybe even three, if Maria got to Torres, too.

He grunted. Agent Wilson would probably think so.

Still, he didn't want Kenzie in the firing line. And it seemed that's exactly where she was. Again.

12

Sᴜɴʙᴇᴀᴍs sʟɪᴄᴇᴅ through the half-open shades and bounced off her laptop. Kenzie closed the screen and wondered for the umpteenth time why she wasn't out enjoying her Saturday morning like other normal women her age. Then she remembered she didn't have anyone to enjoy it with.

School hadn't been easy after her mother had disappeared, and the only friend she'd kept was now married and living in Fort Lauderdale. She'd made friends at the police academy, but they'd become cops and after her accident, she hadn't felt like socializing with them anymore. Hearing what bust they'd been on, or what arrest they'd made was more than she could bear. That dream had been shattered along with her kneecap and fibula, and no amount of physical therapy could put it back together again.

Reid flitted briefly through her mind, but she couldn't imagine him in shorts with a surfboard under his arm or sipping a cappuccino in the mall. That would mean he had to chill out, and she didn't think he could downshift to that extent. The most relaxed she'd ever seen him was when he'd been with her. They'd held hands and strolled down Ocean Drive like normal couples do. He'd squeezed her hand and smiled into her eyes. He'd looked happy.

Then she'd destroyed that by saying it wasn't working out, by suggesting they'd be better off as friends. He'd accepted it, but she knew it wasn't what he wanted.

You have to open up to people, Kenzie. Not shut them down. The words of the psychologist her father had taken her to see after her mother's disappearance.

He'd thought it would help. That it would help her come to terms with what had happened, and how her life had changed.

It didn't.

Even now, twenty years later, she kept people at an arm's length. It was safer than letting them in.

Look what had happened with Reid. One kiss and it had made working together impossible. He'd even slept outside her condo one night when she hadn't come home—and she'd never thought of Reid as the jealous type before. Relationships changed people, made them irrational, unable to think clearly. She didn't want that.

She and Reid, they were a team. They were friends. It was perfect the way it was.

Taking a deep breath, she got up from the table and pulled up the shade. The sunlight was blinding. It was not a day for wallowing. Perhaps she would go out after all. She didn't need a partner or a bunch of friends to do that.

Putting on a summery dress, even though it was mid-February, she threw her laptop bag over her shoulder and left the condo. It was a short drive to Bal Harbor Beach. She'd pick a scenic spot, power up her computer, and do some research while she soaked up the winter sun. Maybe she'd even sip a cocktail.

At first, she didn't notice the black SUV driving behind her. The traffic was thick, being a weekend, and the car stayed hidden behind two other vehicles. It was only when she changed lanes she noticed it veer across behind her.

Nothing suspicious in itself. Cars did that all the time.

She drove on, keeping an eye on the rearview mirror. It was still there, tucked away two cars back. Was she being paranoid? The SUV was just heading in the same direction as her, that was all, along with thousands of other weekenders.

Testing her theory, she took a right onto a wide avenue to go around the block and back to the main road. "It won't turn," she mumbled to herself. "You're just being silly."

It turned.

Crap.

Driving on, she took a left and then another left, until she was heading back to the main road. The black SUV did the same, but by now, the driver would know it was a test. Kenzie's pulse beat a little faster. Who was following her? And why?

As expected, the black SUV accelerated past her as soon as she was back on the road heading toward the beach. It turned off a couple of streets up ahead, wheels screeching on the asphalt.

Thank goodness.

Kenzie pulled into a strip mall parking lot and cut the engine. Her hands were shaking. After what had happened last year, any vehicle displaying suspicious activity scared the hell out of her.

She reached for her phone, stared at it, then put it away again.

No, she couldn't call Reid every time something went wrong. He wasn't her husband, or even her boyfriend—despite having saved her life several times over the last year. To be fair, she'd done her bit too, helping him solve cases that he otherwise might not have solved. They were a team. But that didn't mean he was her knight in shining armor.

It had become too easy to pick up the phone and call him. It was usually her first instinct, and that bothered her. She must resist, and handle this herself.

She opened the window to get some fresh air, but all she smelled was exhaust fumes, so she closed it again. Was this to do with Maria's memoirs? Was someone sending her a message? First the tires in the penitentiary parking lot and now a not-too-subtle tail.

It must be. Well, she wouldn't be put off. Walking away wasn't an option. They needed the names Maria had promised, and she already had a publisher waiting for the book. It was going to happen whether Maria's cronies wanted it to or not.

Kenzie was about to start up again when her phone rang. Glancing at the screen, she saw it was Raoul. She frowned. What was he doing calling on a weekend?

"Hello?"

"Kenzie? It's Raoul."

"I know. What's up?"

He hesitated, put off by the agitation in her voice. "Sorry to interrupt your weekend, but I've found something. I thought you'd want to know."

"Where are you?" Suddenly, the appeal of the beach had vanished.

"At work."

If he was working on a weekend...

"Hold that thought. I'll be there in twenty minutes." She hung up and turned the car around.

Newspaper offices almost never slept. The staff went home at the end of the day, but there was always someone there This was the case when they were working on an ongoing feature where there were constant updates, in which case the entire news team stayed in until the crisis was over.

Large television screens mounted to the walls were tuned to the news channels, the sound down so as not to distract. CNN. BBC. Al Jazeera, RT, and CNC. You could take your pick.

Raoul sat at the desk next to Kenzie's, his laptop in front of him. She could tell by his hunched shoulders he was concentrating hard.

"What did you find?"

He jumped.

"Sorry, didn't mean to startle you."

"It's okay." He looked at her dress. "I hope I didn't interrupt your day?"

What day?

"It's fine, let's see what you got." She sat down at her desk but angled her chair so she could see his screen.

He tabbed to a different browser and pulled up a scanned copy of an old newspaper article. It was faded at the edges, but along the top she read El Mexicano.

Her eyes widened. "What's this?"

"It's an interview Federico Lopez gave to a provincial newspaper back in 1998. He was in prison at the time. GBH, I believe, although the details are sketchy. I searched the local papers in Mexico for any reference to him when he first took over the cartel. Prior to his arrest, he was quite active in the local communities, buying and distributing supplies, building railways and road networks, that kind of thing. According to my source down there, he was something of a local Robin Hood."

Kenzie studied him. Damn, why hadn't she thought to do that?

"Anyway, the interesting thing is he mentions his wife being away. Listen to this." He read from the article, translating as he went.

'My wife, Maria, is currently in France with my son, Matteo. They're spending the summer there with friends.' There's even a family photo with their teenage son.

Maria had her arm around the boy's shoulders, a proud smile on her face.

Kenzie tried to make sense of it. "So what? She spent the summer in France. Lots of people do that."

"She was gone for almost six months."

Her eyes narrowed. "How do you know that?"

"It was on her visa application." Raoul looked pleased with himself. "Back then, all US citizens had to obtain a visa to travel to France, particularly for long stays."

Rubbing her forehead, she asked, "Do you know someone at the visa agency?"

"Not exactly."

Then she got it. "Okay, I don't think I want to know how you got hold of that information, but I'm taking your word that it's reliable. We can't make a mistake about this."

"It's correct. Maria Lopez flew back to the United States on September 17th, 1998, a full six months after she left."

Keith's words echoed in her head. *Double source, Kenzie. Always double source.*

"We need to double-check those details." Although, she had to admit the visa application was compelling.

"I have," he retorted, as if that was a given. "But first, there's something else."

"Oh, right. Okay." She may have misjudged Raoul. "What's that?"

"In the article, Federico mentions she was on vacation with her son."

"Yes?"

"Well, Matteo Lopez didn't go overseas for six months."

"He didn't?"

"Nope. He didn't go at all."

Kenzie shook her head. "And how do you know that?"

"Because he was arrested in California on April 21, 1998." He pointed to a picture on the screen. "Like father, like son."

She looked at the handsome teenager with his mother's dark eyes rimmed with long lashes, his mouth pulled back in a thin line. He couldn't be older than fourteen. "Shoplifting," Raoul explained. "His father's solicitor bailed him out."

Staring at the mug shot, her brain worked overtime. What did it mean, if anything? "I'm not sure any of this is relevant," she said eventually. "Maria could have been visiting friends in France, and her son decided not to go."

"True." Raoul paused for a moment. "But that's not the interesting part."

"There's more?"

"Oh, yeah. Much more." Cheeks flushed, his fingers flew over the keyboard, bringing up yet another tab. "Maria's visa application asked for her hotel details, so we know she stayed at a place called Saint Marcel in Giverny. I looked it up, and they're on Google, but they don't have a website. In fact, the entire village only has about 600 residents."

"Wow, that is small. Unfortunately, I doubt the hotel will have kept records going back twenty-four years."

"Actually." Raoul spun around to face her. "They did."

"Seriously?" Kenzie couldn't believe this guy.

"Well, kind of. They had a guest book that they asked everyone to sign. It was just something they did. I called the hotel and asked for a copy. There was no Maria Lopez staying there during the summer of 1998."

Kenzie's heart sank. "You mean she wasn't there? It was all a farce?"

"She was there, all right," he said, beaming. "Just not under her name."

Her head was beginning to hurt. "How can you possibly know that?"

"Because I sent the hotel a photograph. The owner recognized her immediately. Apparently, she was high maintenance. 'The most glamorous but difficult guest we've ever had,' and that's a direct quote."

Kenzie burst out laughing. "That doesn't surprise me."

"There's something else."

"What?" Raoul was full of surprises.

"Sandrine, that's the owner, emailed me a picture in return. It's a framed photograph that hangs in the reception area of the hotel. It was taken by an amateur photographer after a concert on the grounds in 1998." He clicked his mouse and brought it up on the screen. "Recognize anyone we know?"

Kenzie leaned in. The photograph was in black and white, but her eyes were drawn to a stunning dark-haired young woman in an off-the-shoulder dress. She was smiling, a haughty tilt to her head.

"Maria," she murmured.

She was also heavily pregnant.

13

STEELING HIMSELF, Reid strode into the Miami PD headquarters and flashed his badge.

"Garrett," greeted the officer on duty and waved him through security.

Reid took the elevator to the fourth floor, same as he had every day in the twelve years he'd worked there. The squad room was frantic as usual, with phones shrieking, computer screens glowing, and printers splattering out page after page of case notes.

Lieutenant Perez's voice hollered over everyone. "Ortega, where the hell are we on the Coral Gables homicide? I need an update. I've got the DA breathing down my neck."

Ortega, with whom Reid had a difficult relationship, yelled back. "I'm chasing ballistics. Give me an hour, and I'll have something."

Reid nodded to Detective Ryan, a female officer still earning her stripes. He'd met her last year during the Swamp Strangler case. She was a good cop, and he had a lot of respect for her. She smiled broadly in return. "Good to see you, Lieutenant."

The layout, the sounds, the smells of the squad room still felt familiar, but it wasn't home anymore. Sweetwater was home now.

Perez spotted Reid over the desks and beckoned to him.

"Garrett," grunted Ortega, as he walked past.

Reid gave a curt nod back. It wasn't a warm welcome, but at least they weren't punching each other across the room anymore.

"Come inside." Perez held the door open for him. Reid walked in and eased his tall frame into the chair opposite the Miami PD Lieutenant's desk. As usual, it was covered in reports, printouts, and multicolored pens scattered around like crayons. Reid remembered the LT liked to underline possible follow-ups in red and highlight any salient details he could feed back to management in yellow.

"It's good to see you." Perez leaned back and studied him. "You look well. Driving a desk suits you."

Reid didn't miss the little smirk. His old boss knew very well that despite being a lieutenant, like him, Sweetwater Police Department was understaffed and in addition to driving a desk, Reid also worked on active cases, followed up leads and interviewed suspects. In that respect, the job suited him very well.

He'd never be able to order people around, read reports and schmooze with the higher-up's day in, day out. It'd drive him crazy. No offense to the LT, but leaving Miami PD was the best decision he ever made. Going to work at Sweetwater was the second.

"Thanks. How are things here?"

Perez shrugged. "Same as always. Homicides are on the rise, drugs are rife, nobody respects us cops, and we like to pretend we have a handle on it, when in fact we're screwed."

Same old shit.

Reid snorted. "I hear you."

Perez got up and poured them each a cup of coffee. "It's my special blend," he said, handing it to Reid. "Let me know what you think."

Taking a sip, Reid grunted appreciatively. "It's good. Where did you get this?"

"I can't divulge my sources, you know that."

"Now you sound like Kenzie," he scoffed.

"How is she?" Perez asked. "Last time I saw her, she was black and blue from that awful car wreck she had."

"She's fine." Reid frowned. "Although, her tires got slashed last week at the women's penitentiary, which isn't good."

"A warning?" Perez knew about Maria's memoirs and the deal they'd made with the cartel boss.

"Could be. I might have to assign her some protection."

"Do you think she's at risk?"

"Maybe. I'd tell her to back off, but you know what she's like."

"Hell would freeze over," Perez muttered.

"Exactly."

Glancing at the time on his phone, Perez said, "Let's get down to why you're here. I've got a meeting with the exec committee in ten minutes." He rolled his eyes. "We need to adjust our quotas for the quarter, since the crime stats aren't coming down."

Reid pursed his lips. "Better you than me.".

"Your time will come."

Reid rolled his eyes. "Okay, I'll get to the point. We found a woman in the swamp last week. She'd been eaten by a python."

"I heard. That's not something you see every day."

Reid acknowledged that with a tiny nod. "I think she might have been Cuban or Haitian." The words lingered.

Eventually, Perez frowned. "You think she was illegal?"

"Yeah. She was wounded. Shot in the leg. We found her in the middle of the Glades, miles from anywhere. It's my guess she was trying to get away from someone."

"Except they shot her," Perez finished.

"Well, they shot her, but they didn't kill her. The injury wasn't fatal. It was while she was wading through the swamp bleeding, that a reticulated python wrapped itself around her and squeezed her to death."

"Talk about bad luck," Perez murmured.

Reid grunted in agreement.

"What do you want from me?" He was fidgeting now, eager to go to his meeting.

"I took the airboat down to the coast yesterday," Reid spoke faster, getting to the point. "Through the Glades. I think the traffickers are coming in that way, dropping their cargo off in the Southern Glades, near Homestead. I want to organize a search of that area. They must be keeping the refugees somewhere while they extort money from their relatives. Otherwise, how did this woman escape?"

Perez stared at him. "Do you have any idea how enormous that area is? It's a national park, for Christ's sake. You can't just grab a few guys to help you search it."

"I know, that's why I'm talking to you. Miami PD has the resources to organize such a search."

"You want me to pull my cops off a hundred other cases to search a swamp?" He laughed. "Garrett, you've had some crazy ideas, but this tops them all."

He folded his arms over his chest. "I take it that's a no."

"Damn right it's a no. Now if you don't mind, I must get going. I've got..."

"Yeah, I know. A meeting."

Perez gave him the kind of look he used to give him when he worked there.

"Good luck," Reid called after him.

He was walking back to the elevator when Ryan beckoned him over. "I heard about your snake victim," she said. "Nasty surprise."

He didn't deny it.

"I don't know if this is relevant." She hesitated as if she were trying to decide whether to proceed or not. "But a young boy was admitted to the hospital last week for treatment. They found him wandering in the Southern Glades, dehydrated and malnourished. He kept asking for his mother, although nobody knows where she is. He was alone when they found him."

"Is he Cuban?" Reid asked, his brows shooting up.

"Yeah, I think so. His English is limited."

"Okay, thanks." A surge of adrenalin shot through him. The boy could be related to his snake victim, or if not, perhaps he came over with her. It was worth checking out. "Which hospital was he taken to?"

"Jackson Memorial."

"Thanks. You're a star."

She grinned. "I hope it's a lead."

"I'll let you know."

The boy, Sebastian, was recovering in a ward with three other kids. He was older than Reid had expected—maybe seventeen or eighteen —with dark, curly hair and huge, wounded eyes. He reminded Reid of an injured stallion about to bolt.

"Hola. I'm Detective Garrett." He pointed to himself. "This is Detective Vargas."

Vargas, who spoke fluent Spanish, smiled and took over the questioning. "We'd like to talk to you about what happened? Is that okay with you?"

Sebastian gave a tense nod and peered suspiciously at Vargas, then Reid, then back at Vargas. It was clear he wasn't a fan of the police.

Reid let them speak. He trusted Vargas to get as much information from the boy as possible. No translation needed as Vargas would fill him in later. For now, Reid was content to watch the boy's reactions. Concern. Exhaustion. Fear. Each emotion flitted across his taut features at one point or another. Trying to be brave, but he was a mess inside.

At first, the boy spoke in short, stubby sentences, swallowing his words, but as Vargas drew him out, he became more animated. The kid had spirit; Reid could see it in his flashing dark eyes and the stubborn tilt of his chin. He'd escaped from wherever they'd been kept and made it through the swamp. That's why he was still alive.

An hour later, a nurse came to check on him and politely suggested they wrap it up. Even Reid could see the boy was flagging as exhaustion set in. Vargas wrapped up the interview.

"Gracias." Vargas patted the boy on the shoulder.

He gave a terse nod, then fell back onto the pillow and let the nurse take his blood pressure.

Reid and Vargas left the ward and walked back to the car. "I'll drive while you fill me in." Reid took the keys from his sergeant.

Normally Vargas was the designated driver.

"They came over in a boat," Vargas began, fastening his seat belt. "He didn't know the men who brought them. Four men, all armed with assault rifles."

Reid raised an eyebrow.

"The kid knows guns," Vargas explained with a shrug. "He's also into boxing, martial arts, that sort of thing."

"Is that how he got away?" Reid asked.

"Yeah. They were imprisoned in a cabin in the jungle. I think he's talking about the Glades because he said it was marshy and wet. They were locked in a giant cage, unable to get out. He says they were there for three days."

A cage. Jesus.

"How many of them were there?" Reid asked.

"Ten in total. He was traveling with his mother."

"How did he escape?"

"A man came to the cabin. He was the first person they'd seen since they arrived. He didn't get a look at him," Vargas said before Reid could interject. "His face was covered by a balaclava."

"Convenient," grumbled Reid. What they needed was a lead. Something that would tell them who this guy was.

"He fed them, then unlocked the cage and tried to take Ramona, that's the kid's mother, away. Sebastian went crazy and lashed out, throwing open the cage door. The man fell back onto the floor allowing his mother to escape. Sebastian followed, darting out into the night. He ran, not knowing where he was going, desperately trying to find his mother. Then he heard a gunshot and his mother scream. He knew then that she was dead. So he hid. He was going to go back and kill the man who'd shot his mother, except he got lost."

"Brave kid," Reid murmured. He understood vengeance. Knew what it was like to want to hunt down the person responsible for killing someone you loved. He'd been there.

"A fisherman found him wandering around incoherent two days

later. The kid hadn't had anything to eat or drink for several days. He was barely conscious."

Reid shook his head. Nothing he could say or do would make up for what that boy had been through. "He's a survivor. He'll get through this." That much he did know, although the scars would last a lifetime.

"What's going to happen to him now?" Vargas asked.

"He'll be placed with a foster family until we've verified his mother is indeed dead." He didn't want to think about it, but it was a real possibility that the woman lying in the morgue with a bullet wound in her leg was Sebastian's mother.

"I'm going to get CSI down here to take a DNA swab," he said. "We can match it to the snake victim and see if they're related."

Vargas nodded grimly. "I'll get on it."

14

KENZIE STARED at the image of a much younger Maria Lopez on the screen. There was no mistake. That was her alright. "Oh my God. She's pregnant."

"Correct." Raoul gave a smug smile.

Her brain went into overdrive. "Maria's never talked about another child. As far as anyone knows, Matteo is their only son." She thought about all the articles she'd read on the Morales cartel, Federico Lopez, and his wife. Nowhere was a second child mentioned.

"Perhaps she got rid of it," Raoul suggested.

Kenzie clicked her fingers. "You're right. She got rid of it because it wasn't her husband's."

Raoul shrugged. "We can't know that for sure. Perhaps she wanted to spend her pregnancy in France."

"Think about it." Kenzie jumped out of her chair and paced up and down the aisle. "She goes to France for six months, checks into a hotel under a false name, and then keeps the newborn baby a secret. It has to be an illegitimate child. I'd stake my career on it." Excitement surged through her. "Oh, my God, Raoul. This is huge."

The researcher contemplated this for a moment. "I don't know, Kenzie. He may have known all about it."

Kenzie whirled around to face him. "Did she come home with a baby?"

"I—I don't think so, but I'll have to check. It would need a visa to enter the States, so I doubt it."

"Could you? I'll wait."

She sank back into her chair, tapping her fingers on the desk. Of course, Maria may have flown back with the baby and it died of natural causes in the States, and that was why it had never been mentioned. There could be a completely rational explanation. Except her gut was telling her otherwise.

Raoul tapped away at the keyboard. She didn't watch him, but instead browsed unseeingly through her emails. She couldn't focus on anything else, not until she knew for sure.

Raoul cleared his throat.

"Well, is there?"

He shook his head. "I can't find any visa issued for a newborn baby in September 1998," he said.

"I knew it!" She was up again, pulse racing. "She left the baby in France."

"If she'd aborted it, she'd have been home a lot sooner," Raoul said, warming to her theory. "She must have given it up for adoption."

"That's what I think," Kenzie whispered. "I don't think she had any choice. Federico would have killed her."

"He obviously never found out." Raoul ran a shaky hand through his hair. "But the baby daddy is out there somewhere."

"So is the child," Kenzie croaked. "A child nobody knows about."

"Yet," said Raoul.

Kenzie contemplated this, her head spinning. "I think we should sit on this for a while, just until we've verified everything. The consequences are potentially huge. We need to be sure before we go public."

"Okay, I'll do some digging into what happened to the baby."

"Be discreet," Kenzie urged him. "We don't want anyone to find out about our inquiries. It might make them suspicious."

"Gotcha."

"Also, find out where the son is now. He must be about thirty-eight. Let's see if he's affiliated with the cartel, or if he's managed to get out."

"Will do."

Kenzie put her hands on her hips. There was so much to process. "Do we know what name Maria was going under?"

"Not for certain, but there's only one guest who stayed at the hotel for the entire summer. A woman who went by the name of Nora Molina."

"Nora Molina." Kenzie ran it off her tongue.

"I'm going to crosscheck that name with the clinics in the village. Giverny is a small town, so it won't be hard to find her. There must be a record of the birth somewhere."

"Great idea." Raoul was good. No, scrap that. He was excellent. She was grateful Keith had pushed her to use him. "Thanks, Raoul."

He glowed.

"Let me know as soon as you find something."

"Will do."

Reid woke up with the sun shining in his eyes. He'd forgotten to close the drapes, and it was another blistering day. He blinked, squinting as it burned his retinas, then rolled out of bed to escape it.

The cabin was stuffy as hell. Walking semi-naked into the living room, he opened the sliding doors to the deck and stood there, hoping for some fresh air.

Except it was warm and dry. The weather stations were talking about an entrenched La Niña, which was contributing to a warmer and dryer winter than usual. He couldn't remember when last they'd had rain.

Even the choppy water shimmered as it shot laser-like rays back into the eyes of anyone watching. Reid turned away.

Coffee. Then he'd call Vargas.

After they'd spoken to Sebastian yesterday, they'd decided to search the Glades themselves. The cabin must be somewhere in that vicinity. The Southern Glades was a vast area, but they knew where the snake had been found, and where the fisherman had discovered the boy, which narrowed it down substantially.

Vargas agreed to meet him at his place and from here, they'd take the airboat to the spot where the python had been found. It was the easiest and fastest route, being so isolated. They'd look around for the cabin using the data they had. Maybe they'd get lucky.

Vargas arrived on time and, like Kenzie, walked around the house and approached from the narrow strip of soggy grass at the front. He whistled a greeting, but Reid already knew he was there. He'd heard his Ford Mustang pull up.

Vargas had treated himself to the sports car after their last case had closed. He'd said it was his dream car but secretly, Reid thought it was to impress his girlfriend, the fiery Shannon.

"Sorry to hijack your weekend," he said when Vargas had hopped onto the deck. The young detective was wearing colorful shorts, and a faded green T-shirt with a surf logo on it.

"It's cool. I want to find these guys as much as you do."

Reid nodded. There wasn't much Vargas wouldn't do for the job, which was one of the reasons they got along so well. He went way beyond the call of duty, and Reid pushed him hard.

"Okay, good. Let's go."

They climbed onto the airboat, and Reid started the engine. Vargas cast off, and they were away, heading down the canal and out into open water.

"How far away is it?" Vargas asked. He hadn't been present when the gator hunter had cut open the snake. Reid had sent Dwayne to man the scene, but at that point, he hadn't really thought they'd find a human body inside, let alone a murder victim.

"An hour south," Reid replied, opening the throttle. The engine screamed, and they sped over the windswept surface, barely touching it. The sawgrass turned into a blur underneath the boat. Vargas gave a yell of delight and settled back to enjoy the ride.

"First time?" yelled Reid.

"Yay! this is great!"

Reid chuckled, the sound lost amongst the roar of the engine.

Reid turned the boat, and it drifted out to the side, seemingly weightless, before surging forward again. At speed, that maneuver could be dangerous, but he wanted to show Vargas a good time. It was the least he could do.

"Yeah!" Vargas was loving it.

On they sped until they reached the mangrove forest, where Reid slowed to navigate through the narrow waterways. On either side, roots entwined with branches, twisting into a chaos of foliage. Above them, the trees arched, forming a mystical green tunnel. He often thought it was like something out of a fantasy novel.

"No wind," Vargas commented, as the stiff breeze halted. The white crests disappeared, making the water look like it had been ironed out. Over the soft chug of the engine, they heard the birds clacking as they called to each other. An inquisitive raccoon scampered out onto an overhanging branch to check them out, then, finding nothing of interest, disappeared again. Behind the boat, a flash of a tail was followed by a shallow splash.

The narrow channel widened, the roots gave way, and they broke through the other side. Unhindered, Reid accelerated again. "Not far now," he shouted over the drone.

Fifteen minutes later, they cruised to a stop. Reid let them drift while they absorbed their surroundings.

"It all looks the same," Vargas said, standing up.

"The python was found over there." Reid pointed to an area of hard ground. The water lapped up over the grassy edges, but the raised portion was dry. Apparently, they like it around here.

Vargas peered into the murky shallows. "Are we going ashore?"

"Yeah, let's try to trace the woman's footsteps back to where she came from. This piece of land juts out into the swamp, so there's only one way she could have come."

Reid pulled on a pair of heavy rubber boots and threw a second set to Vargas. "You might want to put those on. Wading through the swamp in tennis shoes isn't advised in the tourist brochures."

Vargas didn't hesitate. "Thanks."

Reid secured the airboat to a sturdy tree, and they set off. At first, the ground beneath them was squelchy and wet, but as they progressed along the peninsula, it got firmer. He pictured the mystery woman running for her life, wounded and in pain, stumbling over hidden roots and small bushes, grazing her hands and knees. "Come on, let's pick up the pace."

Vargas was in better shape than he was, and they hiked for forty minutes before they came to an open area covered in sawgrass and invading cattails. The sun-dried foliage bristled in the midday heat. Beneath their feet, the ground had become soggy again.

Reid spotted a dark shape in the bushes to their left. "Gator," he breathed.

Vargas jumped back. "Shit."

Luckily, the gator was more interested in sunning itself than lunch and didn't move as they sidestepped around it. They waded through the ankle-deep water, weaving around tangles of trees and clumps of bush. "This is like hiking through a jungle," Vargas murmured, as a branch whipped across his face.

"At least it's the dry season," Reid remarked. "And we don't have the humidity to contend with." He took a drink from his water canister, then wiped his mouth on his sleeve. Unlike Vargas, he'd worn a lightweight long sleeve shirt to protect his arms in case they had to fight their way through vegetation. It was coming in useful now, but he could feel the perspiration running between his shoulder blades.

"According to the coordinates we've been given, they found Sebastian around here." Vargas glanced at his phone. "He couldn't have come from the south, which means the cabin must be somewhere north of here."

Reid had come to the same conclusion. "Let's head that way."

"It's getting deeper." Vargas said as the marshy water lapped at their knees.

Reid had studied the map before they'd left. "It gets shallower again further north, and then we're back in the jungle."

They pushed on, pausing every few hundred meters to take their bearings and have a drink of water. Dehydration was a very real risk out here in the middle of nowhere. Sebastian was a case in point.

Sure enough, the water level dropped and soon they were trudging over dry ground again, although the rambling bushes and tall grass made it hard to see where they were going.

"I know we've passed the place where Sebastian was found, but I don't think his wounded mother would have made it this far." Vargas stopped and squinted up at the dappled sunlight. It etched through the cracks in the trees, slicing towards the ground.

"Agreed." Reid stopped a few yards up ahead. "Let's spread out and search this area. I think we're in the right zone."

"It's pretty isolated." Vargas consulted his phone. "But there is a rough track of sorts about three miles east of here. They could be using that as an access point."

"Makes sense," Reid agreed. "The smugglers drop the refugees off by boat, hike to the cabin, then lock them up like animals. Luca, or the ghost, as he's known by Border Patrol, then takes over the management of the prisoners and contacts their relatives to ask for money."

"And when they don't pay up," Vargas muttered. "It's game over."

Reid nodded. "Out here, nobody will ever find them. It was a pure coincidence that gator hunter discovered that engorged python, otherwise, we'd be none the wiser."

They split up. Reid went west while Vargas went east. The plan was to search a mile in each direction, then make their way back to the middle.

Half an hour later, they were back where they started. "Nothing on my side," Vargas said, wiping sweat from his forehead. His dark hair was damp and swept back off his face.

"Same. Let's try northwest and northeast."

They set off at right angles to each other. Reid trod carefully, trying not to make too much noise. He was about to turn around when he heard rustling behind him. He spun around, his hand reaching for his weapon, but it was only Vargas. "Shit, you scared me."

"Sorry," Vargas croaked, his voice hoarse. "But I've found the cabin."

Reid's eyebrows shot up. "Where?"

"Half a mile out. We'd better call for backup. I think there might be someone there. I heard voices from inside."

Reid trailed him as they marched over the knotted ground in the direction Vargas had come from. Sure enough, the trees parted, and in the middle of a small clearing stood a wooden cabin. There was a rickety porch out front, two windows and a door. They drew closer, their weapons drawn. On closer inspection, the structure was sturdier than it looked.

"Can you see inside?" Reid whispered.

Vargas crouched down beneath one of the windows, then tilted his head upwards to take a peek. "No, it's boarded up from the inside."

To prevent intruders from getting in, or to prevent those inside from getting out? He was betting on the latter. A chill ran down his spine. Was this where the trafficked refugees were being kept? Were they in there now? Caged, like animals?

Suddenly, there was a rush of hot air, and Reid smelled smoke.

"What the—?" He glanced around, sensing they weren't alone. "Vargas, did you feel that?"

"Fire!" yelled Vargas, running away from the cabin. "The place is on fire."

That's when he saw it. Giant yellow flames licked at the concrete structure and spread to the surrounding bush. The dried-out vegetation went up like kindling.

"Holy shit," muttered Reid. "Call the fire department. This whole place could go up. It's as dry as hell out here."

"I can't get a signal." Vargas held his phone in the air. The heat from the fire felt like a furnace, fueled by the wind.

"Did you say there were people in there?" Reid ran towards the cabin.

Vargas followed but they couldn't reach the door, the heat was too intense.

"What about the window?" Reid yelled. The bush around them was flickering dangerously. They didn't have long.

Vargas picked up a rock and smashed one window. The glass toppled outwards, as did the rock, landing at their feet. A large wooden plank had been nailed across the window on the inside.

"Shit," muttered Vargas. "What now?"

"Hello?" shouted Reid, hoping someone inside would hear him. "Is anyone there?"

There was no reply. Just the roaring of the fire as the flames got higher.

"It could be empty," Vargas said, rapping on the other window. "Hello? Can anyone hear me?"

Still no reply.

By now, the entire cabin was engulfed in flames and Reid and Vargas had to move back. They turned around, but there was nowhere to go. The bush behind them had gone up in flames. Smoke stretched high into the sky, creating a giant plume.

"Jesus, Mary and Joseph," Vargas hissed. "Now what?"

They were trapped in the middle of a raging inferno.

15

KENZIE HUNG UP. "ANOTHER DEAD END."

She and Raoul had called every hospital and clinic in Normandy, hoping they'd have records going back twenty-four years. Not many did.

"We need a French speaker," he said. "No one can understand my accent." It had been an exercise in frustration.

"I have a contact in Paris," Kenzie said. "I'll call him on Monday and ask him to help us. Right now, I'm going home while there's still some of the weekend left." She glanced out the tinted window at the muted blue sky. It would be sunny for a while still.

Driving away, Kenzie remembered she still hadn't thanked Dr. Murray, the vet, and South Kendall wasn't far from where she was now. She had no idea if he worked Saturdays, but it would be easy enough to stop at the animal hospital on her way home.

A sleek midnight-blue Porsche 911 caught her eye as she pulled into the parking lot. The personalized Miami number plate read ANML DOC. Cute. Was that his?

She parked next to it and walked into the clinic. The front desk was empty, and the waiting room was devoid of people. Perhaps they weren't open.

"Hello?" she called.

There was no answer.

Maybe she shouldn't be here. She checked the operating hours on the door and saw that Saturday afternoons were "by appointment only." Oops.

"Can I help you?"

She spun around to see the man from the roadside pulling off a pair of bloody surgical gloves. For a second, her heart skipped a beat, then she realized he'd been in surgery. Duh.

"Hi. I'm sorry to walk in," she rushed. "I didn't know you were closed."

"We're not, technically speaking." He stared at her for a long moment, then recognition dawned. He broke into a wide smile. Instantly, his eyes crinkled and his face relaxed. "Kenzie Gilmore."

She smiled back. "Guilty as charged. I hope I'm not disturbing you."

"No, I've just performed an ovariohysterectomy on a cocker spaniel, and I'm taking a breather before my next appointment."

It wasn't often Kenzie was rendered speechless. "Oh..."

He laughed. "Surgical sterilization to the layman, or woman."

"Right. Well, I just wanted to say thank you for coming to my rescue last year. I'm sorry it's taken me so long to track you down."

"That's alright. I didn't expect you to. Thanks for returning my jacket."

"Oh, you got it. That's good."

"And your note. I knew who you were, by the way. Or rather, I found out when that news story about the Governor hit the papers. Impressive reporting."

She flushed. "Thanks, although it was a team effort."

"Was that why you were run off the road? They wanted to silence you?"

"Yeah, something like that." They wanted her dead, but she didn't want to seem overly dramatic.

He cocked an eyebrow. "Wow, and I thought my job was exciting."

That made her smile.

"Do you want to join me for a coffee? There's a small cafe across the road. They don't make a bad cappuccino."

"Sure."

They went out into the sunshine and ordered coffees. In the bright light, she noticed the freckles across the bridge of his nose like she had when she'd first opened her eyes by the roadside. His dark hair was lifting in the wind.

"How have you been?" he asked. "You had a nasty concussion when I saw you last."

"It turned out to be mild," she replied. "No lasting effects."

"I'm glad to hear it." He took the coffees and handed her one. They sat down at a wooden table. There was a brief pause.

"How long have you been a vet?" she asked.

"Twelve years now." He nodded toward the clinic. "But I started the practice with a friend from college five years ago. It was always my dream to run an animal hospital."

Judging by the Porsche, he wasn't doing too badly.

"It was busy when I stopped by the other day," she said. "You seem very popular."

He shrugged it off. "We offer a good service, and we're the only veterinary hospital for miles around. That helps."

Modest, too. He must know those women were there because of him, although to be fair, she hadn't seen his partner yet.

"Do you have any pets?" he asked.

She narrowly avoided spluttering on her coffee. "N—No. My job isn't conducive to having a pet. I'm always jetting off somewhere at the drop of a hat or getting myself into trouble. I never know when I'm going to be home."

"Must make relationships difficult."

She glanced at him, surprised by the question, but his expression remained neutral. "Um, yes, I suppose it does."

"Does that mean you're single?" His brown eyes, the color of his cappuccino, were sparkling.

Was he hitting on her? Kenzie hesitated, unsure how to respond. She was saved by her phone ringing. "Excuse me. I'd better get this."

He hid a smile and turned away.

It was Detective Diaz, calling from somewhere noisy. "I can't hear you," Kenzie shouted into the phone. "Can you repeat that?"

There was a roaring in the background, like she was in a wind tunnel.

"Reid and Vargas are where?"

She strained to hear, then her heart skipped a beat. "Where?"

"Oh my God! I'm on my way."

She hung up, her hands trembling.

"Is everything okay?"

"Um, no. I don't know. Sorry, I've got to run." She scrambled to her feet, almost knocking over her paper cup. "Thanks for the coffee."

Without waiting for a reply, she ran off in the direction of her car.

Kenzie drove like a madwoman down the Ronald Reagan Turnpike towards Florida City, before turning west on Ingraham Highway into the Southern Glades. The road was barely more than a dirt track, and she bounced over the grassy ledges, trusting her sat nav programmed with the coordinates Diaz had given her.

"It's bad," the woman detective had warned. "They're trapped near a cabin deep in the Glades. The wildfire is raging all around them. Fire services are on the way, but it's already out of control. The wind is making it worse."

"Please let him be okay," she prayed, as the engine of the Bolt strained and shuddered. The trip had taken a good hour and a half, and these narrow roads surrounded by vegetation were slowing her down even more. In the distance, she could see a plume of lethal black smoke twisting into the sky.

The radio reported hundreds of acres already on fire and spreading fast. This was what the national park services had been worrying about for weeks. The dry conditions, the strong wind, the hot air—perfect conditions for a wildfire.

"We wanted to do a controlled burn," a park official was saying on the radio. "But some idiot beat us to it."

Some idiot? It was arson?

She pushed the accelerator to the floor, willing the electric vehicle to go faster. Finally, she ran out of road and saw a makeshift parking area to the right. She pulled in next to a fire engine and several police vehicles.

A crew of firefighters carried equipment down a path into the bush. Above them, smoke stretched into the air and there was a strong smell of burning.

She took off down the path, following the crew.

"What are you doing? Are you crazy?" A man in a fire helmet yelled at her. "Get back!"

Kenzie skidded to a stop. In front of her, a wall of fire stretched up to the tallest tree. The heat was intense, stinging the hairs on her arms and face. She took a few steps back.

Oh, good Lord. Was Reid on the other side of that?

"I'm with the police," she shouted. "Where's Detective Diaz?"

"Over there." The man nodded towards a cluster of police officers. "But we're warning everyone to get back. If the wind changes direction, we're in serious trouble."

Kenzie swallowed. If the wind changed direction that raging inferno would come straight for them. She ran up to Detective Diaz. "I just got here. What's the latest? Have you heard from them?"

"Yeah, I've got Vargas on speaker. We're trying to pinpoint their location. They've had to retreat down the peninsula to the water, but the sawgrass is burning all around them. I'm not sure they can get back to their boat."

Oh, God. "Is there anything we can do?"

"I'm sending in a chopper," Diaz said. "I had to get clearance from the captain, but we've got to get them out of there."

"How much time do they have?" Kenzie stared at the growing cloud of black smoke hovering overhead like something from an apocalyptic feature film.

Diaz's expression was grim. "Not long."

16

"KEEP WETTING YOUR CLOTHES," Reid told Vargas as they moved further and further south. The ground in front of them smoldered from the heat and patches spontaneously combusted as if by magic.

Every now and then, a scalding ember would land on his neck or arm, burning him. At least he had sleeves; Vargas had nothing but a T-shirt on. Still, he didn't complain. He did what Reid told him and bent down to splash yet more swampy water onto his arms and face. His clothes were soaking wet, as were Reid's, and clung to his arms and legs, making it hard to move.

Behind them, the world was on fire. The inferno drew ever nearer, moving as fast, if not faster than they were going. Fueled by high winds, he knew they were fighting a losing battle.

"It's hard to believe there's so much fire when we're surrounded by water." Vargas stomped out an ember with his boot.

"Yeah, it's the grass, it's acting like kindling. It's so dry out here."

The temperature had flared to well over a hundred degrees. Both men were suffering from heat exhaustion. They couldn't take much more of this.

"Will we make it to the boat?" Vargas held his phone above his head. The signal was weak.

Reid didn't want to give him false hope. "Doubtful. Our best bet is to stay close to the water. To get back to where we moored the boat, we'd have to get over that high ground. If it's not on fire already, it will be soon."

Vargas glanced at the single bar. "I'm losing reception."

"Have they located us yet?" Reid asked. Diaz had been trying to pin-point their location.

"I freakin' hope so. It's still on, but if we lose the signal, they won't be able to find us."

"Yet another reason to stay put," Reid remarked. "They'll send a chopper to our last known location."

"If we can." Vargas stared in shocked fascination as a palm tree went up in flames, disintegrating like some fiery apparition. Another flared up, sending sparks flying in all directions.

"Duck!" Reid pulled him down into the water. They stayed under for as long as possible, while smoke billowed overhead.

Reid popped his head up and took a tentative breath. It wasn't great, but it was doable. Vargas emerged, spluttering. "There goes my phone."

Reid glanced up at the smoke-filled sky. No sign of the chopper. His heart sank. If that bird didn't get here in the next few minutes, they were toast. Literally.

As it was, there wasn't anywhere to land.

The sawgrass around them flared and burst into flames. Shit, now what? There was nowhere left to go. The wind swirled around them, driving the temperature up, making it impossible to breathe. Reid sank down so he was just above the water level. It was slightly better there. He motioned to Vargas to do the same. All around them, the Glades were burning. If they hadn't been stuck in the middle of it, it would have been quite mesmerizing.

Vargas was coughing, smoke invading his lungs. Reid could see by his eyes he was terrified, but fighting not to give in to the panic. His respect for his second-in-command skyrocketed.

"Hang in there," he rasped, hoping he could do the same. His vision was getting hazy. Just as he was about to black out, he heard the faint whop-whop of rotor blades. He glanced up. Sure enough, a big fat chopper was making its way towards them.

"Vargas, it's here!"

The sergeant's blackened face turned skyward, and Reid saw a flash of white teeth. They both stood up and waved, ignoring the flames licking at their legs. Seconds later, a long rope ladder uncoiled towards them. The helicopter hovered just above the flames, fighting the updraft.

"Get on," Reid yelled, pushing Vargas towards the ladder.

His sergeant grabbed hold and began to climb. There wasn't time for him to get up before the flames engulfed Reid, so when his partner had cleared the first rung, Reid jumped for it. He wrapped his arms around the rope and hung on for dear life. Both men dangled dangerously above the flames. There were no harnesses to clip them in, no time for that.

The chopper banked, and Reid felt the heat of the inferno lessen as they gained height. He heaved a sigh of relief, but his strength was ebbing. It was all he could do to hold on. Above him, he was aware of Vargas having the same problem, his legs searching for leverage, finally wrapping around the side of the rope ladder. It stabilized him, but Reid wasn't high enough to do the same. His legs dangled free; he was relying on brute strength to keep him on the rope.

Luckily, they didn't have to go far. The chopper pilot, realizing he was about to lose his cargo, lowered the machine into a fire-free clearing behind where the police vehicles and fire service had converged.

Reid let go feet from the ground and collapsed in an ungainly heap. Through his watering eyes, he saw Vargas dismount, then double up in a fit of coughing. When he was done, he grinned at his partner. "We fucking made it."

Reid was about to reply when the corners of his vision blacked out and he sank back onto the ground. The last thing he saw was a paramedic running towards him, then nothing.

"Reid, can you hear me?" She was pleading now, tears pricking her eyes.

A paramedic had administered oxygen, but he wasn't responding.

"Blood pressure dropping," the paramedic said, his eyes on the monitor. "Let's hook him up to the high-flow oxygen."

"Reid, please wake up."

She saw his eyelids flicker. Yes, that's it. You can do it. She reached for his hand only to find it covered in blisters, so she held his arm instead. His shirt was scorched where embers had scalded him, and there were dark patches on his combat pants where the fire had burned the material. He was likely to have a bunch more burns under that.

Vargas had already left in an ambulance to get checked out. He had some minor burns on his legs from where the flames had reached them, but other than that, he was in good condition. Reid seemed to have inhaled far more smoke and couldn't clear it from his lungs.

He moaned, and his hand reached up to the tight-fitting mask that had been placed over his nose and mouth. "No, don't touch it," Kenzie said. "You need the oxygen."

His hand fell back onto the gurney. They'd moved him into the ambulance, but wanted to get him stable before they took off. The bumpy road meant they couldn't treat him effectively should the need arise.

"Heart one hundred and fifty beats per minute and coming down. He's not showing signs of hypoxia."

That was good. She squeezed his arm. "Breathe," she told him. The oxygen would help clear out his airways. He coughed, which the paramedic took to be a good sign, then gave a ragged rasp before his chest began to rise and fall in a steady rhythm.

"Blood pressure stabilizing," said the paramedic with a smile. "He's conscious."

Kenzie heaved a sigh of relief. The ball of tension in her stomach dissipated. Reid was going to be okay.

"Don't ever scare me like that again," she told him sternly. He'd yet to open his eyes, but she saw his lips curl up underneath the oxygen mask.

"Right, we're ready to go," the paramedic told her. "You coming with us?"

She had her car here, so she reluctantly refused and said she'd meet them at the hospital. Before she got out of the ambulance, she leaned over and kissed him on the cheek. "I'll be there as soon as I can."

All she got was a nod in response, but considering he'd been unconscious only a few minutes earlier, that was good enough.

Kenzie leaped out of the way as more fire trucks hurtled into the clearing, their sirens piercing the air. This was the closest they could get to the blaze. Even so, they had to carry their equipment a good mile to reach the burning cabin.

The sky was alive with the sound of rotor blades as helicopters in rotation dropped water onto the burning national park. It seemed like too little, too late. The sky was an apocalyptic black and the hot wind whipped her hair across her face.

Press vans arrived, including one from the *Herald*. Crap, she had a job to do. She'd been so preoccupied with what was happening to Reid, that she'd forgotten she was a reporter. Keith would kill her if he knew she was here and didn't get the story.

Police officers had cordoned off the rough path leading to the cabin, which meant the media were kept out. That gave her an advantage. She traipsed back down the track, careful to stay out of the way of striding firemen carrying heavy equipment and grim-faced police officers.

She was almost there when a white-clad forensic team overtook her. "Excuse me. Excuse me," came an urgent plea as they stepped past.

"Is someone hurt?" She called after them but got no reply. She quickened her step, not wanting to miss out on the action.

Her phone started ringing. It was Clive, the *Herald's* photographer.

"Yeah?"

"Kenzie, was that you I saw behind the cordon? Can you get me in? I want to take some shots of the blaze and these bastards won't let me pass."

"Something's going down. I'll call you back." She hung up and hurried after the paramedics.

Diaz and an officer from Homestead PD exchanged a few words with the CSI team, and then the police officer led them around the back of the cabin.

"What's happened?" Kenzie asked, trying not to sound too interested. "Is someone else injured?"

"Fatality," Diaz murmured, wiping perspiration off her face and leaving a sooty smudge in its place. "We managed to pull her away from the blaze, but she's been dead for a while."

Kenzie caught her breath. "Another refugee?"

"Possibly. We'll have to get her to the morgue before we can speculate." She looked exhausted, and her job was nowhere near over. Kenzie knew that once the cabin and surrounding vegetation had stopped burning, teams would go in and gather evidence. This was now a crime scene. Diaz wouldn't be getting home before daybreak.

Kenzie put a hand on her arm. "Can I do anything?"

A small smile. "No, thanks Kenzie. Why don't you get yourself home?"

"I'm going to the hospital," she said.

"Give him my best." Diaz smiled. "I'm just glad we got to them in time."

"That was due to your fast thinking," Kenzie said. If Diaz hadn't commissioned the chopper, Reid and Vargas wouldn't have stood a chance. Not in the middle of a blaze like that.

The urge to see the body was too strong to ignore, and she knew Keith would want details, so she crept around the back of the cabin and approached the paramedics. They were hoisting a woman onto the stretcher.

"Do we know how she died?" she asked, in her best police academy voice.

"Multiple bullet wounds," the medic replied, mistaking her for a detective. It was a fair assumption, given that no one other than cops were allowed beyond the cordon. "She was shot several times in the chest."

Interesting. Another homicide in the Glades. And all in the vicinity of the burned-out cabin. "Got an estimate on the time of death?" She'd been around Reid long enough to know how these things were done.

"Minimum, twelve hours maximum twenty-four. You'll have to ask the ME for a more accurate TOD."

"Thanks." She took a couple of photographs with her phone before they took the body away, then had a good look around the crime scene. But of course, the woman hadn't died here. She'd been moved to preserve her body from the fire. Like the mystery woman and Sebastian, she'd been running into the jungle to escape her captors. Like the mystery woman, she hadn't made it.

Another life extinguished, and for what? The pursuit of a dream? A new life in America.

Kenzie sighed, a heaviness settling in her chest. The air was acrid and smokey, making her feel sick. It was time to go. She took a few more photographs of the smoldering cabin and surroundings. It wasn't Clive's standard, but it would have to do. They still weren't letting anyone else in.

The firefighters had doused the cabin in water, subduing the blaze, but the surrounding swampland was still burning. Now it had taken hold it would be hours, if not days, before they got it under control.

She had a quick word with one of the firemen on her way back to the clearing. "Any idea what caused the blaze?"

"This time of year, it's usually lightning." He adjusted his helmet with gloved hands. "But the cabin reeked of kerosene."

She gasped. "It was deliberate?"

"Yes, ma'am. No doubt about it. Someone wanted to burn that

place to the ground, and they damn well succeeded. They also managed to set the Glades alight." He shook his head. "Fucking idiot."

"How bad is it?" Kenzie asked.

"Over two hundred acres already." His voice was grim. "And it's spreading faster than we can contain it. The dry weather hasn't helped. This place was a tinderbox. All it needed was a spark."

It found it in the form of a deliberate fire aimed at destroying evidence.

Perhaps the perpetrator was hoping the body would be destroyed, along with the place the captives had been held. Except the police had arrived faster than expected, thanks to Reid and Vargas, who'd called in the fire. Without their alert, the whole area would have burned to the ground before anyone realized it was ablaze.

It was bad enough the cabin had been destroyed, but at least the firefighters had prevented the inferno from spreading northwards towards the road. Thanks to Reid and Vargas, those communities weren't at risk of losing their homes, although the residents might need to move out of the area for a while to get away from the smoke. It was all-encompassing.

Kenzie's throat burned, and her mouth was dry and dusty. It was time to go. She thanked the fireman before hurrying back up the path to the clearing. With every step, the smoke became less dense, and she began to feel better. She couldn't imagine what it must have been like for Reid and Vargas, surrounded by the fiery inferno with nowhere to turn. How terrifying.

He's okay, she told herself as she got into the car. The air-conditioning was a welcome relief, and she aimed the vent at her face, turning it up as high as it would go. In her rearview mirror, she saw Clive running after her, but she didn't want to waste any more time. She'd forward him the photographs, and he could do with them what he pleased. Right now, she needed to get to the hospital. She needed to be with Reid.

17

REID PULLED the oxygen mask off his face. "I don't need this," he growled at the nurse, who tutted at him.

"Your saturation is still on the low side," she warned him, but he ignored her.

"Where are my clothes?"

"I'm sorry, sir, you can't leave yet. Doctor's orders. You're to stay put until he gives you the all-clear." Reid let out an unsavory exclamation and fell back onto the bed.

"Are you being a difficult patient?" Kenzie walked in grinning. "I'm so sorry," she told the nurse. "I'll talk to him." The nurse shot her a grateful smile and exited the ward.

"Thank God you're here." He pushed himself into a sitting position. "Tell them I'm okay, so I can get back to work."

"You're not going anywhere," Kenzie ordered, sitting on the foot of the bed. "You were in bad shape when they got to you. You need time to recover. It's only been a few hours."

"Vargas doesn't have to," he moaned.

"Vargas didn't inhale as much smoke as you," she pointed out, rubbing a soot smudge off her arm. He knew she was right. Dammit.

He felt so helpless, and he hated hospitals. They smelled like the morgue.

"You look almost as bad as I do," he said, taking in her grimy hair, smudged face, and soiled clothing. "What the hell happened?"

"I took a look around the cabin," she said. "You know, while I was there. They weren't letting reporters through, so—"

"So you took advantage of your relationship with me to poke around."

She grinned. "Something like that."

He shook his head. Typical Kenzie, but he wasn't going to berate her when he was desperate for an update. "What did you find? Tell me everything." He couldn't keep the eagerness out of his voice.

"I was going to."

He slumped back. "Sorry, I just want to get out of here and back to work." He mustn't take his frustration out on Kenzie. He remembered her pleading with him.

Don't ever do that to me again.

"Did they save the cabin?"

He could tell by her expression it was worse than he thought. "No, it was completely destroyed. Unfortunately, it's still too early to go in. Whoever started the fire doused the building in kerosene. It was deliberate, Reid."

He gave a grim nod. "Yeah, we figured as much. I could smell the fuel when we got there. They must have done it moments before we arrived."

"Do you think they knew you were coming?"

"Must have. Or they knew it was just a matter of time. Either way, they got there before we could get inside. Vargas said he thought he heard voices."

She paled. "I hope nobody was inside. It's bad enough they found that woman's body nearby."

"A body?" He jerked upright. This was the first he'd heard.

"Yeah, sorry, I thought you would have heard by now."

"No one tells me anything," he muttered. "What body?"

Kenzie pulled up the photos on her phone and handed it to him. "A woman. She'd been shot in the chest."

Reid zoomed in on the photograph. "It's not point blank. Looks like she was shot trying to get away," he said. "Interesting that it was her chest, and not her back."

Kenzie frowned. "You mean if she was running away, she would have been shot in the back?"

"Yeah."

"Maybe she turned to face her shooter or perhaps she was pleading with him. Who knows?"

Reid gave a slow nod. That was something for forensics to determine. Hopefully, more would be revealed during the autopsy. "I wonder if it was the same caliber bullet," he murmured, thinking out loud.

Kenzie was quick to catch on. "You mean the same as the bullet you found in the snake woman?"

"Same gun, yeah."

"That would make sense. The two bodies were found within a couple of miles of each other, both within easy distance of the cabin."

"That's the connection." Reid reached for the glass of water next to the bed, then realized he couldn't grab it because of the bandages around his hands.

Kenzie's gaze dropped to them, and her expression softened. "Are you okay? That must hurt like hell."

It did.

"I'm fine. Doc says these must stay on for at least twenty-four hours to keep the skin sterile until it starts to heal. It's a pain in the butt, though. Makes doing anything with my hands impossible."

"At least you can still man a desk." A flicker of a smile played on her lips.

"Don't joke," he grumbled. "I hate being out of action."

"I know."

His brow wrinkled as a thought struck him. "How come she wasn't burned?"

Kenzie knew he was referring to the body. "The firemen got to her before the fire did. They moved her out of the way of the blaze. It means evidence around the body has been lost, but at least she's intact."

That was the main thing.

"What about the fire?"

Kenzie grimaced. "The fire is out of control. I was listening to an update on the way over. Most of the Southern Glades is burning, and they're warning the rest will follow. There's a planned controlled burn south of Highway 4 in the hopes it will stop the fire, but that's about all they can do for now."

Reid shook his head. It was unthinkable that one person had set half the state alight.

The doctor came in to check his vitals and take his oxygen saturation again. "You're improving by the minute. I'll be happy to discharge you this evening."

Reid grunted. Not soon enough, in his opinion, but it was better than spending a night in the hospital.

"That's great news." Kenzie smiled at him.

"You'll have to come back tomorrow evening for your dressings to be changed," the doc said, glancing at his hands. "Same goes for those burns on your legs, but I don't think it's reason enough to keep you here."

"Thanks, Doc."

"I'll give you a ride home," Kenzie offered.

"Are you sure? It's pretty far out of your way. I can always get a cab."

"No, I want to." Her lower jaw jutted out which meant she wasn't going to take no for an answer. It would be pointless arguing with her.

"Okay, thanks."

"I am going to find a restroom to freshen up," she told him, getting up. "And a decent coffee, but I'll be back."

"Cool."

He watched her walk from the room, her lopsided ponytail swaying as she went.

Kenzie drove a grumpy Reid home from the hospital. His hands were still bandaged, which made it look like he had enormous paws. It was kind of cute.

"I can't even open the front door," he complained, dropping his keys.

"Here, let me."

They must have given him a wash at the hospital, because he was much cleaner than she was. Her hair and clothes reeked of smoke, but at least she'd managed to clean the smudges off her face. She was desperate for a shower, but she wanted to see to Reid first. He was standing in the middle of his living room, looking a little lost.

"What can I get you?" Kenzie asked.

"A glass of water, and my phone." He pulled a face, and she knew how he hated depending on someone else for his needs.

"Sure."

After she'd done that, he thanked her and sank into one of the wicker armchairs. He didn't have a television, but there was a stereo system and CD player plugged into a wall socket. It was easy enough to switch on. Even he could do that with his bandaged paws. He'd have to listen to whatever was in there, though.

The laptop lay on the table, along with a couple of manilla folders. Case files, no doubt. There was more than enough to keep him busy.

"Okay, if there's nothing else, I think I'll go home," she said.

"Thanks for your help today, Kenz." The way he was looking at her made her stomach flip.

She took a steadying breath. "You're welcome. Are you sure there's nothing else you need me to do?"

"No, you've done enough. I'm sure you're beat as well. Go home, and we'll talk tomorrow."

Tiredness swept over her, but her day wasn't done yet. In all the drama, she'd completely forgotten about Raoul and what they'd discovered. Had he found out anything more?

"Okay, but if you need a lift to work, give me a call."

"I'll get a squad car to pick me up."

He didn't want her help, or he didn't want to ask for it.

There was a slight pause.

"Okay. I'll be going then."

Just leave. Now. Walk out the door.

It was that look.

Okay, she was going.

"Bye."

She opened the door and stepped out into the warm, smoke-filled night. Crazy to think that the wildfire was still burning, only a few miles south of here. A thought struck her, would it spread past the burn line? Would it extend up to Highway 75, eating up everything in its path? If so, Reid's cabin was right in the danger zone.

Nah, she was being overly dramatic. It had been a long day. What she needed was a shower and some food, and then she'd catch up with Raoul before falling into bed.

The drive was uneventful, and by the time she got home, she could hardly keep her eyes open. Fumbling for her keys, she thought about Reid dropping his and smiled. She liked that he'd needed her. It was a change from all the times he'd come to her rescue.

Kenzie was about to put her key into the door when she realized it had been forced open. Someone had jimmied the lock.

What the—?

She reached for her phone to dial 911. The worst thing she could do was go inside. The intruder or intruders might still be there. She hurriedly backed away.

"Hello, 911. How may I help you?" came the operator's voice.

She gave her name and reported the forced entry.

"Are you in the property now?" asked the operator.

"No, I'm outside."

"Stay there. A police officer is on the way."

The lights were off, the place was in darkness. It didn't look like anyone was inside. She couldn't see the telltale glow of a flashlight from outside on the lawn and they wouldn't be able to see anything without one.

No thumps or voices. Just a heavy silence, made heavier by her trepidation.

Eventually, a squad car pulled up. An officer she didn't recognize jumped out and approached the building. "Are you Mrs. Gilmore?"

"Miss, yes."

"You make the 911 call?"

"I did."

"This is the property?"

"That's right." She showed him the front door and stood back while he entered. "You see anyone come out?"

"No, it was in darkness when I got here. I don't think there's anyone inside. I've been here for about fifteen minutes."

He nodded and moved in, his weapon in one hand, his flashlight in the other. Slowly, he moved into the living room. Kenzie followed.

"Stay back, please miss," he told her. She stopped walking but didn't go back outside. This was a waste of time. Whoever had been here had already gone.

She switched on the light, and the officer grunted and turned off his flashlight. "Thanks."

"No problem."

Then she gasped. The living room was in shambles. The sofa cushions had been pulled out, the photos on the sideboard had fallen over, the drawers were open, even the television cabinet had been emptied, wires spilling out onto the floor.

On the wall, someone had written:

BACK OFF... OR ELSE.

18

Kenzie and the police officer stared at the ominous message for a full minute before he turned to her and said, "I'd better call this in."

She nodded, her head spinning. First the slashed tires and then the black car following her. What did it mean? Was it one of Maria Lopez's enemies who didn't want her to publish the memoirs for fear of what they might contain?

"What?" snapped Reid when she called to tell him what had happened. "I'm coming over."

"No, that's okay, you're exhausted. I'll stay at a hotel tonight."

"Don't be ridiculous." His tone was firm. "I'll be there as soon as I can. And put the uniformed officer on the line, I want him to post a man outside tonight."

"I'm not sure it's worth all this fuss," Kenzie replied. "Whoever was here has gone now."

"They were looking for something specific, that much is obvious. If they didn't find it, they might decide you're the appropriate person to ask."

She hadn't thought of that.

"Okay," she said, suddenly feeling vulnerable. "You can come over."

. . .

"Sorry about all this." She pulled a face as Reid strode into the condo an hour later.

He shrugged it off. "It's not a problem."

She glanced at his bandaged hands. "How did you get here?"

"Uber." He sidestepped a forensic expert who was looking for fingerprints and studied the writing on the wall. "Capital letters. Written in... What is that? Red marker pen?"

"I'd guess lipstick," Kenzie supplied.

He raised an eyebrow. "A female intruder?"

"Or working for one."

He turned to face her. "You think Maria Lopez is involved?"

She sighed. "I don't know. I wouldn't have thought so except she's been getting death threats, so maybe whoever is sending her the masks is also trying to scare me off."

"Back off... or else," Reid read out loud, then he looked around at the mess. "If their aim was to leave a message, why ransack the place? Any idea what they were looking for?"

"Notes on the book? Anything Maria might have told me?" She shrugged. "It's anyone's guess."

"Has she told you anything confidential? Anything other members of the cartel wouldn't want getting out?"

"No. We've talked about her childhood and how she met Federico. We haven't even gotten to the organizational stuff yet." Kenzie thought about the six-month vacation in France. The unwanted pregnancy. The baby left behind. Surely it couldn't have anything to do with that.

"What?" said Reid.

"Nothing."

"You've had a thought. What is it?"

She exhaled. He knew her too well. "Nothing. It can't be related. Nobody knows about it."

"Knows about what?" He put his hands on her shoulders. "Kenzie, tell me what you know."

Glancing at the forensic techs peeling tape off the side of the cabinet, she lowered her voice. "Not here."

They went into the bedroom and Kenzie closed the door. "Promise you won't repeat a word of this." Her eyes bore into his.

"I can't—"

"Promise, Reid, or I can't tell you."

He sighed. "If it has to do with Maria, I need to know."

"It's not. Well, it is, but it's nothing to do with the case. It's a personal matter."

Reid sat down on the edge of the bed. "Kenzie, you're not making any sense."

She stood in front of him, looking down. "In 1998, Maria spent six-months in France. Federico didn't accompany her."

"So?" His forehead furrowed in confusion.

"We found a photograph of her taken at a hotel during her stay there. In it, she's heavily pregnant."

Reid's eyes widened.

"When we contacted the hotel, we discovered she'd checked in under a false name."

"You don't think the child was Federico's?" He'd connected the dots immediately.

"She left the baby there," Kenzie said in answer to his question. "Federico couldn't have known about it, although that is not confirmed."

"Wow." There was a pause as that sank in. "That's a big secret."

"I know." Kenzie flopped down beside him. "No one knows what became of the child. Raoul, my assistant, is looking into it."

Reid digested what she'd told him.

"What about Maria?" He cocked an eyebrow. "Does she know you know?"

Kenzie shook her head, her voice a whisper. "No, nobody does. That's why it can't have anything to do with this." She waved her hand towards the door.

"Unless someone is trying to warn you off before you find out."

It was a possibility. "But who? It can't be Maria. She wants the book written. It's going to make her famous. It's also going to get us the list."

Reid scratched his chin with the back of his bandaged hand. "That depends on who the illegitimate child is. Now that Federico is dead and Maria's incarcerated. . ." He left it hanging.

Kenzie gasped. "You think the illegitimate child is making a play for the cartel?"

"I don't know. I'm just speculating."

Kenzie dwelled on this for a while, then shook her head. "I don't know. If nobody knows who the child is, then it probably doesn't know who its birth mother is either."

He grunted in agreement.

"And even if it found out," she continued with her train of thought. "Maria used a fake name. There'd be no way to trace her."

"Except you did."

"It's a stretch," Kenzie said after a beat. But then there were the slashed tires and the black SUV.

"Yeah. A big one."

She bit her lip. "Hey, Reid."

He looked up.

"Could you do me a favor?"

"If it's within my power."

It was just like Reid not to agree right away. Not because he was difficult, but because he didn't want to make a promise he couldn't keep.

"I need to tell you something first, and please don't be mad."

He frowned. "I hate it when you say things like that. Why would I be mad?"

"Because I didn't mention this earlier."

He didn't reply.

She took a deep breath and told him about the SUV that had followed her home.

Deep lines appeared on his forehead. "You're absolutely sure it was tailing you?"

"Yes, I drove around the block to check, and it followed me.

When we got back on the highway, it zoomed off into the distance. Whoever was driving knew that I was on to them."

"Shit, Kenzie. You should have said something. First your tires were slashed, then you were followed, and now this. You need protection."

"I need to find out who slashed my tires and who's following me," she reasoned. "Then I'll know who broke into my apartment and why."

He scowled at her. "I don't like this. We can't fight an invisible enemy."

She shot him an appeasing smile. "That's where you come in. It happened on Saturday morning around ten o'clock. If you track my movements on those license plate recognition cameras, you'll see who was tailing me. It was a black SUV. That's all I know."

"You didn't get a plate."

She was still kicking herself about that. "It stayed two cars behind me, and I wasn't sure it was following me until I took the detour. By then, I was too frazzled to take down the plate."

"Don't worry. I know it's scary, particularly after what happened last time. Let me see what we can do, okay? There are a couple of cameras on that route. One of them might have caught them."

She touched his arm. "Thank you."

They waited until the CSI investigators had gone before they collapsed on the couch. There was a nature documentary on the TV, but Reid had already leaned back and closed his eyes. He was shattered. Kenzie was going to get him a pillow and blanket, but her eyes were drooping, too.

I'll just shut them for one minute.

It was her last thought until she woke up with her head on Reid's shoulder, the sun filtering in through the semi-open shades, throwing stripes of light across the red lipstick on the wall.

19

REID OPENED his eyes and felt Kenzie's soft hair against his cheek. He lay still, savoring the silky texture and warmth of her head against his shoulder. For a fleeting moment, he wondered what it would be like to wake up like this every morning.

But she hadn't wanted that. Friends, that's what she'd said. No complications, nothing to derail their partnership. So be it.

Shifting, he tried to wriggle out from beneath her without waking her up. It didn't work. She murmured something and snuggled into him.

He froze, unsure whether to extricate himself and stand up or stay put and wrap his arm around her. While he was deciding, she snaked an arm around his waist, and shifted her head onto his chest.

Could she hear his heart pounding?

He fought the urge to touch her, to stroke her head. Then he remembered the way she'd looked at him after he'd spent the night in his car outside her condo. Disappointment. Her eyes seemed to say: Why are you doing this?

With his bandaged hand, he moved her arm off him and sat up. Her eyelids fluttered open.

"Sorry," he murmured. "I didn't want to wake you."

"Oh, God." She bolted upright. "I fell asleep on you, didn't I?"

"Yeah, but it's okay, I was too tired to notice."

She gave him a strange look, and he grimaced. That hadn't come out right.

Looking away, he asked, "Mind if I freshen up?"

"Go ahead." She ran a hand through her disheveled hair. "What time is it?"

"It must be about eight." The sun was shooting rays across the room.

"Crap, I'd better call Raoul." The awkwardness already forgotten.

Reid strode to the bathroom. In the background, he could hear her on the phone, crisp, focused. Her mind on Maria Lopez, not the break-in that had occurred last night.

"Coffee?" she asked when he got back.

"Yeah, thanks."

Her gaze dropped to the splash marks on his shirt, and his damp hair.

"Washing one's face in forensic gloves without fingers is quite challenging," he explained.

She laughed, easing the tension. "I can imagine. How are you feeling?"

"Much better, but I can't wait to get these damn things off." He held up his bandaged hands.

"How are you going to drink your coffee?" she teased. "Do you need a straw?"

"Actually, that's not a bad idea." He chuckled. "But I think I can manage." He had to pick the mug up with both hands, but it wasn't as hard as he thought.

"I need to get ready for work," she said. "Do you need a ride home?"

"I'm good." The Glades was out of her way. "I'll catch a ride with the officer outside. They'll send a replacement tonight." As she opened her mouth to complain, he held up a hand. "I insist. Just until we know who's intimidating you and what their intention is."

Kenzie relented. "Okay, fine.

Reid looked around for his phone. He'd taken it out of his pocket last night before falling asleep and wasn't sure where he'd left it.

"It's probably down the side of the sofa," Kenzie said. "It's like a black hole down there. Sucks everything in."

He felt between the cushion and the side. Sure enough, his phone was there.

"Holy shit," he exclaimed, after pawing at the screen to turn it on. "Twenty-seven missed calls and twelve text messages."

Kenzie frowned. "Is everything alright?"

"Something's happened." He clenched his jaw. "Damn, I knew I shouldn't have turned my phone off. For once I wanted a good night's sleep, you know?"

"I know."

"Jesus!" The bottom fell out of his world.

"What is it?" Kenzie put a hand on his shoulder. "You've gone white."

"I—" he drifted off, unsure how to put into words what he'd read.

"Reid? What is it?" There was genuine panic in her voice now.

Fuck.

Blood roared in his ears. White noise, preventing him from thinking clearly. "I didn't hear it..." he muttered, his head spinning. "I didn't know."

Kenzie grabbed the phone out of his hands.

"Oh, my God." She looked up at him, horrified. "Your cabin burned down last night."

He nodded, his throat burning. "If I hadn't turned it off... I could have been there. Done something."

There were other messages, which she read out loud.

From Vargas: *Reid, the blaze is spreading. Are you okay?*

Monroe, the duty sergeant: *Lieutenant Garrett, please respond. The wildfire is approaching Highway 41.*

Vargas again: *Reid, please call me when you get this.*

His latest recruit: *Boss, it's Hamilton. If you're at home, please evacuate. The fire is coming your way.*

And finally, several from the crisis alert team at the fire department. EVACUATION NOTICE. PLEASE LEAVE YOUR HOMES AND EVACUATE THE AREA. THIS IS A FIRE ALERT.

And he'd ignored every single one of them.

He hung his head.

"You didn't know," Kenzie said quietly.

"I should have been there."

"If you'd been at home, you could have died in the blaze."

He stared up at her, his brain glitching out. Was that true?

"Think about it," she urged. "You were exhausted. You went out like a light, there's no way you would have heard those texts. Your phone is set to silent anyway."

"They would have gone door to door. Made sure everyone was out."

"You never hear anyone knocking on your door," she reminded him. "Seriously, Reid. It's a blessing you were here."

Kenzie never used that kind of language, but she was serious now. Her blue eyes boring into his, pleading for him to understand, to get it.

"Ugh!" He punched the screen in annoyance, then ripped the bandage off his right hand to make a call. Right now, his damaged hand was the last thing on his mind.

"Hamilton, it's Reid. Where are you?"

Boss, thank God. We were so worried. Are you okay?

"I'm fine. What the hell happened? How'd the wildfire spread so fast?"

He listened while Hamilton filled him in on the details. The wind had increased to ninety miles per hour, fueling the fire. Emergency services couldn't contain it. The burn-line didn't work, and once it jumped the road, there was no stopping it. The river of grass went up like kindling.

"I need to survey the damage. Can you pick me up? I'm at Kenzie's place in Bay Harbor Island"

A pause.

Sure, no problem. I'm leaving now.

Kenzie rested a hand on his shoulder. "I don't know what to say except I'm sorry."

"It's not your fault." He sank back down onto the sofa but couldn't get his brain into gear. He was still in shock. Everything was gone. His house, his belongings, the few items he cared about.

"What are you going to do?" she whispered.

"I'm going to survey the damage, first and foremost." He looked wearily up at her. "Then I'm going to go to work and find the fucker who did this."

Kenzie bit her lip. "Is there anything I can do to help?"

"Stay away from Maria Lopez for the time being." His tone was harsher than he meant it to be. "Until we figure out who's targeting you, don't visit the penitentiary. It's not safe."

Kenzie stuck out her chin. "What about the agreement? If I don't write the book, she's not going to give us the list."

"To hell with the list," he growled. "Your life is more important."

She stared at him for a long moment. "Okay."

What? No argument?

"Good."

Reid paced up and down the living room, downing copious amounts of coffee until Hamilton arrived. By then, he was buzzing with an angry energy. "I'll call you later," he said to Kenzie, before he left the house.

"I'm sorry, Reid," she murmured, as he left.

"Not your fault." Neither of them could have seen this coming.

"You know you can stay here until you sort something out."

"Thanks." He hadn't thought further than the next hour yet, but it was nice of her to offer. Perhaps it wasn't so bad. There was a chance the fire had only grazed the house, not burned it to the ground. Some residences had been spared; others obliterated.

At first, he'd used the remote cabin in the Glades to hide away from the world, now he enjoyed living there. The wide-open spaces, the wildlife, the views. So different from the urban sprawl and crime-ridden messiness of the city. It had become his sanctuary.

Now it could be gone.

As they drove across town, Reid had one thought in his mind: To find whoever had done this—and make him pay.

20

KENZIE THOUGHT LONG and hard about going to the prison to see Maria. Reid had been emphatic, and she didn't want to go against his wishes, but she was conscious of all those cartel members out there who were still operating, still importing drugs into the United States.

Once this book was out, they could arrest all of them like they'd done with the Florida group. She thought about the lives that would save. Maria wanted fame and fortune, and she would get it. Kenzie wasn't going to break her promise.

Another part of her was glad she wasn't backing down. To hell with those who sought to intimidate her. Kenzie Gilmore did not intimidate easily. She didn't like bullies, and she wasn't about to let them get the upper hand.

On the flip side, however, she would be more cautious. If she saw that black SUV tailing her again, or any vehicle for that matter, she'd take down the license plate and report it to the police.

That settled, she got out of her car and walked into the prison.

Maria was in a better mood today and they got through a lot of material. She talked about her relationship with Federico, how he worked his way up through the ranks with his wife by his side.

"We were a good team," Maria said, not without a touch of nostalgia.

"Let's talk about when your husband got arrested for GBH." Kenzie watched the cartel boss's reaction. Her expression remained impassive.

"That was a terrible time. He was imprisoned for a year, and let me tell you, Mexican jails are no joke."

"So I've heard. How did you cope without him?"

A flicker of an eyelid, so slight, she almost missed it. "Fine, although the heat was on, so I left the country for a while. I went overseas."

"France, wasn't it?"

Maria's eyes narrowed. "How do you know that?"

"My researcher dug it up. I think it was mentioned in an interview your husband gave before he went to prison."

She relaxed. "I stayed with friends in Bordeaux. My son came with me."

Liar.

"I've always wanted to go to France," Kenzie said wistfully. "It sounds so romantic."

Maria didn't comment. Instead, she gazed at Kenzie, a steely glint in her eye.

"It can be dangerous," she said after a beat. "Especially for a woman alone."

"Is that right? What a shame. It's such an intriguing place."

"Bad things have been known to happen there. Very bad things. I'd reconsider if I were you."

There was a pause. You could cut the tension between them with a shiv. "I'll take that under advisement."

Maria tilted her head. "That would be wise."

Kenzie put her hands in her lap so Maria wouldn't see them trembling. "Okay, moving on..."

It was toward the end of the interview that Maria dropped her final bombshell. "This'll be our last face-to-face meeting. I'm being transferred to another facility."

"What?" Kenzie was thrown. How had she only thought to inform Kenzie now? "How are we going to discuss the book?"

"The prison will give me remote access." A nonchalant shrug. "It's the modern age. We can conduct these interviews via Zoom."

It took a moment to sink in. Remote visiting hours. Was that even a thing? Would they make special allowances for Maria? "Are you sure? Will that be allowed?"

Maria flashed her an enigmatic smile. "Don't worry so much, Kenzie. You still get to finish the book. I will make sure of it." Maria wanted these memoirs published as badly as she did.

Kenzie felt like the carpet had been yanked out from under her. This was all so sudden, she couldn't get her head around it. "W— When are you leaving?"

"Soon." She wouldn't say any more than that.

"Is this to do with the death threat?" Kenzie thought of the sinister painted mask left in Maria's cell.

"Yes, they want to move me out of the state, somewhere where I'm not so well known." She smirked. "Like it's going to make a difference."

This was a blow. It would be much harder getting Maria to open up over a Zoom call, even harder getting her to give them the names they needed to make the arrests.

"Do you know where?"

"They wouldn't tell me for security reasons. Nobody knows. Orders from above." She laughed. "Whoever that might be. Maybe you should ask your detective friend."

Reid didn't know, or he would have said something. Agent Wilson was Kenzie's bet. Reid had spoken to him about the rumors regarding Torres and the subsequent death threats Maria had been getting, and he'd decided to act. Taking her out of the state would also get her away from any friends or sympathizers inside the penitentiary, anyone who could be feeding her information.

"Well, nobody informed me."

"I just did."

Kenzie forced a smile. "Thank you."

The guard called time, and Kenzie glanced up in alarm. "How will we get in touch?"

In a rare gesture, Maria reached out and touched her hand. "Don't worry. It'll be fine, you'll see."

Kenzie nodded, then watched her rise and walk back to the guard.

"They're moving her," Kenzie told Reid after she'd left the prison. She sat on the stairs outside, her phone in her hand and the sunshine on her face. It always felt warmer after a meeting with Maria. "Did you know about this?"

"No. Wilson didn't say anything. Not that he would. It's outside my remit."

"I would have thought he might have mentioned it since he agreed to the deal," she pointed out. "My interviewing her is going to be much more difficult now, if not impossible."

"I'm sorry, Kenzie. I can't deal with that now."

Shit, how could she have forgotten?

"I'm sorry," she blurted. "Is it really bad?"

"Yeah, there's nothing left." His grim tone said it all.

"I'm so sorry. Is there anything I can do to help?"

"Not unless you can rewind the last twenty-four hours, no."

She bit her lip. Reid sounded as dejected as she'd ever heard him. "What are you going to do now?"

A sigh. "I don't know. Call the insurance company, I guess. In the meantime..." He trailed off.

"You can always stay at my place," she offered again.

"Thanks, but I don't want to put you out. I'll find somewhere near here. I'm still rummaging through the remains." It sounded like he was talking about a body.

"Okay, but call if you need to talk."

He hesitated. "Thanks."

Like hell he would. That wasn't Reid's style. He'd never opened up to her about anything in the year and a half she'd known him, not really. He'd talked about Bianca, his ex, who'd died in the botched op, but in matter-of-fact terms. No emotion. Like he'd filed it away so it couldn't hurt him. That was how he coped.

One day, she worried, it would all come flooding back, and he'd have to deal with it.

"I've got Hamilton looking into those traffic cams you asked about. I'll let you know as soon as we find something."

"Don't worry about that now," Kenzie stressed. "It can wait."

"Your safety is a priority," he barked. She could tell he wasn't in the mood for arguing.

"Okay, thanks."

"Speak later." And he hung up.

She could only imagine what he must be going through. His entire life reduced to rubble. How would she cope in those circumstances? She'd be devastated.

Part of her wanted to go to him, to be there for him, but she knew he wouldn't accept her help. He couldn't get away from her fast enough this morning. Ever since they'd had 'the talk,' he'd distanced himself from her. Perhaps she'd been foolish thinking they could just go back to how they were before they'd kissed. Before feelings had gotten involved.

Nothing was the same after that.

Putting thoughts of Reid aside, Kenzie placed another call. This was to someone she hadn't spoken to in a while.

Carlisle Harrington.

Source. Fixer. Nefarious deal broker.

Carlisle knew everyone worth knowing in Miami. His reach extended to Arab oil magnates, Russian oligarchs, and Czech arms dealers. He brokered deals worth billions, taking a small cut for himself in the process.

They'd crossed paths last year when Kenzie had investigated a particularly nasty loan shark. Since then, they'd worked together a few times. It was turning into a mutually beneficial relationship, and one Kenzie didn't want to abuse.

It was always like this. She'd leave a message, and he'd get a hold of her in due course, probably using an untraceable burner phone. Carlisle didn't believe in taking chances.

My business depends on discretion, he'd told her once. *That is why I am a ghost.*

She left a message requesting a meeting, and then got to her feet. Darn, she was stiff. Sleeping on the sofa hadn't done her neck any favors. Or Reid's chest, she couldn't be sure which one.

A text message came through. Keith wanted her back at the office. They had features to discuss, promotional material for the book release, and she had yet to give him an update on the trafficking organization.

"We've got to capitalize on the momentum from her arrest," Keith boomed from behind his desk. Kenzie stood in the doorway; she hadn't even said hello yet.

"I thought that's what we were doing."

"Online readership is petering off. People are getting tired of Maria Lopez. We need something fresh, something to renew their interest."

Like an illegitimate love child?

Except she didn't say that. Some secrets had to be kept—at least for the time being.

Bad things have been known to happen there.

"I'll come up with something," Kenzie said, sighing. "How about life inside Miami's largest women's prison?"

"Good. Good." Keith clicked his fingers. "I like it. Let's run with that this week. Send it to Sonya to summarize for the website." The content on the blog was always shorter than in the paper itself. Online viewers had shorter attention spans.

Raoul was waiting for Kenzie when she got back to her desk. "I found it," he announced.

"Found what?" She sat down, spinning her chair around to face him.

"The clinic where Nora Molina gave birth."

Kenzie gaped at him. "You're kidding!"

He grinned. "It's a small nursing home just outside the village, run by a bunch of nuns."

"It's Catholic?"

"Yeah."

That made sense.

"How do you know she gave birth there?"

"I called them."

Kenzie shook her head. "You spoke to a French nun?"

He gave her a funny look. "Yes, her English was pretty good, actually."

"Okay." Raoul was a godsend. It was something she'd have done, if she'd had the time, but was amazed he'd taken the initiative.

"Sister Michelle remembered Nora," he added. "Feisty lady, she said. Lots of spirit."

That sounded like Maria. "What happened to the baby?"

"Nora gave it up for adoption. The nuns arranged it, although they wouldn't give me the adopted parents' details."

That was understandable. "Did you get the child's name?"

His shoulders sank. "No, that's the disappointing part. They decided to let the adoptive parents name the child, so there is no name in the register."

Damn. That would make finding out who the child was even harder. "Do we know what sex the baby was?" Kenzie asked.

Raoul grinned. "We sure do. Maria Lopez gave birth to a baby girl."

21

THE SUN BEAT DOWN, glinting off glass shards. All that was left of his house was a smoldering stack of wooden boards, smashed windows, and debris. It was as if the fire had sucked in the entire structure, then spat it out again, discarding the remnants over the scorched ground.

There were some unrecognizable items that could have been furniture, but it was impossible to know for sure. They could also have been part of the deck or the boarded walkway. The only thing that remained unchanged was the murky water, lapping at the singed edges of the canal as if to say, what's all the fuss about?

"There's nothing I can do here," he snapped, turning away.

Vargas grimaced in sympathy. "It will have to be rebuilt from scratch."

Reid felt reality ebb away. How could his house be gone? How could he be standing here on this charred patch, staring at what was once a wooden structure—three wooden structures, in fact—containing everything he owned? At any moment, someone was going to come and wake him up and tell him it wasn't real. That it was all a terrible nightmare.

Even his truck had been totaled. He kicked a twisted mass of smoldering metal and snorted in disgust. Damn his blasted hands. If he'd been able to drive, at least he would still have his pickup.

"You staying at Kenzie's, boss?" Vargas asked him, as they got back into the squad car.

Kenzie. The break-in. The writing on the wall. Perhaps he should stay with her, but not because he wanted to, but because it would be protection against whomever was intimidating her.

He thought about her warm head on his chest, the scent of her hair.

Things he couldn't have.

"No," he said. "Take me to the Gator Inn."

By some quirk of fate, the sleazy, flea-bag motel had miraculously escaped the blaze, along with Smiley's, a rowdy dive bar, and the small Everglade community that lived alongside it. Everything to the east was destroyed, including a hiking tour company, a gator farm, and the Miccosukee Indian gift shop. The fire had come dangerously close to Kendale Lakes, a neighborhood northwest of Miami, but thanks to the aptly named East Coast Buffer Water Preserve area, it had lost traction and died out.

They stopped at a nearby supply store so Reid could buy some new clothes, bandages, and a toothbrush, along with a duffel bag to keep them in. In the motel room, he stared at it lying on the bed.

His worldly possessions reduced to one bag.

The troubling thoughts were interrupted by his buzzing phone. "Yeah?" he snapped, without looking at the screen.

"Lieutenant Garrett, it's Carlton here from the forensic lab. We've got the results of that DNA test you ordered."

He caught his breath.

"Oh, yeah. Was it a match?" He wasn't relishing telling Sebastian that he was right, his mother wasn't coming back.

"No, sir."

"Wait." He frowned. "It wasn't a match?"

"No, sir. The person that DNA belonged to was not related to the boy."

He exhaled. That was something, at least. The boy's mother might still be alive.

After a long, hot shower, he redressed his hands as best he could—the nurse at the hospital was not going to be pleased—and took an Uber to work. He'd organize a vehicle from the police carpool until he could get a replacement.

"I hope you have insurance," Monroe said to him as he walked into the precinct.

He grunted. "Yeah, but I'm not sure it'll cover that."

"Sorry to hear about your place, boss," said Dwayne. "Beatrice is cooking a pot roast, and she'll bring it over later."

"Thanks," he replied, moved by the gesture. Beatrice was the nurturing type, and this would be the second time she'd come to his assistance. He had to endure several other murmurs of sympathy before he got to his desk. It seemed everybody knew about his current predicament.

"Where are you staying, boss?" asked Hamilton, a rookie cop fresh out of the academy.

"The Gator Inn."

It would mean nothing to the young detective who hadn't stepped foot in the Glades. Not many people did unless they had reason to. He hadn't until he'd moved there.

He got to work, reading reports and trying not to think about his house. After a while, Diaz came over. "Here's the autopsy report on the victim found near the cabin." The new detective had been amazing coordinating the fire department and CSI teams at the crime scene. He told her so now.

"Just doing my job, sir," she said stoically, in classic Diaz style. "They're still filtering through the evidence."

"Anything useful in the autopsy?" Reid asked.

She pulled up a chair. "Yeah, there were a few things. Sorry about your house, by the way."

He grunted in acknowledgement.

Diaz wasn't one for sentiment either and surged ahead with the report. "The victim was in her mid-twenties. We haven't identified her yet, but she died from multiple bullet wounds to the torso. You were right, she was facing the shooter. She would have looked her killer right in the eye."

"Poor woman," he muttered. At least it was quick. With that many gunshot wounds, she wouldn't have known what hit her.

"She's not in any system in the US, which makes me think she could be a Cuban refugee, like the last vic. Her clothes are pretty good quality and available in many stores in Havana."

"We can assume she paid her killer to smuggle her into the States." Reid clenched his jaw. They needed to find this fucker before he killed any more innocent people.

"Agreed," said Diaz, matter-of-factly. "There is one other thing. She had a dove tattoo on her right shoulder."

Dove tattoo.

His heart sank.

"Get Rosa, the maid from The Miami Herald in here. Didn't she mention something about a tattoo?"

Diaz paled. "God, yes. You're right. A bird tattoo. Her sister had one."

Reid gave a tired nod. "We may have found Daniela Martinez."

Reid watched as Rosa collapsed into Kenzie's arms. This time, the body she'd come in to identify was the right one. Or the wrong one, depending how you looked at it. Great sobs wracked her frame, her legs barely holding her up. Kenzie led her out of the viewing room and into the sterile corridor. There were four connected plastic chairs, the only chairs in the whole corridor, positioned outside the door. They also seemed to be clinging to each other as if for support. The two women sat down.

"I'm so sorry, Rosa." Kenzie stroked the woman's back.

"She was so young," the woman moaned. "All her life she dreamed of coming to America."

It was tragic. Reid couldn't stand to look at her anymore. Her pain was too visible, too raw.

"Will you see she gets home safely?" he asked Kenzie.

She gave a small nod, her blue eyes clouded with sorrow.

As Reid emerged into the morgue parking lot, his phone buzzed. It was the insurance company calling to discuss his claim.

"Which one's that?" he barked. "The house or the car?"

By the time he got back to the police department, he was fuming. The home insurance company had told him his coverage didn't include acts of God.

"God wasn't the one who burned down my fucking house," he'd yelled at the astounded operator. "It was a murdering scumbag people smuggler."

Too much information. He ought to know better.

His claim was being transferred to the disputes department. Little did he know, his day was about to get a lot worse.

"Boss?" Diaz hurried up to his desk.

"Yeah?"

The detective's eyes were haunted. "They've found more bodies at the cabin."

His stomach lurched. He'd been afraid of this. Vargas had said he'd heard voices before the fire had propelled them back into the bush. "How many?"

"A lot." Her voice shook.

Reid leaped out of his chair. "You're driving."

22

Kenzie sat outside a coffee shop nursing a cappuccino. The scene with Rosa at the morgue had left her shaken. In an instant, she'd been catapulted back to when her mother's body had been found. Knowing it was her, but not wanting to believe it. She'd kept her eyes closed so tight because if she opened them, it would become real.

The sun was warm, the air filled with the scent of magnolia. People were going about their day. Mothers pushing babies, friends meeting up, shoppers heading to the grocery store, bags tucked under their arms. The normality was comforting.

Her thoughts turned to Maria's illegitimate child.

A baby girl.

What had become of her? Did the child know who her real parents were? Had she ever tried to find them? Lots of adopted children were curious about their real parents, and some even tracked them down. Was Maria's daughter one of those?

Kenzie did the calculation in her head. If the child had been born in 1998, she'd be 24 now. Old enough to travel to America to track down the mother who gave her away. Was that the person sending Maria death threats?

It was a stretch. Maria's daughter had been born in France. How would she have gotten the death masks into the prison? It was much more likely one of Maria's adversaries, someone afraid of what Maria knew, of what she might reveal.

She took a sip of coffee, distorting the heart the barista had made with the foam. Everything was fuzzy at the moment. The people following her, the lipstick threat on the wall, Maria's transfer, Reid's sudden displacement. None of it made any sense. She sighed and finished her drink. Time to get back to work. Keith would be wondering where she was.

Slinging her purse over her shoulder, she set off down the street to where she'd parked her car. As much as she loved the Bolt, finding a charging station wasn't always easy, and sometimes it meant parking further away than she would have liked.

Still, it was a beautiful day, so she shouldn't complain.

Halfway there, she heard heavy footsteps behind her, and glanced over her shoulder. It was just a heavyset man in a bright Hawaiian shirt holding a sun umbrella. Beachgoer. He hurried past, giving her a rueful shrug.

Kenzie exhaled. Her nerves were taut. Not everybody was out to get her, even though it was beginning to feel that way.

The street had emptied out, turning more commercial. Looking around her, she picked up the pace. The parking lot was only a block away.

She was almost there when a man stepped out from a side alley and grabbed her arm. Stumbling, she opened her mouth to scream, but a beefy hand clamped down over her mouth.

"Don't say a word," he hissed.

She froze.

A flash of color caught her eye. The man in the Hawaiian shirt.

What was going on?

He shoved her down the side street in front of him, one chubby hand still over her mouth so she couldn't shout for help, the other gripping her wrists at the small of her back. She tried to stall, digging her heels into the pavement, but he propelled her forward with his bulk.

It was no good. He was too strong for her.

She tried to remember the self-defense she'd learned at the police academy, but it was impossible to implement any of the moves when she was being ushered forward at a frantic pace. Her kidnapper was more muscular than she'd thought. He might look pudgy, but he was solid, with a barrel chest and a grip of steel.

"Where are you taking me?" she tried to say, but it came out as, "Mmmaarghee." Also, he was tilting her head back, which made talking difficult.

Where was a cop when you needed one? The alleyway was deserted. On one side, the breeze kicked up dust eddies in a fenced off parking lot; on the other, the back of an apartment block loomed menacingly. No balconies, no windows, nobody to shout up to for help.

They got to the end and Kenzie saw a black car waiting, the engine running. She panicked and kicked out. Blacked out windshield. Nondescript design. No idea who was inside.

"Noooh!" It was a muffled moan. If she got into that car, she was history.

The man held her hands behind her back in his large one, the other still covering her mouth. When she wriggled, it felt like her shoulders would pop out of their sockets.

"Get in," he growled, releasing her mouth for long enough to force her head down into the car.

She opened her mouth to scream, when a cool voice said, "I wouldn't do that, if I were you."

Carlisle Harrington!

"Sorry for the subterfuge," he said in his rounded diction that made him sound European. "I had to ensure nobody saw us."

"Jeez, Carlisle! You frightened me half to death." Was he out of his mind? "I thought I was being kidnapped."

"No, Kenzie dear. Just a little chat."

She shot him an annoyed look. "If he'd said it was you, I would have come without the fuss." Men! Couldn't they have a normal conversation?

"Couldn't take the chance," he said. "You're being watched. You know that, right?"

"I am?"

The black car, the slashed tires, the break-in.

"Darling girl. You have problems."

She rolled her eyes. "Don't I know it."

Carlisle glanced at the Hawaiian shirt guy who was now in the passenger seat. "Thanks, Leonard. Gregory, let's take a drive."

They set off, the black car gliding down the road like a sinister, silent beast. Carlisle pressed a button, and a screen hissed down between the front and back seats.

"Soundproof," he said. "We may speak freely."

Kenzie shook her head. "You definitely have a flair for the dramatic."

He responded with a sliver of a grin. "One can't be too careful in my profession."

A career fixer, Carlisle organized everything and anything for the wealthy and powerful. He put people in touch, forged deals and negotiated clandestine meetings between governments and less desirable elements of society.

He'd told her once it had taken close to forty years to get where he was today, and he guarded his contacts with cold-war secrecy. He also had several identities, yet didn't exist on any database. Kenzie knew, because she'd tried to find him—after they'd first met.

He was a mystery. An enigma. Carlisle Harrington wasn't even his real name. All she knew was he was incredibly well respected in his field.

"Your mystery child," he began, regarding her intently. He had very pale blue eyes that could turn icy at any given moment. "Born in Giverny in a Catholic nunnery, shrouded in secrecy. I'm impressed you found her."

"My researcher is excellent," Kenzie said, feeling smug.

"Yes, Raoul is a man of many talents. A dangerous man, given the right motivation."

"How did you—?" She frowned. Nothing escaped Carlisle. "Raoul wouldn't hurt a fly," she said, but she knew he didn't mean that.

"A word of warning." His tone was light, casual. "Keep him happy. He could do a great deal of damage on the other side of the divide."

She hated it when he spoke in riddles.

"I plan to." She stretched her neck that was still tense from being held at a strange angle down the side street. Leonard had a lot to answer for. "What are you doing looking into Raoul, anyway?"

"He works with you, my dear." A pause. "I work with you."

Enough said.

"Do you know who's following me?" It would be great if he could tidy up that little mystery.

"Sadly, no, but I drove past your apartment the other night and saw a black SUV parked outside. Unregistered plates. Very suspect."

"They followed me home," she whispered. "Until I made them."

"Be careful, Kenzie." He drew an envelope out of his inside pocket. Carlisle was always immaculately dressed, no matter what the weather. Today he wore a silver suit jacket over a white shirt. It brought out the gray in his salt and pepper hair, and made his eyes appear more incandescent than ever.

He handed it to her.

Unable to contain herself, Kenzie ripped it open. Inside was a color photograph of a young woman.

She glanced at him. "Maria's illegitimate daughter?"

"Meet Emmanuelle Lenoir. A twenty-four-year-old French model living in New York. She's been there for the last five years, since she signed with Capital Models Inc."

Kenzie studied the photograph and scrunched up her forehead. "She looks familiar. I must have seen her in a magazine or something."

"Could be." His pale eyes twinkled. "But it's more likely you saw her in a newspaper, maybe even yours."

She gave him a quizzical look.

"She's engaged to Warner Sullivan."

Kenzie gasped. "No way!"

He gave a stiff nod. "I wouldn't joke about something like that."

Kenzie blinked at the image, then turned her shocked gaze to him. "Warner Sullivan, President Sullivan's son?"

23

It was like a scene from a dystopian science fiction movie. The floor was thick with ash and debris, the walls blackened by fire damage, and a mutilation of wires dangled from exposed sockets. Reid wrinkled his nose. An acrid smell of God-knows-what hung in the air.

"Mind your step," Diaz warned him. The water and fire-retardant foam had turned everything into a seething mess.

They were dressed in full forensic gear. Overalls, booties, masks, and gloves. This was a live crime scene, and they couldn't risk contaminating any potential evidence. He glanced around for signs of human remains, but found none.

"Where are they?"

Diaz pointed to the left. "There's another room."

A wardrobe, or what was left of it, had been pushed aside to reveal a door in the wall. From where he was standing, it looked like yet another piece of burned debris, which was why he hadn't noticed it. The forensic team had pried it open, and now it lay discarded on the floor.

"They were burned alive," the frazzled medical examiner told them. "Every last one. It's not pretty."

Reid took a deep breath and ducked through into the secret room. Water dripped off the door frame onto his forehead, but he hardly noticed.

Jesus Christ.

Charred bodies lay everywhere. Their contorted positions indicative of the painful deaths they'd suffered. Most were curled in the fetal position, trying to protect themselves from the merciless flames. Others were splayed out, mouths open in silent, blackened screams as if pleading with someone—anyone—to open the door.

"Is it bad?" came Diaz's voice.

"Yeah." It was a croak. He counted them, slowly, one by one, giving each his or her due. Five men, three women, and one smaller frame that could have been a child or teenager. "Nine bodies total."

Diaz climbed down, then came to an abrupt halt.

"Oh, geez," she whispered. He'd never seen her turn so pale.

"You okay?"

"Yeah." She stared around the room for a long moment, soaking up the horror. It changed a person, something like this. They'd both carry it with them. Pulling herself together, she said, "I'm going to take some photographs for our records."

"We'll get the forensic photographer's images," he told her. "You don't have to do this."

"That'll take ages," she said, and she was right. By the time the CSI team had documented the victims, taken the bodies to the morgue and the evidence to the lab, it would be days, if not weeks, later. Then would come the write-up and the report, including the photographs.

They didn't have that long. They didn't want to wait.

He gave her a stiff nod.

She got to work, her hands trembling a little as she held the camera.

Reid studied the faces of the victims, gasping their last breath. What a way to go. His own brush with smoke inhalation made him relate to them even more. He *knew* what it felt like to gasp for air, to feel the hairs on your body singe as the fire got closer. He only hoped they died of asphyxiation before the flames got to them.

He exhaled, pushing the memory aside so he could concentrate.

"Do you think they have relatives in Florida waiting for them?" Diaz wondered out loud.

"Probably. The smugglers were extorting money from their families. That's why they were holed up here. If they couldn't pay..." He left the sentence hanging.

"Disgusting," she muttered. "Animals."

She wasn't wrong there.

"We'll get them." For these people, for Daniela, for destroying half the Everglades National Park, countless wildlife, the environment, not to mention his house and truck. His voice was firm. "We'll nail them, no matter what it takes."

"This one's wearing a necklace." Diaz zoomed in on the pendant around a petite woman's neck.

Reid bent down to look. "What is it? I can't make it out."

Diaz zoomed in on the camera screen. "It looks like a musical symbol. I think it's a treble clef."

"What's that? Like a note?"

"Yeah, kind of. It's used at the beginning of a piece of music to set the pitch."

He blinked at her.

"What? I used to play the piano at school."

Reid raised an eyebrow. "One of our victims was musical? That may help to identify her."

They continued working their way around the crime scene, photographing anything and everything that might be important.

Reid was glad to get out of the death chamber and back into the sunshine. He shrugged off the feeling of gloom and turned his face skywards. There was still a lingering smell of smoke in the air, even though the blaze was under control now and confined to a small area in the northern Glades.

"Excuse me, Detective Garrett?" shouted a male voice.

He turned around. At the cordon, a group of reporters and

camera operators were impatiently waiting for news. "Clive Daniels from The Miami Herald. Kenzie sent me."

He walked over. "I'm afraid I can't let you through. This is still an active crime scene." And no way did he want the victims' gruesome corpses displayed all over the front page of the newspaper, even if it was the *Herald*.

"What have you found, detective?" called another voice.

"How many victims?" yelled another.

He scrutinized the crowd for the speakers, but they didn't appear to be anything other than eager reporters.

"We can't give out any information at this stage." He kept his voice neutral. "A press release will be issued later today."

Often, the perps came back to the crime scene, but everyone here looked legit. Still, you couldn't be too sure. He gestured to a shaky Diaz standing behind him gulping air. "Could you video the onlookers, just in case?"

"Sure." She knew the drill.

While she took out her phone, a man wearing a baseball cap and holding a camera turned around and walked away. Casually, like he'd got his shot and was going home.

"Excuse me!" Reid ducked under the cordon.

The man didn't turn around, just kept walking across the clearing to a dirty pickup truck. The wheels were caked in mud and the windshield wasn't much better. The man got in and closed the door, obscuring his face from view.

Reid broke into a run. "Hey, you! Stop!"

The engine coughed to life, and the truck took off, gravel spraying over Reid's shoes. He scowled at the departing vehicle, straining to make out the license plate, but that too was obscured by sludge.

Dammit.

Was this one of the smugglers? Had he been keeping tabs on the investigation? Looking to see what they'd found. If they'd found... the bodies?

He clenched his fist. If so, he'd been right here within their grasp.

Please let Diaz have managed to get a clip of him on her phone, something they could analyze.

"I'm coming for you," he muttered, as the pickup sped around the bend and out of sight. He thought of the nine corpses lying in the cabin, the pain and terror they must have experienced, and felt a surge of adrenalin. "You won't get away with this, you bastard. We *will* hunt you down."

24

Kenzie gaped at Carlisle.

"You're absolutely sure this is the right girl? *This* is Maria Lopez's illegitimate child?"

He gave a curt nod. "One hundred percent."

"But... how?" How did she get from a tiny French village to New York? How did she meet Warner Sullivan? There were so many questions spinning around in her head it was hard to think straight.

The Mercedes eased around a corner and onto a wide residential avenue. Outside, the trees tilted in the wind, their fronds waving like a cheerleader's pom-poms, but there wasn't a sound inside the car as Kenzie waited for him to speak.

"I had a friend obtain the records from the convent, and we traced the child's adopted parents. After that, it was easy." A practiced smile. He was good at this.

Obtain.

Kenzie didn't want to know what that meant.

"They gave you their daughter's name?"

"It was simple. Her mother loves to talk, misses her daughter terribly." He smiled, except it was more like a smirk. "She's very proud of Emmanuelle's modeling career in Le Big Apple."

Kenzie shook her head.

"Okay, that's great, but can we prove it? We'll need a DNA test." She was thinking out loud.

Carlisle's eyes glittered. He reminded her of a cat sitting in the shadows, waiting to pounce. "Emmanuelle inherited a rare blood disorder called thalassemia. Something to do with hemoglobin, but non-life threatening. It was diagnosed when she was younger, and there's a record of it at the Centre Hospitalier Intercommunal Eure-Seine." The French words rolled off his tongue.

Kenzie blinked at him. "And I thought Raoul was good."

He tilted his head to the side, acknowledging the compliment. "Like I said, her maman likes to talk."

The police had Maria Lopez's DNA on file. She was a convicted felon. Kenzie's pulse rate escalated. Once they ran a comparison, they'd be able to prove Maria and Emmanuelle were related.

Carlisle lowered his voice, not that there was anyone to hear. "Kenzie, you do realize that there are a lot of very powerful people out there who won't want this coming out."

She paused, the reality setting in.

Holy shit.

Carlisle was right. This was the President's son they were talking about. A shiver shot down her spine.

Carlisle added, "Especially with an election coming up. . ."

He didn't need to elaborate. she could join the dots herself.

"Is that who is following me?" she croaked. "The secret service? Someone affiliated with the President?" The disbelief was evident in her tone. Surely not. She was being overly dramatic. This wasn't a thriller movie, this was real life. Her life. Kenzie Gilmore, investigative reporter for the Miami Herald.

Back off... or else.

Is that what they meant? Back off before you discover something you'll regret. Like a secret love child? Like a possible threat to the presidency?

"Could be." Carlisle's pale blue eyes bore into hers.

She went cold. "How could they know that I know? You only told me a few moments ago."

"But they don't know that." He tapped a manicured finger against his chin. "Maria could have told you. It would make a terrific addition to her memoirs. A shocking reveal in the final chapters..."

"We're assuming the White House knows who Emmanuelle's biological mother is."

"If I can find out..." He shrugged. "They would have vetted her when she got engaged to Warner Sullivan. It's standard protocol."

"Yet they haven't warned her off?" Kenzie raised an eyebrow. "If they really knew who she was, surely they would have tried to break them up?" Was she grasping at straws here? Hoping...

"Maybe they did. Perhaps Warner refused to listen? I believe he can be quite strong willed."

It was a possibility, still... How likely was it that anyone associated with the President or his campaign would come after her?

"What about the opposition?" Carlisle interrupted her thoughts. "They would pay dearly to get their hands on this kind of information."

Kenzie gasped. "Carlisle! You're not suggesting I sell it to the opposition?"

She didn't like his smile.

"Those are the kind of games I play," he said coyly. "I can help you if you want to remain anonymous."

"No thanks," she said. "I'm not doing this to topple governments."

"Why are you doing this, Kenzie?" His gaze was probing. "For fame? The Pulitzer?"

She shook her head.

I just want to get drug dealing scumbags off the street.

But he wouldn't believe that. His mind didn't work that way. In his world, everything had a price.

"I'm a reporter," she said. "I want to tell the truth."

"You could sell that truth and become very rich. Have you ever thought of that?"

Her look said it all.

Carlisle gave a slow nod. "A word of advice, my dear. Think very carefully how you proceed. Making this public is the safest course of action. Bring it out into the open. If it's no longer a secret, you don't need to be silenced."

He had a point there.

"It'll destroy the presidential campaign," she whimpered. Not to mention Warner Sullivan's relationship with Emmanuelle, assuming he didn't know.

"They'll take a knock," he admitted. "But there are things you can do to mitigate the damage."

"Like what?"

"You could speak to them first. If they leak it to the press, at least they're controlling the flow of information. As a couple, they can distance themselves from the campaign. Emmanuelle can denounce her mother. You get the picture. At least they'll have fair warning."

"Is that what you'd do?" she asked.

He chuckled. "No, I'd sell it to the highest bidder, but that's just me. Right now, I'm looking out for your best interests."

"Why?" She raised a suspicious eyebrow. "Why didn't you take the information and sell it as soon as you found out about it?"

"I like you, Kenzie." For once, his gaze was soft. "Let's just say I'm enjoying our symbiotic relationship and don't want to ruin it by hijacking your little secret. Although I will admit, it is tempting."

"Thank you, Carlisle." She bet that if he needed the money, he'd sell her out in a heartbeat. His indulgent smile said as much.

Her phone buzzed.

Glancing down, she saw it was Reid. "I'm sorry, I'd better take this."

He nodded and tapped on the window. The black car pulled over and the doors unlocked. Until that point, Kenzie didn't know she'd been locked in.

"Take care, Kenzie."

"Goodbye, Carlisle, and thank you." She climbed out, still reeling from what he'd told her.

"Hello?"

"Kenzie, it's Reid. I'm calling from the cabin."

"Oh, yeah." Her eyes followed the svelte black car down the avenue until it was out of sight. They were back where they'd begun, near the parking lot. The driver had timed it perfectly. "What's up?"

A pause.

"There was a hidden room."

She heard the heaviness in his voice. "What?"

"Adjoining the cabin. There was a hidden room."

Oh, God.

"How many?" she whispered. He didn't have to explain. She knew exactly what was coming next.

"Nine."

Nine people dead. With Daniela that made ten.

The wind lifted the hair off her neck, making her shiver. "I'm on my way."

Kenzie spent the next hour at the crime scene, watching as they took the bodies away.

"It's appalling," she whispered once the last victim had been loaded into the medical examiner's van. "Who would do such a thing?"

Reid told her about the man in the clearing.

"Do you think he was involved?"

"Maybe. We'll analyze the video footage when we get back to the station." At her quizzical look, he elaborated. "Diaz filmed the group of onlookers and reporters—that's when he fled."

"License plate?"

"Muddied up."

"Crap. Did you get a description?" she asked. "Height, build, hair color?"

Reid shook his head. "No, he was wearing a baseball cap pulled down over his eyes. I couldn't tell what color his hair was. He was average height, slender build and holding a camera."

"Good disguise," she murmured. She ought to know, she'd used it enough times herself.

Clive came up to them. "I've got plenty of shots of the burned-out cabin." He tapped his trusty Canon. Reid wouldn't let them photograph any of the bodies, and quite frankly, Kenzie agreed. They weren't a macabre discovery to be gawked over. They were real people who deserved respect—and justice.

Clive swung his camera over his arm. "Also, Kenzie, the boss wants you back at the office ASAP, and he didn't sound happy about it. Something to do with what Raoul was looking into."

Kenzie went cold.

Please, no.

Had Keith wrangled the information out of Raoul already?

She huffed quietly to herself.

Reid shot her a quizzical look.

"I'll call you later. We'd better go."

Kenzie drove as fast as the speed limit would allow, then took the stairs two at a time to the *Herald's* newsroom.

"I don't know what you've done, but Keith's furious," Lexi, the copyeditor, told her as she threw back the office doors, breathing hard.

Great. She was going to get it now.

Raoul was nowhere to be seen. Chicken shit.

"Kenzie, get in here!"

Lexi wasn't joking. She'd never seen Keith so upset. He was almost purple.

"I'm here." She steeled her shoulders. "What's up?"

Raoul would have told him about Maria's illegitimate love child, but even he didn't know who she was. Nobody knew about that other than her and Carlisle.

"You know what's up," he fumed. "Maria Fucking Lopez is what's up. Raoul told me about her kid. A goddamn illegitimate kid."

"We wanted to double-source it," Kenzie tried. "You always tell me..."

"Don't..." He warned, eyes flashing. "This is monumental. You come to me with something of this magnitude, and then *we* double-source before we print. We call her for comment. We verify the source of information. You know the drill."

Kenzie averted her gaze. "It's too important to get wrong," she murmured. "I wanted to be sure."

"Raoul seemed pretty damn sure. Besides, I've seen the photograph. It's her alright, and that stomach is not the result of too many croissants. The woman is definitely pregnant."

Kenzie tilted her head in acknowledgement. When Keith was in this mood, it was best to let him rant. When he'd exhausted himself, she'd try to reason with him.

"The convent confirmed it. She was there under a fake name. The same name she used for the hotel in Giverny. There is no doubt she had a child, and it was given up for adoption. That is double-bloody-sourced." Kenzie let him continue, watching him pace up and down behind his desk.

He swung around. "Do you know who this woman is?"

"Not yet." It was amazing how easily the lie slid off her tongue.

"Well, find out. In the meantime, we're going to press."

"You can't." Kenzie gasped. "Not yet. We don't have all the facts."

"Of course we can, and we must. If anyone else gets hold of this, we'll have missed the scoop of the season. With her memoirs coming out next year, this is gold dust."

"There might not be any book if this comes out."

He fixed hard eyes on her. "The book is your deal, Kenzie. Not the *Herald*'s. We have no vested interest in the publishing contract. We said we'd publish supporting articles, which is good for both of us, but I'm not holding back on this. And we can't sit around and wait for someone else to scoop us."

"Don't you think it's too gossipy for the *Herald*?" she tried. "Maria Lopez's secret love child? I mean, come on."

He scowled. "Now you're telling me what content to publish? I thought that was my job."

"We're not a gossip mag," she stressed.

"No, but Maria's life has been threatened in prison. She's been moved to a different facility—nobody knows where—and now it transpires she's got a secret daughter out there somewhere. A daughter who would be in her twenties by now."

"Coming for her?" Kenzie raised an eyebrow. She didn't admit she'd had the exact same thought herself.

"It'll sell newspapers, and that's all I care about." He ran an agitated hand through what was left of his hair. "And we're one step ahead of the tabloids."

Thanks to Raoul.

He had a point, though. By the time the memoirs were published, the news about Maria's secret baby could be out. If they found out about it, there's no telling who else might. Maria Lopez was newsworthy. A dozen papers were looking into her background. Eventually, one of them might also come across the article containing the interview with Federico Lopez.

She massaged her temple. "It's going to put me in an awkward position. Maria's trust in me will be destroyed."

"Not my problem. If you want, we can use Raoul's byline. It doesn't have to come from you."

"It's the *Herald*. She'll know it's me."

She's been keeping tabs on you.

Kenzie swallowed, remembering the look in Maria's eye when she'd warned her off.

"At least let me talk to her first?" she begged. If she could give her a heads up the article was coming out, it might mitigate some of her anger. Maybe she could still salvage the book.

"I don't want to hold off on this," Keith said. Then his tone softened. "But for the sake of your relationship with Maria, I'll give you twenty-four hours."

"Thank you." Kenzie rushed from the room.

Kenzie stared at Warden Branigan, the man in charge of Miami-Dade County Women's Correctional Center. "What do you mean she's gone? She was supposed to be transferred at the end of the week."

He shrugged, running a hand over his thick, fleshy neck as if ironing out the folds. "They collected her this morning."

"Who? The DEA?"

"The U.S. Marshals Service." With his bushy mustache and protruding canines, Warden Branigan reminded her of a walrus. "They're transporting her to a different institution, that's all I know."

"Did they tell you where she was going?"

"No, they don't tell you Jack shit if they don't wanna. The whole point is to give her anonymity." He glanced at her like she was stupid. She felt it.

"Well, who does know? Her lawyer?"

"You'll have to ask him," Branigan replied, already losing interest. His gaze dropped from her face to the untouched chocolate bar on his desk. She could tell he was dying to take a bite.

Maria Lopez employed a top-notch defense attorney by the name of Nigel Simpson. He'd won some high-profile cases during his career, but not this one.

No one could save Maria Lopez.

It had taken a jury less than six hours to condemn her.

Then again, Simpson wasn't in it for the win. He was there for the massive retainer he got from the Morales cartel and their ongoing business. He had four daughters and a demanding ex-wife, as well as a much younger girlfriend with a taste for the finer things in life.

"I'll do that."

If Simpson knew, he wasn't telling. "Maria will call me if she needs me."

Kenzie swatted at a fly in irritation. It had somehow buzzed in through the double-glazed office window and was frantically flying kamikaze-style into the walls in a useless attempt to get out. Kenzie knew how it felt.

"Did you know about the transfer?" she asked the poker-faced lawyer.

"She told me a couple of days ago, that's the first I heard. I believe it was a very sudden decision."

"Yes, but a decision by whom?"

He shrugged.

"Do you know where she's being taken?"

He shook his head. "I'm as much in the dark as you." His gaze followed the fly around the room. Why did she get the impression he wasn't telling her something?

"Look, Mr. Simpson, if you know how I can get in touch with her, please tell me. It's vitally important I speak with her. You could say it's a matter of life and death."

Mine.

He regarded her coldly. "Has someone died?"

"No."

Not yet.

He regarded her curiously. "Do you know who's threatening Maria?"

"It's not about that. It's a...a personal matter." Perhaps that would get through to him, but his eyebrow barely raised. She got the impression he'd heard it all before.

"I'm sorry, I can't help you." His voice was flat.

She asked a couple more questions, but Simpson was frustratingly tight-lipped. He answered in short, staccato sentences and said the bare minimum. Kenzie got to her feet. "If you hear anything, here's my card." She placed it on the desk.

He didn't touch it. "My assistant will see you out."

Ugh! That man was infuriating.

Kenzie stomped up the road to her car. Now what?

She couldn't get in touch with Maria. The article about her illegitimate daughter was going to be in tomorrow's edition of the *Herald*, and there was nothing she could do about it. Perhaps she should warn the publisher? This would surely jeopardize the book deal.

Reid.

Crap. He wasn't going to be happy about it, either. Neither would Agent Wilson of the DEA. Their carefully brokered deal was about to go up in smoke. At least nobody knew who Maria's daughter was, or what ties she had to Washington. It would be catastrophic if that got out.

Kenzie didn't want to think of the repercussions. That was a secret she had to keep to herself, at least until she'd had a chance to speak to Emmanuelle Lenoir.

25

REID GLANCED up as Kenzie raced into the squad room.

"We have a problem." She was flushed and out of breath.

"What's happened?"

"I've messed up. I've ruined the book deal, everything."

He frowned. It wasn't like Kenzie to be a defeatist. "Maria?"

She pulled a face. "Who else?"

He gestured for her to sit down. She did so, leaning forward so only he could hear her. Vargas and Diaz, who'd seen her rush in, were hovering expectantly. "We found something in her past, something she didn't want anyone to know about."

"I'm sure there are a lot of shady things in her past."

"This is big, Reid. Huge."

Leaning forward. "I'm listening."

"Maria had an illegitimate child back in 1998 in France when her husband was in prison. It was given up for adoption. Nobody, not even Federico knew."

Reid stared at her. That was not what he'd been expecting. "Are you sure?"

"One hundred percent. We, or rather my researcher, spoke to this old nun at the convent and she confirmed everything. She remembered Maria, or rather Nora, which was the false name she was going by."

Reid raked a hand through his hair. "Why do you think you messed up?"

"I hinted to Maria that I knew." At his look, she threw up her hands. "I was trying to get a reaction out of her."

Narrowing his eyes. "What did she say?"

"She warned me off. In fact, she hinted France could be a very dangerous place."

He shook his head. "A veiled threat?"

"Yeah, and she's keeping tabs on me." Kenzie gulped, reaching for the bottle of water on his desk. Without asking, she took a sip. "Sorry, you don't mind, do you?"

"No, go ahead." He'd already had half the bottle, and he liked that she didn't care. "What do you mean, keeping tabs on you? Did she admit to having you followed?" His eyes widened. "The lipstick on the wall, was that her?"

"I don't think the break-in was her." Kenzie frowned. "But I'm pretty sure it was her men in that black SUV."

Reid reached for a folder amongst the pile on his desk. Vargas and Diaz, unable to hear what was being said, went back to their desks. "I have something on that," he said, finally finding it at the bottom of the stack. "Here."

She waited while he opened it and thumbed through some paperwork.

"We picked up the SUV on Byron Avenue, just like you said. See, here's your Chevrolet, and there's the black car following you." He pushed a photograph across the desk.

"That's the one." Kenzie lifted her gaze to him. "Who does it belong to?"

"That's the weird thing," he said. "Those plates aren't registered to anybody."

Her brow creased. "I don't understand."

"It's a front, a dummy corporation. We don't know who the owners are." He paused, wondering how much to say. At her quizzical gaze, he added, "It could be a government organization."

"Government? As in the DEA? CIA?"

He shrugged. "Maybe, but why would they be tailing you?" It didn't make sense.

"What about the cartel?" she asked. "Could it be a dummy corporation set up by the Morales cartel?"

"That's possible," he acknowledged. "Although this was a slick job. Usually, there'd be illegible scrawled signatures and faded copies of company documents, but in this case there was nothing. The application had been seamlessly approved."

Kenzie went very still.

"What is it?" he asked. "You know who it is, don't you?"

"It's Maria." Her reply was a fraction too quick. "It's got to be. The cartel must have someone on the inside, someone who smoothed the way."

"Yeah, that is the most likely scenario." He could almost see the cogs moving in her brain. "That doesn't explain the break-in or the message on your wall," he pointed out. "Forensics haven't managed to find even a partial at the scene. Your apartment was clean."

"They wore gloves," she said.

"They certainly knew what they were doing. There wasn't a single hair or skin fragment. Nothing to tell us who the perps were." He gave her a hard look. "These guys were forensically aware, Kenzie."

Like a government agency.

She wouldn't meet his gaze.

"What are you into, Kenzie?" He rested his elbows on the desk.

She tucked a stray hair behind her ear. "I wish I'd never got Raoul involved. It was Keith's fault. He hired him to help me."

"What are you talking about?"

"Raoul, my researcher. He's too damn good. Now we have this information that's going to destroy my relationship with Maria. Keith's publishing it in tomorrow's edition." She looked flatly at him. "We're screwed."

Reid got the feeling she wasn't telling him everything. "Can't you stop him?"

"No. I've tried, believe me. I got a twenty-four-hour extension, but Maria's already been moved, and I can't reach her. I was trying to salvage the deal, your deal." She sighed. "But it's too late."

He remembered her telling him that, but he'd been staring at the remnants of his burned house at the time and hadn't acted on it. Damn, he was slipping. "Did you find out where she's being transferred to?"

"No, I was hoping you could find out. Nobody's telling me anything. I've spoken to the prison warden and Maria's attorney. Neither of them knows. Apparently, it's for her own safety."

He rubbed his chin; it felt rough. He needed a shave, but holding a razor was awkward. His hands were still bandaged. The bulky dressings meant he'd paired down his personal grooming to the bare minimum. Same with everyday tasks. He must look like a big old grisly. "The death threats?"

"Yeah, must be. If we could only find out who authorized it, we might be able to find out where she's been taken."

He gave a curt nod. "Leave that with me. I'll give Wilson a call. He must have ordered the transfer."

"The entire deal is on the hook," Kenzie stressed, getting to her feet. "It's imperative I talk to her before the paper hits the stands tomorrow morning."

"That doesn't leave us with much time."

Her eyes were clouded with worry. "I know."

She still hadn't answered his question about what she was into, but perhaps it was nothing. Perhaps it was all to do with Maria Lopez. That woman had a way of causing chaos wherever she went. In his opinion, she should be serving her life sentence without the luxury of a book deal, of the fame and fortune that would inevitably come with that. Even rotting in obscurity was too good for her. But he kept his mouth shut. He knew how Kenzie felt about freedom of speech.

"Boss, Sebastian is here." Vargas approached the desk. "Hi,

Kenzie. You rushed in here like you had a swarm of bees behind you. Is everything okay?"

She glanced at Reid. "Yes, just a bit stressed. How are you, Willie? Still with Shannon?" Kenzie was one of the few people who called Vargas by his first name.

"Yeah." Color seeped into his usually impassive face.

"That's great. Good for you." Reid knew she was genuinely happy for him. Vargas was a good guy, and despite their differences, Shannon seemed to make him happy.

The awkward teenager sauntered up behind Vargas, his hands stuffed into his pockets. Reid was pleased to see he looked much better than he had a couple of days ago in the hospital.

"Take a seat, Sebastian." Reid pointed to the chair Kenzie had just vacated.

"I'll leave you to it," Kenzie said.

Reid gave her a distracted nod. "I'll talk to Wilson and call you later." When he got back to the Gator Inn. Right now, he had an unpleasant task to do. He needed the boy's help in identifying who the multiple burn victims were. How many had come over on the boat with him? Did he know their names or where they were from?

Before he had a chance to ask, the boy gave a muffled cry and pointed to a photograph lying on Reid's desk. On top of the forensic reports and other documents was the close-up Diaz had taken of the pendant one of the victims at the burned-out cabin had been wearing. Treble clef, she'd called it.

Kenzie paused, turning around.

Vargas frowned. "¿Qué pasa?"

The boy prodded the photograph, his face crumpled in distress. He barked out a sentence that Reid didn't understand. Kenzie did, and her hand moved to cover her mouth.

He got the message.

"He recognizes the necklace," Vargas hissed. "Says it belongs to his mother."

Kenzie closed her eyes.

"This is your mother's necklace?" Reid pointed to the high-res photograph. Thank God you couldn't see the distorted features or charred remains of the body, only the neck area where the pendant hung.

The boy whispered, "Si," and began to gabble in Spanish.

Vargas translated. "She was wearing it at the cabin. It's important to her. His father gave it to her. She would never take it off."

Reid nodded at Vargas, whose face dropped. He put a hand on Sebastian's shoulder and in case there was any misunderstanding, broke the news that his mother was dead. The boy stared at him, then got up and ran from the room.

Vargas started to go after him.

"No, leave him," said Reid. "Give him some space."

Vargas nodded and sat down. "Poor kid."

"What's going to happen to him?" Kenzie asked.

Reid shrugged. "I'll call immigration services, and they'll process him, but until he's granted refugee status, he'll be taken into foster care."

"Isn't he old enough to take care of himself?" Kenzie asked.

"He's eighteen in two months," Reid said. "Until then, he has to go into the care system. That's the way it works."

Kenzie frowned. "He's just lost his mother. What he needs is stability and a place in which to grieve, not social workers, processing, and strangers."

"It's not my decision," Reid argued. He didn't like it either, but that's just the way the system worked.

But Kenzie's gaze was unwavering. "Can't you do something?"

"Where am I supposed to put him?" Reid asked. "Even if I could do something, there's nowhere for him to go. He has no relatives here, no family friends that we know of. His best bet is with a religious charity or refugee organization."

"How long will that take?"

"A while. These things don't move fast."

"So until then, he's stuck in a dingy hostel with a bunch of other displaced kids?"

"I don't make the rules, Kenz."

She got up. "I need some air."

Reid watched her walk out. His heart was breaking for the kid. Just seventeen and he'd found out his mother had been killed at the hands of the traffickers who'd smuggled them into the United States. People they'd paid good money to, and who'd betrayed them, taken advantage of them.

He met Vargas's gaze, and he saw his own anger reflected there. His sergeant was seething, too. "We have to get these guys," he said.

"We will." Reid had never been more determined. "I guarantee it."

26

KENZIE WENT AFTER SEBASTIAN. She'd been where the young boy was now. She knew that feeling, like someone had sucker-punched you in the gut. The nausea that swept over you when you realized your mother wasn't coming home, that she was gone for good, and you were all alone in the world.

She *knew*.

Sebastian sat hunched over on the steps of the precinct, his face in his hands. Kenzie thought he was crying, and she didn't blame him, but when he glanced up, his face was dry.

"Are you okay?" she said.

He shrugged.

No, of course not.

"Do you mind if I sit down?"

He stared at her as if to say, why, who are you?

"I'm Kenzie," she said, reading the question in his expression. "I'm a friend of Reid's. I work with the police on some of their cases."

He gave a slight nod. Disinterested.

She sat down without waiting for him to say so. Not too close. She wanted to give him enough space to breathe so he wouldn't feel trapped. "I know what you're going through," she said quietly.

He looked over. Doubt was written on his face.

"Really, I do. I lost my mother when I was twelve."

"You did?" It was a whisper.

"Yeah. It was hard. For a long time I didn't know what had happened to her, but now I do."

"Was she dead?" Deadpan eyes; acceptance was setting in.

"Yes, she was dead."

He nodded like it was inevitable.

"That's why I want to ask you something," she continued.

He stared straight ahead, lost in his own personal grief.

"I have a spare room at my place." He glanced up, surprised. "You're welcome to come and stay with me."

He hesitated.

"Reid might be able to arrange it if we asked him," she added. "You could have your own room. I wouldn't bother you, I'm out a lot."

His brow creased. "Why you help me?"

"Because I want to," she said. "You seem like a nice kid, and I know what it feels like to lose someone."

"But you don't know me."

"No, I don't. Does that matter?"

He shrugged. "I don't know anyone who would take in a stranger, that's all."

She smiled. "Now you do."

"How do you know I won't rob you?"

"Are you going to?"

"No."

"Then I have nothing to worry about."

The corners of his eyes creased ever so slightly. "Are you crazy? Willie said you were a nice lady, but I think you might be crazy."

"A little, maybe." She stood up, smiling. "Shall we talk to Reid?"

He gazed at her for a long moment, then nodded. "Okay."

"You don't know this boy, Kenzie. You have no insight into his background, or what he's done. I can't allow him to stay with you." As expected, Reid wasn't happy with the suggestion. She'd taken him aside to have the conversation, away from the rest of the squad.

"I know he's lost his mother. I know what he's going through." She jutted out her chin. "He can stay in my spare room, the one I use as an office. There's a sofa-bed in there that's not too uncomfortable. I'm hardly ever home anyway, so he'll have plenty of space."

Reid looked doubtful. "I don't know, Kenz."

"It's only for two months," she insisted. "Once he turns eighteen, he can move out."

Reid studied her. "That's if immigration services agree he can stay with you. You're not a registered foster parent."

"I'll become one." She wasn't giving up. "You can sign off on the paperwork."

Reid rubbed his stubbly chin. "You can't just use me to cut corners. It's not right."

"It's right for Sebastian." The more she thought about it, the surer she was. The boy needed a safe place to call home. He needed a sanctuary.

"But is it right for you?" He frowned, and she knew he was worried.

"You said yourself that it would be better if I had someone staying with me, with the break-in and everything."

"I meant me, or a uniformed police officer, not an orphaned kid."

"He's almost a man," she pointed out. "Plus, he'll be able to alert the authorities if anything happens."

She was pushing his buttons now.

Reid huffed. "What are the chances of you shutting up about this?"

She broke into a grin. He knew the answer to that.

"Okay, I'll see what I can do."

"Thank you." She hugged him, catching him off guard. He stiffened and pulled back. One of his officers walked past and raised an eyebrow.

"Sorry," she murmured. "I didn't mean to do that in front of your team."

"Um, it's okay." He walked back to his desk. "I'll give them a call now. You'd better hang around."

Two hours and a mound of paperwork later, Sebastian was released into her care.

Reid met Wilson at the same live-music venue as before. This time there was a guy rasping out old Muddy Waters tracks while the crowd lounged in booths and low tables around him. It was about half capacity but full enough to have to raise your voice to be heard.

"Thanks for coming," Reid said. They sat at the bar again, down the one side where it curved towards the wall.

Wilson turned to him. "What's this about? I don't have a lot of time."

"Maria Lopez," Reid said.

Wilson shrugged. "What about her?"

"Why didn't you tell me you were having her transferred to another facility? Kenzie needs to conduct interviews for the book. It's not done yet."

For a moment, Wilson looked stunned. "Transferred?"

Reid felt the stirrings of doubt. "Yeah. Kenzie tried to meet with her today, but she's been transferred out of the state. Apparently, it's got something to do with the threats she's been getting."

Wilson scrunched up his forehead. "First, I've heard."

Reid frowned. "Who'd authorize her transfer, then? The Feds?"

"Can't see why. She's working with us."

"Well, someone thought her life was in danger." The stirring became a loud siren in his head.

"I'll get the warden on the phone." Wilson yanked out his cell-phone and strode towards the exit. Reid followed, after throwing down some money for the bartender.

"I need to speak to him now," Wilson was saying. The sea was a pastel pallet of peaches, pale yellows and pinks thanks to the sun that had set only moments ago. Under normal circumstances, Reid would have taken a moment to appreciate it, but right now his focus was on the DEA agent.

"What's this I hear about Maria Lopez being transferred?" he barked into the phone.

Reid stood a short distance away, wondering what the warden's response was.

"Who authorized it?"

Another pause.

"It most certainly did not come from my office."

Uh-oh. That didn't sound good.

"For fuck's sake," he bellowed. "Get them on the phone right now and tell them to turn around. That's an order. Damn right I'll hold."

He rolled his eyes at Reid. "It's a fuck show. They said the Miami DEA office authorized her transfer. The U.S. Marshals who went to collect her had all the official documentation. Someone's got their wires crossed."

Reid feared it was worse than that.

"Text me the number." Wilson hung up, took a few deep breaths, and then glanced at his phone as it beeped. "I'm calling the U.S. Marshals who have her in transit."

He dialed and waited for them to answer.

"This is DEA Agent Wilson speaking. I believe you have a Maria Lopez in transit?"

"I'm afraid there's been a mistake, I need you to turn around and bring her back."

"Yeah, I said turn around. Now."

"I don't care if you're twenty minutes from Atlanta. I need her brought back here ASAP."

He sighed. "Okay, call me when you get to Atlanta. I want a full sitrep, and then you turn that coach around and bring her back to Miami. Is that clear?"

He snapped his phone shut and pocketed it. "I want to know who the hell authorized that transfer!"

Reid rubbed his temples. Damn, he was tired. The stress of the last week was weighing on him. When he wasn't working, he was yelling at insurance companies, and while he still hadn't got a payout for his house, they had covered the airboat and his pickup, so at least he could get around, even if he didn't have a place to stay. The Gator Inn was good enough for now.

If Kenzie hadn't invited Sebastian into her home, he might have taken her up on her offer. It had been an enticing prospect for a few minutes. But as usual, the moment passed, and things went back to normal.

Now it was too late. Story of his life.

Wilson's phone rang again. The DEA agent answered it, still standing in the street outside the bar. More visitors filed in as the band heated up. Reid could hear the music from outside now. It drew people off the street like a throbbing magnet.

"I thought I said..." Wilson stopped, mid-sentence.

Reid held his breath.

The DEA agent listened, the color draining from his face. Reid braced himself. Something had happened, and it wasn't good.

"Are you armed?" he snapped.

Reid scowled. Definitely not good.

"Well, shoot at them," he insisted.

"What's happening?" Reid mouthed, but Wilson ignored him. He was concentrating on the call.

Wilson listened intently for a few moments, then hung up. Tension radiated through his body.

"What?" asked Reid.

"It's an ambush," Wilson told him, raking a hand through his hair. "It was a setup. They're going after Maria."

27

"WHAT INCIDENT?" Kenzie asked, letting Reid in. He seemed even more disheveled than earlier, if that was possible. Standing in her living room, shoulders taut, the veins in his neck standing out, she'd never seen him so stressed.

"The vehicle transporting Maria Lopez was ambushed this evening. She's gone."

Kenzie balked. "Gone? What do you mean, gone?"

"They got to her, Kenz."

"Who got to her?" Her mind was spinning. Was it a friend or foe? Had her own men helped bust her out of prison, or had her enemies grabbed her with intent to kill?

Sinking into an armchair, he said, "I'm guessing Maria orchestrated the whole thing. From what we can gather, it was her people who boarded the prison van and took out the marshals."

"You mean they were shot?" Kenzie gasped.

"Yeah. One is dead, the other is in critical condition in a hospital. They don't think he's going to make it."

Geez. Kenzie shook her head. Maria had just added a murder charge to her rap sheet, along with a possible attempted murder. "What about the driver?"

"The driver was hit on the head and is still unconscious. He's not going to be saying anything until tomorrow."

She paced up and down in front of him. "How could this happen? I thought it was a legitimate transfer?"

"It was, at least from the Marshals' side. They didn't know it was a setup. They got orders to move her, and they did."

"What a mess!"

"There is some good news." Reid didn't sound very happy about it. "One of the marshals managed to get off a shot before he was killed. We saw it on the in-van camera. He may have grazed one of the perps."

"So you've got DNA?"

"Not yet, but we will."

Kenzie stopped pacing and put her hands on her hips. "This makes things even worse. The article comes out tomorrow, and I have no way of warning her. She's going to be livid."

"It doesn't matter now." Reid hung his head. "She's in the wind."

Flopping down next to him, she said, "We underestimated her. She never planned on giving us the list, did she?"

Reid shook his head.

"Dammit." Kenzie clenched her hands into fists. "I feel so stupid."

"It's not your fault," he said. "You weren't to know. She fooled all of us."

"Here I am busting my chops to write her memoirs, and all the while she was playing me for a fool. Did she even want the book written?"

"Probably." Reid stretched his legs out in front of him. "She's a narcissistic psychopath. She wants the fame and fortune that go with her notoriety. I'll bet she fully intended to get the book published."

Kenzie looked up. "Well, she can think again. I'm not writing her memoirs after this."

Reid gave a weary nod. "It's for the best. She's dangerous, Kenzie. The less you have to do with her, the better."

Knowing he was right didn't make it any easier. The publisher would be disappointed, and so would Keith. He was relying on the fervor attached to the book to sell newspaper copies. Then there was her own reputation to think about. She was passing up on a chance to win a Pulitzer. Maria had crossed her, and that stung. She wouldn't be quick to forgive her.

The fact that she'd been about to do the same thing to Maria wasn't relevant anymore. The article on her love child would be in the morning's papers, but somehow Kenzie didn't feel so bad about that anymore.

Reid stifled a yawn. He looked bushed.

"When last did you eat?" she asked, concerned by his pallor.

He glanced up through bloodshot eyes. "Not for a while."

"Why don't you stay for supper? I've got slow-cooked braised beef in the oven." At his raised brow, she added, "It's for Sebastian. He needs a good meal."

"Ah, in that case, yeah, I'll stay. Thanks." But he wouldn't meet her gaze.

"Great."

While she set the table, Reid said, "'Maybe we can use this to our advantage. If Maria contacts you, we might be able to draw her out."

"But why would she? Do you think she'll still want the book written?"

"It's a possibility."

Kenzie waved a fork in the air. "Well, I'm not going to do it, not unless she gives us those names."

Reid thought for a moment. "What if it meant catching her?"

"You mean like a sting operation?"

"Something like that. It would have to be off the record, though. I'm not convinced there isn't a leak in the DEA. Someone must have told her about Torres."

Kenzie gasped. She'd forgotten Maria had been fishing for information about Alberto Torres.

"Shit. We need to warn him. Now she's out there, there's no telling what she'll do. Reid, she could go after him."

"She doesn't know where he is," Reid said evenly, although she could tell by his demeanor he was worried, too.

Kenzie scowled. "We underestimated that woman before. It's only a matter of time before she finds him."

A grunt. "I'm sure Wilson will tighten security around him or move him again."

The undercover agent had been displaced so many times, she felt for him. They hadn't gotten to know each other very well, but she liked him. He was a good man. He deserved better.

"She's smart," Kenzie said, thinking about drawing her in. "I doubt she'll fall for it twice."

"Depends how it's done. She might trust you, to a point. If she wants the book written—" He left the sentence hanging. At this point, it was all they had.

"If she gets in touch, you'll be the first to know. But I wouldn't count on it."

Kenzie watched Reid struggling with his knife and fork all the way through supper. His palms were still bound, but even with his fingers free, he couldn't grip properly.

"Let me do that," she said, when he tried to help her clear up. "You're exhausted."

She took the plate from his hand. For a split second, he looked vulnerable, and her heart went out to him. He was going back to that two-bit motel in the Glades, and if that wasn't bad enough, he had to drive past his burned-out house to get there.

"You can stay here tonight." Her voice was low. "If you want."

Sebastian had gone back to his room. The teenager appeared to have settled in well, and despite red-rimmed eyes, was holding it together.

He shook his head. "No offense, but I don't think I can handle another night on the couch."

Hesitating, she put her hand on his arm. "Then stay with me?"

He went very still, his eyes boring into hers. "I thought you wanted to be friends."

Christ, she was so confused. "I do, but—"

He sighed wearily. "I'm too tired to play games, Kenzie. Either we're having something or we're not. You can't have it both ways."

Blinking, she realized he was right. What was she thinking?

"It was just an idea," she said, backtracking frantically. "To save you driving all the way to the Gator Inn."

He nodded. "I'm good. Really. Thanks for supper."

"You're welcome."

And she stood there, his plate still in her hand, as he picked up his jacket and walked out of the apartment into the night.

MARIA LOPEZ'S SECRET LOVE TRYST screamed the headlines the next morning. Kenzie cringed when she read it. Even though she'd written the article, the byline said staff reporter, which offered some degree of protection. It wouldn't fool Maria, however.

It can be dangerous.

Should she be concerned for her safety?

Was Maria still watching her? If so, she could pounce at any time.

"I don't have a follow up," she snapped at Carla, the style editor, who was a sucker for any kind of celebrity gossip. Kenzie's nerves were so fraught, she was jumping at the sound of the photocopier. "No one knows who she is."

Not strictly true, but that was a secret she wasn't about to share. Not yet, anyway.

Keith had asked her to do a piece on Maria's escape.

"It's freaking gold," he yelped when she told him. "This woman could keep us selling papers for the rest of the year."

Kenzie called Reid to get an update on the ambush, but he wasn't available. She spoke to Vargas, who gave her a few more details. "A truck was blocking the road," he told her. "When the transit van stopped, two black SUVs pulled up on either side and four men got out, each with semi-automatic rifles. They boarded the transit vehicle and there was a brief firefight. One of the marshals got off a shot before he took a bullet in the chest. We think he may have injured one of them."

"Reid said there was blood."

A pause, and she knew Vargas was contemplating how much to tell her.

"Did you get it analyzed?" she asked.

"Yeah, it belongs to one of the men who used to work with Maria, Romeo Herrera. He lives in California now."

"He obviously went in person to spring her," Kenzie asked. "How's the driver?"

"He surrendered without a fight, which is the only reason he's still alive. We debriefed him this morning, although he can't describe the men. They were wearing balaclavas."

"Convenient. Did Maria appear to go willingly?"

"According to the driver, she walked off the bus with a big smile on her face."

Kenzie gritted her teeth. That sounded very much like Maria.

"She fooled us all," she said.

"She sure did," Vargas replied. "She sure did."

"Kenzie, you've got a visitor in reception."

She glanced up. She'd been so engrossed in the article that she didn't realize Lexi, one of the copy editors, was speaking to her.

"Oh, who?"

"A cute guy who drove up in a Porsche." Lexi smiled at her.

Kenzie knew exactly who that was.

"You tracked me down." She smiled as she walked into the lobby.

"I was concerned. After you rushed off the other day, I thought something might be wrong."

She shrugged it off. "Only a problem at work, nothing serious."

"Must have been quite a problem. Are you sure everything's okay?"

"Absolutely. You really didn't have to come and see me."

"I wanted to." He hesitated, shuffling slightly. Was he nervous? "We didn't have time to chat the other day, so I thought I'd ask you out to make up for it. That is, if you're available." His light brown hair was ruffled, his shirt open at the neck exposing smooth, tanned skin. Attractive, no doubt about it. Good build. Nice smile. The faint smattering of freckles across his nose was endearing.

She thought of Reid's sullen expression.

Either we're having something or we're not. You can't have it both ways.

"Sure." She smiled back. "I'd like that."

"Great." His shoulders relaxed, and his natural charm was back. "How about Friday?"

If nothing untoward happened at work. It had been a long time since she'd gone out on a date. The last one was with Alberto Torres, but that was work related. She'd been acting a part, playing a role. Something she was very good at. Was she acting now?

Reid had taken her out once, but that was work too. They'd been scouting out a salsa bar near South Beach. They'd held hands. He'd smiled at her...

She pushed the thought from her mind.

"Friday's good."

As she walked back into the office, Raoul bounded up to her, glasses askew, cheeks bright pink.

Her good mood disintegrated.

He knew.

It was there, written all over his face. The excitement, the elation, the need to tell someone.

She should have realized if Carlisle could find out, so could her brilliant researcher.

"I traced the adopted family," he stage-whispered.

"Hush..." She grabbed his arm and led him into the photocopy room.

He could barely stand still. "You're never going to believe this. You're never going to believe who she is."

Fuck.

Kenzie closed her eyes. Everything was tumbling down and she couldn't stop it.

"Raoul, I know."

"Maria's daughter. She lives in New York, she works as..."

"I know!" She put a hand over his mouth. "Hush." Someone was likely to hear them and ask what was going on. Nothing was sacred in a newsroom.

A mumbled reply. "You know?"

Removing her hand, she nodded.

His eyes were huge. "But...but... how?"

"I have my sources."

At least she could still shock him. He stared at her, frozen to the spot, his back to the photocopier that was still warm from its last print job. The pungent smell of ink hung in the air.

"Then you know who she's dating?"

"You mean who she's engaged to? Yes."

He glanced around, puzzled by her reticence. "This is big news, right?"

"It's massive." How to put this so Raoul wouldn't suspect her of wrongdoing? "It's just that it's sensitive information. There's an election coming up, and the stakes are high. Something like this could have major ramifications."

It was clear he hadn't thought it through.

"You mean it could be used against the President?"

"Of course. The opposition would give the skin off their backs for that kind of information. I think we need to be very cautious as to how we use it."

Just then Keith walked in. "Kenzie, what the fuck is going on?"

Raoul took one look at the expression on his boss's face and raised his hands. "I'll leave you two to discuss this." And he scurried from the room.

Kenzie turned to Keith. "I'm not sure what you mean?"

"Don't play dumb with me, Kenzie. I know when you've got something. Besides, Raoul is running around like a virgin on prom night. Now fill me in."

She tried to keep a straight face. "Fill you in on what? Raoul was just confirming what we already know."

"Bullshit. You've found her, haven't you? The daughter?"

Kenzie said nothing. Why couldn't the photocopier swallow her up?

"Who is she, Kenzie?"

"Nobody," she lied. "She's absolutely nobody."

He gave her a hard look. "Okay, I'll go and ask Raoul, but if I find you're lying to me, you can kiss your job goodbye." He spun around.

She grabbed his arm. "Wait."

He stopped.

"I'll tell you, but not here. Let's go to your office."

Intrigued, he followed her across the newsroom floor to his fish-bowl office. "Spill," he demanded, before he'd even closed the door.

"You're going to want to sit down for this," Kenzie warned.

He sank into his desk chair with a creak of leather and swiveled to face her. "I'm sitting."

Kenzie took a deep breath, then she told him.

28

REID DROVE his brand-new gun-metal gray Ford F-150 truck into the Sweetwater PD parking lot and cut the engine. His hands still hurt, but they were healing. Scabs had formed over the worst parts, and the nurse at the hospital had just removed the bandages.

"Any signs of infection, and you come right back," she'd told him sternly.

He took a seat at his desk and brought up the camera footage Diaz had taken at the cabin that awful day they'd found the bodies. They'd analyzed it before but hadn't been able to identify the cameraman who'd run from the scene.

He slowed it down and watched it frame by frame, his eyes glued to the hazy figure of the mystery man. He'd been smoking a cigarette in the first few frames, the orange glow from the tip visible on the screen. Then when he'd realized Diaz was filming, he'd flicked the butt onto the ground, turned and walked away.

Combat pants, a gray T-shirt, and a white baseball cap. Was that a logo on the front? He zoomed in, but all he got was a pixelated blue blur. It could be anything.

The man kept walking until he was out of the frame. That's when Reid had taken pursuit. Up the overgrown track to the dusty clearing where the vehicles were parked. A white truck, so dirty it looked brown. Mud conveniently splashed on the undercarriage, the tires, and the plate.

Reid pictured the man getting into it, his face turned the other way. He was careful, very careful. The windows were filthy. You couldn't see anything through them. The engine growled, and the truck took off up the road, spraying pebbles behind it.

He watched the video again. That flick of the cigarette butt, almost arrogant, as if to say, you're never going to catch me.

Reid glared at the image. They'd see about that.

The man walked away, holding the camera in his right hand.

The camera.

He zoomed in on the device, squinting. "Hamilton," he called to the rookie cop sitting nearby.

"Yes, boss?"

"What do you know about cameras?"

He shrugged. "Not a lot. Monroe is better at that."

"Monroe, really?"

"Yeah, he's won a few competitions."

Reid had no idea.

"Get him to come over here."

Monroe oversaw the rookie cops, fresh from the academy. It was a supervisory role on account of his age. He couldn't chase criminals anymore, not with his bad hip and back problems, but despite being out of shape, there was nothing wrong with his mind.

"You wanted to see me, LT," Monroe said, a short time later.

"Yeah, take a look at this." Reid turned the screen in his direction. "What do you make of that?"

"The camera?"

Reid nodded.

Monroe leaned in and studied the image. "I'd say that's a Nikon. Probably a D810 judging by the shape and size. Nice piece of equipment."

"Expensive, too, isn't it?" Reid didn't know much about cameras, but it looked like it was in good condition.

"Top of the range," Monroe agreed. "Who is he? A reporter?"

"Maybe."

"Figures."

"Or he could be one of our smugglers."

Monroe did a double-take. "Seriously?"

"Yeah. If I wanted to trace this guy through his camera, how would I go about it?"

Monroe's bushy eyebrows curled upwards like two caterpillars. "You'd ask the stockists, I guess. But these days you can buy equipment like this online. There's no guarantee he went into a store."

Reid sighed. He was afraid of that.

"Will you give it a try?" he asked, reluctant to let it go. "I know it's a long shot, but you never know."

Monroe looked doubtful. "Sure."

"Thanks, I'll send you the image."

There was one more thing he needed to do. "I'm going for a drive," he told Vargas, who was going through camera footage that he didn't recognize. He stopped to take a closer look. "Where's that?"

"It's outside the refugee charity. I've been keeping tabs to see if Gabby Rosenbaum came back." They'd gotten her full name from the DVA database.

Reid gave an approving nod. "And?"

"No sign of her. She's still on the run. We've distributed her photograph to the local police departments," he said. "But nothing so far."

"We need to find her," Reid said. "She's a link to Luca."

Was he the mysterious cameraman at the crime scene?

Reid drove down to the cabin, enjoying the feel of his truck on the open road. While he was driving, his phone buzzed, so he put it on speaker.

"Mr. Garrett?" Most people referred to him as Lieutenant.

"Yeah? Who is this?"

"Capital Insurance. We've discussed your claim, and I'm happy to inform you that the company has agreed to cover the costs of your property that was destroyed by the fire. You'll get full compensation."

He fist-pumped the air. Yes! At least now he had options.

"That is good news."

They went over the details, and by the time he pulled into the clearing in the Glades, he was whistling to himself. The heavy cloud that had been hanging over him since the wildfire was lifting. Maybe he would rebuild. He'd become attached to the environment; he felt at home there. He wasn't sure he'd be able to settle anywhere else.

Reid parked where the dirty white truck had been and walked down the path until he got to the police cordon. It was still there, designed to keep onlookers away from the derelict cabin, now a charred shell of scorched wood and ash. The bright yellow plastic was out of place among the green palette of the Everglades, a warning that something untoward, something unnatural had happened here.

Reid glanced around the clearing. Where had that guy been standing?

He imagined the video Diaz had taken. She'd been over there, about a hundred feet from the cabin. He'd been standing next to her, peering out at the crowd of reporters and onlookers. The guy with the baseball cap had been standing at roughly eleven o'clock, according to his line of sight. Reid moved a little to his left, his eyes fixed on the ground.

There it was.

The cigarette butt he'd flicked away before he'd made his quick exit.

A lawyer would argue it could be anyone's cigarette butt, that it was circumstantial at best, and they'd be right. But the guy had been standing here, and he had flicked his butt onto the ground in that devil-may-care way. It might not stand up in court, but it could be a lead.

Reid took an evidence bag out of his pocket, and using it as a glove, he bent down and picked up the stub. Then he folded the bag around it.

Who are you?

Hopefully, the DNA would tell them.

29

Kenzie landed at John F. Kennedy International Airport at ten o'clock the following morning. She'd never forget Keith's face when she'd told him who Maria Lopez's daughter was, or to whom she was engaged. The disbelief, the realization that she wasn't joking, then the sheer delight of a newsman who knows he'd scored the scoop of the year.

"How long have you known?" he demanded. "Was it before yesterday's article went to press?"

"Of course not," she lied. "I only found out this morning. I wanted—no, I needed—to be sure. This is potentially very sensitive information."

"Call the White House for comment." Keith's eyes were gleaming.

"I'll do one better," she'd retaliated. "I'll go there and ask them myself."

Keith agreed to hold off for twenty-four hours, which would buy her some time. She had no intention of going to the White House. They wouldn't see her anyway. If she was lucky, she'd get a call in to President Sullivan's campaign manager, a spin doctor appropriately named Vulcan Rosso.

"Sullivan owes his presidency to Vulcan Rosso," Trevor, the political editor, told her. "He's the man you need to speak to."

No, not Washington. She was flying to New York. To see Emmanuelle, Maria's daughter. If her life was about to be scrawled across the tabloids, she deserved a heads up at the very least.

In the cab, Kenzie called the model company Emmanuelle worked for and asked if she'd be available to fly to Miami for a shoot. "There are some particulars we'd like to discuss with her," Kenzie said in her best magazine voice. "Could I speak with her directly?"

They were only too happy to hand over her cell number.

A quick call to Raoul resulted in him texting her Emmanuelle's address a short time later. She didn't ask how he'd obtained it.

The luxury condo in Greenwich Village was situated in a nineteenth century cast iron building manned by a suited doorman. It was freezing cold and pouring with rain, and stupidly, she'd only brought a suit jacket.

"I'm here to see Emmanuelle Lenoir," Kenzie said, trying not to shiver. "I'm with the *Herald*." She showed him her press card.

He glanced briefly at it and then at a visitors' book. "Do you have an appointment?"

"No, but her agency sent me over to discuss an upcoming project. I'm sure if you buzz her, she'll be more than happy to talk to me."

"If you don't have an appointment, I can't let you through."

Inflexible oaf.

Annoyed, Kenzie turned on her heel. "Have it your way. I have a few girls lined up, so she'll lose the job. That's on you."

"One moment—" He walked to an intercom on an inside wall next to a Jackson Pollock painting and pushed a sequence of buttons. Kenzie smiled.

"Miss Lenoir will be with you shortly," he said a short while later. "Have a seat."

"Thank you." A frisson of excitement shot up her spine. She was about to meet Maria Lopez's daughter. Would she know who her mother is? Would she care?

Kenzie walked into the adjacent black leather and marble waiting room and sat down on an oversized couch. An enormous vase of white lilies stood on a dark walnut coffee table in the middle of the room. She could smell the fragrance from where she was sitting, or maybe that was perfumed air freshener.

The elevator pinged open, making her jump. She was still edgy and probably would be as long as Maria was out there. Out stepped one of the most beautiful women Kenzie had ever seen. Straight black hair, a willowy, model's body, and features that wouldn't look out of place on a porcelain doll.

"Hello," she said in a soft French accent that only served to make her more exotic. "I believe you wanted to speak to me about a job?"

Kenzie stood up. "Miss Lenoir, my name is Kenzie Gilmore, and I work for the Miami Herald. Can we talk privately?"

The doorman was standing in listening distance, and despite the bland expression on his face, she didn't trust him. Emmanuelle nodded, and they walked across the waiting room to the darkened floor-to-ceiling windows. Outside, well-heeled shoppers hailed cabs, umbrellas open to the sky.

"My schedule is pretty full this month," Emmanuelle began. "I'm not sure I can spare the time—"

"I'm not here to talk about a job." Kenzie had her back to the window. "I wanted to ask you what your reaction is to the story that broke yesterday about Maria Lopez's love child."

Emmanuelle stared at her, azure eyes unblinking. "Who?"

"Maria Lopez, the Morales drug cartel boss."

Her brow creased. "You mean the woman in prison?"

Or rather, the woman who'd escaped.

"That's the one," Kenzie said.

"Why do I care?" Emmanuelle pouted in the way that only French girls can.

Time to drop the bomb.

"Because Maria Lopez is your birth mother."

Kenzie watched her for a reaction. At first she did nothing, just stood there, her arms draped around her waist, her head tilted to the side. As Kenzie's words registered, she straightened her head and her eyes widened. "Are you insane?"

"Not last time I checked." Kenzie smiled disarmingly. "Are you saying you didn't know who your biological mother was?"

"I was born in France," Emmanuelle whispered. "My parents are Jacques and Francine Lenoir."

"They're your adopted parents," Kenzie corrected. "Your real mother was Maria Lopez, the notorious cartel boss."

"Pavel," she croaked. "See this woman out. She's crazy."

"I'm not crazy." Kenzie spoke faster now as the doorman-slash-bodyguard came over. "I'm telling you the truth, and I can prove it. If you want to know about your birth mother, you'll talk to me, otherwise it's going to be all over the Washington Tribune and New York Times tomorrow morning, and there's nothing you can do to stop it."

Emmanuelle held up a hand, and Pavel stopped. His beady eyes flickered from Emmanuelle to Kenzie and back again.

"You don't know what you are saying." A blush had stained Emmanuelle's cheeks, brightening her eyes, already the color of shimmering water. Kenzie could see why Warner Sullivan had fallen in love with her. "My parents live in France," she reiterated, but her voice was strained, the accent stronger.

"I'll tell you what I know." Kenzie gestured to the leather sofa. "Let's take a seat."

"It's okay." Emmanuelle gave Pavel a tiny nod and moved to the sofa. She sank down with a sigh, twisting her body so her legs were crossed elegantly to the side, the soft material of her knee-length dress rustling against the leather.

Kenzie joined her, feeling a lot less elegant in her trouser suit and store-bought heels. But then again, she'd been trying to look like a frazzled modeling agent, not a member of the New York elite.

"Maria Lopez traveled to France in 1998 under a false name." Kenzie took an envelope out of her purse. She opened it and pulled out a photograph of a heavily pregnant Maria. "Here she is at the hotel in Giverny the week before she gave birth."

Emmanuelle stared at the grainy black-and-white photograph. In that moment, Kenzie could see the likeness of Maria. It was the concentration, the focus, the way her eyes narrowed as she gazed at the picture. Then there was the pitch-black hair, dead straight and glossy. The height and aquamarine eyes must come from her father.

"I don't know this woman."

"I realize that. She gave birth to you at a Catholic convent." Kenzie forced a smile, feeling sorry for the model who was hanging on to every word. "You were given up for adoption immediately after you were born."

Emmanuelle shook her head. "How do you know it was me?"

"The nuns at the convent confirmed it was her," Kenzie explained. "There is no doubt. They also put us in touch with your adoptive parents, Jacques and Francine."

"Did they say they'd adopted me?" Her voice rose at the end.

"They denied it at first," Kenzie said. "But after we pressed them, they came clean and admitted it."

"You are lying." Her voice was a hoarse whisper. "Maman would have told me." Emmanuelle flopped back against the couch, shocked.

"The convent kept records," Kenzie told her. "I have a copy of them here." Raoul was able to get it faxed across. It confirmed that in September 1998, Jacques and Francine Lenoir adopted a nameless baby girl.

Emmanuelle gripped it with long, slender fingers. Her nails were painted a bright fuchsia. "Oh, God."

"You suspected, didn't you?" Kenzie asked.

There was a pause as Emmanuelle battled with her emotions. Eventually, she said, "Growing up, I knew I was different. My parents were simple people. They owned a small holding outside of Giverny. I hated the farm. I moved to Paris as soon as I could."

"Is that where you were spotted by a model scout?"

"Yes, I worked in France for a few years and then this opportunity came up in America. My parents didn't want me to go, but nothing was going to hold me back. I'd had enough of France. I needed to spread my wings."

Kenzie understood the urge to flee. To run as far as you could go, to get away from your dull, uninteresting existence. She'd felt like that after her dreams of becoming a police officer had been dashed. Luckily, she'd had a journalism diploma to fall back on, otherwise she'd still be running.

But no matter how far you go, you can never run away from yourself.

"I remember thinking there must be a recessive gene or something," she murmured. "How could I turn out so different from both my parents?"

"Because you were adopted."

"It makes sense now. Still, what proof do you have that I'm the baby they adopted?"

"You have a rare blood disorder," Kenzie told her. "Thalassemia."

Emmanuelle raised a perfectly plucked eyebrow. "So what?"

"Well, there's a record of it at Washington Memorial Hospital where you were treated last year."

"I take iron tablets," she said a tad defensively. "It's no big deal."

"Be that as it may," Kenzie said. "We did a DNA check against Maria Lopez's sample taken when she was arrested. It's a match. There is no doubt, you are her daughter."

30

KENZIE BOARDED the flight back to Miami feeling like a monumental sleaze. It was clear Emmanuelle hadn't known about her biological mother. Sure, she may have suspected she was adopted, but she never questioned it until now. She'd left at seventeen and gone to Paris. New York had followed three years later. She was living the dream in the big city. There was no need to question her birth, not until now.

To be fair, Emmanuelle had taken it remarkably well. Warner Sullivan, on the other hand, not so much.

"You have to be fucking kidding me," he'd said, when Emmanuelle had told him the news. "Did you know about this?"

"No, I swear. I had no idea."

"She didn't know." Kenzie backed her up. "Nobody knows, yet."

"What do you mean, yet?" His eyes narrowed. He'd been playing the political game for a long time. He might be the rebellious black sheep of the family, but he was still the President's son. "What do you want?"

"Want? No, you've got the wrong idea. That's not why I'm here."

"Everyone wants something."

"Not this time." Imagine living in a world where everything had a price. Carlisle would be in his element right now. "I'm afraid it's too late for that. It's going to come out," Kenzie told them. "I can't stop it. I just came to warn you so you can—"

"So we can what? Prepare ourselves for the media onslaught? Warn my father?" he scoffed. "Oh boy, he's going to love this."

Emmanuelle paled. "Does it have to come out?"

"I'm not the only one who knows," Kenzie said, wishing she was. "My editor has the article ready to go. It'll be in tomorrow's paper."

Emmanuelle wavered, like a stiff breeze would blow her over. Warner was glaring daggers at her. "Fucking journalists."

For once, Kenzie agreed with him.

"I'm sorry," she said. "Maybe if you made an announcement yourselves—"

"That's not going to solve this problem," Warner snapped. "Emmanuelle is going to be plagued by reporters prying into her private life. Into *our* life." He put an arm around her. Kenzie was glad to see it. She'd need the support. "It's going to be hell. My father will take the brunt of it. Jesus, it's the opposition's wet dream."

That it was.

"They don't know yet," Kenzie reiterated. "If you come clean now, you still have time to control the flow of information."

Warner thought about this, then gave a curt nod. "Yeah. It's the only way."

Emmanuelle had that glazed look of a deer in headlights. The bottom was about to fall out of her world, and there was nothing she could do. Not to mention, she'd just found out her mother was a notorious felon.

"I'm sorry," Kenzie said again.

As she'd left, Warner got on the phone to Vulcan Rosso. They were going to release a statement declaring Emmanuelle had no prior knowledge of her birth mother, and no connection to the infamous Maria Lopez, who was now a wanted felon.

"I'd suggest beefing up security," Kenzie told Emmanuelle, before she left. "Maria may try to get in touch, now that she's escaped."

"Don't worry about that," Warner snapped. "We'll make sure she doesn't come within a mile of Emmanuelle."

"We could go away," Emmanuelle suggested. "Until everything dies down."

"Running will make us look suspicious," Warner said, through gritted teeth. "If there's one thing my father taught me, it's to confront problems head on. No, we'll stay and show the world we've got nothing to hide." At least he was thinking rationally. They'd be okay, Kenzie was sure of it. They'd get through this.

The plane prepared for take-off. The flight attendant came on the radio asking everyone to turn off their devices and fasten their seat belts. Kenzie took out her phone to turn it to airplane mode when it vibrated. The lady beside her shot her an unapproving look.

Kenzie didn't recognize the number. She was about to ignore it when a sixth sense told her to answer it. "Hello," she whispered.

"Kenzie, it's Gabby. Oh, God, Kenzie, you've got to help me."

"Gabby?" For a moment she was thrown, then she remembered, Gabby Rosenbaum from the refugee charity. "What's wrong?"

"They're after me." Sobbing mixed with frantic gulping of air followed. It was clear she was terrified.

"Who's after you?" Kenzie asked. "Luca?"

A strangled cry. "They know where I am. Oh, God. They're coming for me, I know it."

"Where are you?" Kenzie asked urgently. All she got was more frightened crying.

"Gabby, where are you? I can't help you unless I know where you are."

"The Golden Palm."

"Where is that?"

But Gabby was crying too much to hear.

"Gabby, listen to me." She raised her voice.

"Shh..." said the woman next to her.

Kenzie ignored her. "I'm going to call the police. Lock the door and wedge something under the handle, okay?"

The sobbing was uncontrollable now. "I saw them... parking lot... watching me."

Shit, she'd never felt so helpless.

"Gabby, I'm going to call the police. Stay put and make sure the door's locked."

Without waiting for a reply, she hung up and dialed Reid's number.

He didn't pick up.

"Answer your phone, dammit," she pleaded.

But he didn't. It went to voicemail.

She tried one more time before the plane took off as a flight attendant came and asked her to switch off her device.

"One more call," she begged. "It's an emergency."

"I'm sorry, ma'am. We're about to take off. There's no WIFI on this flight. You'll have to wait until we land."

Reluctantly, she pocketed her phone and thought of Gabby alone in her hotel room. It would be two and a half hours before they landed. She only hoped it wouldn't be too late.

It was dark outside, and most of the squad had left for the day. Reid watched Kenzie's call go to voicemail and turned back to the forensic report he was reading.

"Find anything, boss?" asked Vargas, who was the only other detective, apart from the night duty officer, still at the station.

"Not a damn thing," he growled. The fire had destroyed any evidence at the cabin.

What little DNA they'd managed to retrieve from the victims wasn't yielding any results. "There's nothing in the system either." Vargas gazed at his screen. "They were all refugees."

It was as he'd expected, but they had to check anyway.

"Did Sebastian recognize the man in the baseball hat?" Reid asked.

Vargas had been to Kenzie's place that afternoon to speak with the boy to see if he could give them any more information.

"Unfortunately not." Vargas sighed. "Although he said the height and build was similar to one of the men who took them to the cabin. The others were all shorter or stockier."

Reid thought back to the secret room adjoining the cabin. The death chamber. Like a living, breathing thing, it had sucked the fire in but left the prisoners with no way to escape.

"Did he hear them talking?" Reid asked.

"Yeah, they spoke Spanish," Vargas confirmed. "But he only picked up a few words here and there. The swamp, the cabin, meeting the victims' relatives in the park to pick up the money, and something about a marina."

"A marina?" Reid jumped on it. That could be where they're mooring their boat. "Which marina?"

"That's what I've been trying to find out." Vargas threw his hands in the air. "But there are dozens of marinas in the Miami area alone, not to mention up and down the coastline. It's like looking for a needle in a haystack."

That was true. Reid dropped his head onto the desk. "We need a freaking break. What is it with these guys?"

"They're pros," murmured Vargas. "Destroying the cabin meant there was nothing to find. Charred bodies don't give up much in the way of evidence."

He shook his head. "Let's start with the lesser-known marinas. They're not going to want to hide their vessel in full sight. It would have to be somewhere remote, where they could come and go unnoticed."

Vargas gave an accepting shrug. "I suppose it's better than doing nothing."

Three hours later, it was approaching midnight. Vargas yawned. "I'm going to call it a night, boss," he said.

"Yeah, me too." But he made no move to get up.

Vargas logged off when his desk phone rang. He picked it up. "Detective Vargas, how can I help you?" His sergeant always answered the phone the same way, no matter who he thought was calling.

"Yeah, we're on it. Thanks."

"What is it?" Reid asked as he hung up.

"That was Dispatch." Vargas shook his head. "They got a 911 call from Kenzie. She gave them a location for Gabby Rosenbaum. Apparently, she's in some sort of trouble."

Reid jumped up. Dammit. That's what Kenzie's call was about. Kicking himself, he grabbed his keys and phone off the desk. "Which motel?"

"The Golden Palm."

"I know it. Let's go."

Vargas pushed in his chair. "I'm right behind you."

31

They blue-lighted it downtown to the Golden Palm Motel, a dumpy, beige, two-story building with a functional rather than pretty garden out front. It tried hard but didn't quite earn the three stars displayed above the door.

"Which room?" Vargas asked as they charged up the paved pathway.

"She didn't say."

They burst inside. "Which room is Gabby Rosenbaum in?" Reid barked, flustering the receptionist.

"Uh-um..." She glanced down.

"Sweetwater Police Department," he added, flashing his badge.

"Oh, er, sure." She put her hand on the mouse and clicked through to the bookings. Her brow furrowed. "We don't have a Gabby Rosen-whatever listed."

Of course. She was on the run, hiding out. She wouldn't use her real name.

"This woman." Vargas was ready. He showed the woman a photograph of Gabby, one that they'd used to circulate to the other police stations.

The receptionist bit her lip. "Oh, her. She's in room 204."

"Thank you!" Vargas shouted as they took off up the stairs. Room 204 was the second right along a threadbare corridor. There was a Do Not Disturb sign on the door.

They both pulled out their weapons. Vargas shouted, "Gabby, it's the police. Open up."

No reply.

Reid gave a curt nod and stepped back, covering his partner. Vargas kicked in the door. It tore away from its hinges, not offering much resistance.

Reid switched on the light and they scanned the room.

"The bed." Reid choked out the words. Gabby lay unmoving on the dreary comforter. At first glance, she could have been asleep but there was something about the stillness that unnerved Reid.

He bent over the prone figure, looking for signs of life. The gentle rise and fall of her chest, the flutter of an eyelash, but there was nothing. Reaching out, he felt for a pulse. Her skin was cool and clammy.

"Anything?" Vargas asked.

Reid shook his head.

Vargas thumped his hand against the wall. "Damn, we're too late!"

"Whoever she was running from finally caught up to her," murmured Reid, inspecting the body. "She's been strangled. There's bruising around her neck."

Vargas circled the room. "It looks like she's been here a while. The bin's filled with takeout wrappers and cans of soft drinks." A suitcase full of clothes lay open under the window.

Reid pulled a pair of forensic gloves from his back pocket. Now that this was a murder scene, they had to be careful. "Let's get CSI in here, although I doubt we'll find anything."

Vargas snorted. "In a fleabag motel, no way."

God only knew how many people had stayed in this room, and it didn't look particularly well cleaned. Put together, it was a forensic nightmare.

Reid lifted the victim's hands and inspected her fingernails. "She didn't put up much of a fight," he remarked, but he hoped there was evidence not visible to the naked eye. Skin cells, a hair follicle, fibers from clothing... anything that could give them a lead to whoever killed her.

"Let's go downstairs and talk to the receptionist." Reid straightened up. "She may have noticed something."

"I—I didn't see anything," she stammered, when they told her the guest in Room 204 had been murdered. "Is she really dead?"

"Yeah." Reid leaned over the counter. "I need a list of all your guests, along with any CCTV footage you have available."

The receptionist hung her head. "There is no CCTV."

"What is that?" Reid pointed to the surveillance camera mounted above the front entrance.

"That's just for show," she whispered. "The owner said it would stop people misbehaving."

Reid gritted his teeth. More like he didn't want to spend the money to get them operational.

"Aren't you worried about working here by yourself with no security?" Vargas asked.

She glanced beneath the counter. "I can take care of myself."

Vargas glanced at Reid who shook his head. They'd let that one slide. Illegal or not, firearms were not their current priority.

"You didn't see anyone suspicious enter the motel in the last few hours?" He wasn't sure how long Gabby had been dead for but if she'd called Kenzie three hours ago, it had to be less than that.

"This is a twenty dollar a night motel. Everyone looks suspicious to me."

Fair enough.

"Anyone abnormally suspicious," he amended. "Or anyone acting erratically."

She sighed. "I don't know. Maybe."

Reid gritted his teeth. "Could you be more specific?"

"There was one guy," she said. "He gave me a funny look."

"What do you mean?" Reid asked. He was losing patience.

"I mean he stared at me in a freaky way. Gave me the creeps."

"What room is he in?"

"He isn't a customer. He came with Mr. Piper."

"Is Mr. Piper a guest?"

"Yeah. He stays here long term. Pays in advance for the whole month."

"Does he often have guests?"

"No, not often." She inspected her nails. "Maybe every few weeks he'll bring some guy back."

Reid glanced at Vargas. "Let's check him out."

He turned back to the girl. "Is he still here?"

"I don't know. I don't keep tabs on the guests." There was a packet of cigarettes on the counter, and no ashtray. She went outside to smoke.

"Room number?" asked Vargas.

"307. Top floor."

They took the stairs two at a time. "Hope he's still there," panted Reid when they got to the top.

"This is it." Vargas drew his weapon. "Ready?"

Reid nodded and knocked on the door.

There was no answer. He knocked again.

"Can't you see the Do Not Disturb sign on the door?" came the sleepy reply.

"It's the police, Mr. Piper. Open up."

A pause, then shuffling. Eventually, the door swung open. A well-built, bleary-eyed man with a mop of rusty brown hair glared at them. "Yeah?"

His muscular torso was about to burst out of his tank top. This guy worked out. Reid peered behind him into the darkened room. "Lieutenant Garrett from Sweetwater PD. Are you alone?"

"Yeah, what's going on?"

The man had a barrel chest and fists the size of hams.

Vargas trained his gun on him.

"There's been an incident downstairs, and we need to ask you a few questions. Can we come in?"

The man hesitated, glanced at Vargas's weapon, then nodded. "Sure."

He stood back. Reid kept his own gun holstered. The guy was unarmed. There wasn't much space to hide a weapon in those boxers or that strung-out top.

The motel room was stuffy with an unmistakable tang of sweat and body odor. "Mind if I open a window?"

Without waiting for a reply, he pulled back the blinds and opened the window. Fresh air swept in. That was better.

"What incident?" The man stood in the center of the room, looking at them. Was this the guy who'd killed Gabby? He had the strength. It wouldn't take long for him to overpower the young woman, yet he was too casual, too disheveled to be a killer.

Reid glanced at the crumpled double bed. It was empty.

"Did you notice anything unusual tonight?" A general question to start, to get him talking.

"No, nothing. What's happened?"

"There's been an incident on the floor below."

His eyebrows rose, his mouth dropped open. Classic signs of surprise. "What kind of incident?"

"You didn't hear anything?"

"No, I told you. What kind of incident?"

"A woman was murdered."

"Murdered?" He sat down on the bed. "Jesus. I didn't hear a thing. Who was it?"

Reid's gut was telling him this guy wasn't involved.

"Her name was Gabby Rosenbaum. Did you know her?"

"Not by name. Was that the girl in room 204? I've seen her around, but we've never talked."

Definitely not involved. If he'd wanted her dead, he'd have had ample opportunity before now.

"Are you in town on business, Mr. Piper?" Vargas asked.

"No, I live here. I've recently separated from my partner, so I'm staying here until I find somewhere else to rent."

"So the man you had in your room this evening, he wasn't your partner?" Reid watched him closely. He shrugged. "No, detective. That wasn't my partner. I work at Romeos, I'm a bouncer there. Sometimes I bring a man back to my hotel room. You got a problem with that?"

"Nope, no problem," Reid said. "But we're going to need his name."

The bouncer shifted uncomfortably on the bed. "Graham. His name was Graham, but that's all I know."

"Any idea where we can get hold of him?"

"I don't have a number or anything," he said. "I hadn't seen him at the club before."

Shit.

Reid rubbed his stubble that was fast turning into a beard. "What time did he leave?"

"Around three, I think. I wasn't looking at the time."

It was nearly four now. Gabby had been dead for at least an hour. Her skin had been cold to the touch. This was a waste of time.

"Did your friend leave the room at any time during the evening?" asked Vargas.

"What? You think he—" The bouncer broke off. "No way!"

"Just answer the question," Reid said.

The bouncer blinked as he tried to recall. "No, I don't think so. Oh, hang on—"

Reid glanced at Vargas.

"Yeah, he went out for beer. It didn't take long, though. There's a shop around the corner. He was back in fifteen minutes."

Would it be enough time to strangle Gabby on the floor below? His heart beat faster.

"Can you give me a description of Graham?"

"Sure, he was average height, slim build, dark hair."

"Hispanic?" Reid asked.

"No, but he wouldn't... he'd never... you know."

"I know, but if we could speak to him, we could rule him out of our inquiries."

The bouncer gave a distracted nod. Reid could see he was bothered by the thought. Unsure about the man he'd bedded.

"What?" asked Reid.

"Nothing."

"Something, though. Was there something about him that bothered you?"

"It's crazy," he said. "But I thought I smelled perfume on him."

"Perfume?"

"Yeah, like a woman's deodorant or something." Reid's pulse escalated. If he'd strangled Gabby, he may have inadvertently picked up her scent from around her neck.

"Did you smell it before he went out to get beer?"

The moment dragged out. The bouncer shut his eyes, and when he opened them again, he looked devastated. "No, I don't think so."

32

Kenzie threw her suitcase into the backseat of her car and closed the door with a bang. Damn Reid for not answering his stupid phone. Of all the times not to pick up. Instead, she'd had to call 911 and report Gabby's frantic message. Now she had no idea what had happened, and it was too late to call.

Besides, Reid was obviously avoiding her.

The sun was poking its fiery head above the cityscape as she drove out of the airport and into the dawn. It was on the freeway when she first noticed the black SUV. Her heart skipped a beat. Was it following her?

Tense, Kenzie gripped the steering wheel, her eyes fixed on the vehicle behind her. It weaved in and out of the traffic, gaining on her. On a whim, she slowed down to see if it would pass. It didn't. Instead, it pulled back, cutting in behind a truck in the other lane.

Sweat pricked her upper lip. Was she being overly paranoid or was the SUV following her?

Squinting into the rearview mirror, she tried to make out the occupants, but the sun reflecting off the windscreen made it impossible. It could be one person—she thought she made out the outline of a head—but then again, it could have been two.

There was no way off the freeway, so she continued onto the I-95 N and then right onto 77th Street. When she got to Biscayne Boulevard, Kenzie turned hard left into a street next to a car stereo shop. Heart pounding, she pulled over and waited to see what the SUV would do.

Don't turn, she prayed. Let it be a mistake, a product of her overactive imagination, made worse by the long day.

It kept going.

Thank God.

She scoffed, feeling silly. Her nerves were on edge. A hot soak in the tub and a few good hours of sleep was what she needed. Then she'd try Reid again, or maybe Vargas, and find out what had happened with Gabby.

Turning the car around, she headed back onto the boulevard. At the next set of traffic lights, her phone rang, making her jump. Glancing at the screen, she exhaled. It was Nick, the veterinarian.

"Hi." She put it on speaker. "You're up early."

"I'm on my way to work," he replied. "I remembered you saying you were on the red-eye back to Miami, so I thought I'd call and wish you good morning. How was your trip?"

That's right, he'd texted yesterday with a restaurant suggestion for their date, and she'd told him she'd be back this morning. Sweet that he'd remembered.

"It was okay." She kept her tone neutral. "I had to do a couple of interviews, but they went well." As well as could be expected. She drove past Miami Shores Country Club, the green lawns luminous under the night lamps. A few super keen golfers were already out on the course. Kenzie checked her rearview mirror once more. The stretch of road behind her was bare. No SUV. She relaxed.

"How about you? How's your day looking?"

"Busy." He laughed. "Although not nearly as interesting as yours, I'm sure."

"I don't know. You must treat some weird and wonderful pets."

"Don't forget the wild animals at the nature reserve," he added. "I'm out there two afternoons a week."

She chuckled. "Your job is definitely more interesting than mine."

"So are we still on for Friday?"

"I think so." Her condo came into view and she pulled up outside. "I mean, yes, I'm free." Unless something else came up to drag her away.

"Cool. There's this new restaurant I'd love to try if you're in the mood for Italian?"

"I love Italian."

Kenzie got out of the car, phone to her ear. Opening the trunk, she lifted out her carry-on, then pressed the button on her keyring to close it.

"Great. Me too."

She walked up the path towards her front door, pulling the case behind her, the other bag slung over her shoulder, and her phone in her free hand. Behind her, a car drove by.

"If you send me your address, I can pick you up. How's eight?"

"Eight is good. I'm on Bay Harbor Island, I'll text you the full address." The car appeared to be idling, so she turned around.

An icy fear engulfed her.

It was the black SUV from the freeway. They'd found her.

Horrified, she watched as the door opened and a man got out. Black leather jacket, dark jeans, and a balaclava.

She froze. "What do you want?" Her voice was shaky, unnatural.

The man didn't reply.

"Who's there?" Nick asked. When she didn't answer, he asked, "Kenzie, is everything okay?"

"Oh, God, he's got a gun." She ran for the door.

A muffled shot rang out, embedding itself into the wall next to her. She screamed. "Sebastian!"

Another shot, closer this time.

Kenzie spun around. If she was going to die, she wanted to face her killer. The man in black strode up the path, hand outstretched, gun glinting in the early morning light. She braced herself, waiting for him to pull the trigger, waiting for the bullet to bury itself in her flesh.

But it never came.

Instead, he marched up to her and punched her in the face. Stars danced in her vision as her head whipped back, and she fell to the ground. The grass was soft against her cheek.

Then pain exploded in her side. The bastard had kicked her in the ribs. God, it hurt. She gasped for breath, buckling over. But there was no time to recover. A sudden weight made her look up. He was sitting on her, straddling her, his enormous hands encasing her throat.

What?

He was strangling her.

She bucked and tried to throw him off, but he was too strong. She clawed at his face, but he leaned back, and she swiped empty air. The big hands squeezed. The pressure built and built until it felt like her head was going to explode. His grip tightened, and she began to black out.

No, she screamed, but it was all in her head. *I'm not ready to die.*

Then out of nowhere. . . a flash of red. . . and a figure hurled himself at the man on top of her. The two men sprawled across the lawn.

Sebastian!

They rolled over and over and then got to their feet. A fist connected with skin, but Kenzie couldn't work out who was hitting who. She heard a yell and a series of fast strikes, and the man in black went down.

Kenzie shut her eyes. It hurt to look.

"Sebastian..." she murmured.

Another yell, but it wasn't the teenager. Forcing her eyelids open, she saw the man in black sprinting back to the SUV. A car door slammed.

Had he gone?

She tried to speak, to ask Sebastian if they were safe, but the words wouldn't come out. She felt his hand on her shoulder, before her world faded to black.

33

"Let me get this straight," Diaz was saying. "Gabby Rosenbaum's killer picked up a guy staying at the motel, went home with him, then slipped away under the pretense of buying beer to murder Gabby?"

"It looks that way," Reid confirmed. They were back at Sweetwater PD, the entire team having been called in. The first few hours after a murder were crucial, and Reid didn't want to waste them. Besides, the sun was already up. It was the start of a new day, and they had a killer to catch.

"He knew Gabby was there and needed a way in," Vargas added.

"Going in as a guest's lover would avert suspicion," Monroe agreed, rubbing sleep from his eyes.

"We almost didn't pick it up," Vargas said. "If we hadn't talked to the bouncer in the room above, we'd never have known about Graham."

Reid gave a rough nod. "Mr. Piper's coming in later to give us a description. I'm hoping we can put together an identikit."

Diaz frowned. "Could Graham be Luca? Did you show the bouncer the picture of the guy in the baseball cap?"

"Not yet. I'll ask him when he comes in. He's willing to help. My impression is that he's basically a good guy and is freaked out by what happened."

"Agreed." Vargas nodded. "I don't think he's involved."

"Run him through the database anyway," Reid said. "Just to be safe."

"Will do." Vargas had the guest list from the motel to get through too. It would take a while.

"I'll help," Diaz offered. Vargas shot her a grateful smile.

Hamilton had been tasked with making a list of marinas in the greater Miami area. Reid told him to focus on the lesser-known and out of the way ones.

"I've brought sustenance," called a feminine voice from the door.

They glanced up. Shannon, Vargas's girlfriend, stood there holding a cardboard tray of coffee and a box of donuts.

"You beauty!" exclaimed Monroe, who was still questioning camera suppliers. It was beginning to look like the baseball cap guy had bought his camera online. It fit with everything they knew about this organized crime group. No trace.

She grinned. "I thought you could use it."

The team grabbed at the coffees and donuts. Sugar and caffeine, just what they needed to get going at six in the morning. Even Reid, who hadn't eaten since before they'd left for the motel the previous night, had one. After that, he didn't feel like he could lay down the law and ask Shannon to leave, so she perched at the end of Vargas's desk while he ran names through the system.

The Golden Palm guests, as it turned out, weren't the most law-abiding of citizens. One had a warrant out for soliciting, another had a previous for assault, and a third owed thousands of dollars in outstanding traffic fines.

"Reel 'em in," Reid said to Hamilton, new out of the police academy. "If they're still there." Once the news of the murder got out, he doubted anyone wary of the police would hang around.

Hamilton left, along with another uniformed police officer.

Reid was helping Vargas write the report on Gabby Rosenbaum's murder when his phone rang. He didn't recognize the number.

Frowning, he answered.

"Garrett." A frantic rush of words greeted him, mostly in Spanish.

"Sebastian, is that you?"

More garbled noises. What the hell was going on?

"Vargas, take this." Reid thrust the phone at him.

Vargas listened, his eyes hardening. "Kenzie's been attacked," he said. "Sebastian is with her. They're in an ambulance on the way to the hospital."

Reid felt the floor tilt. "Jesus. Is she okay?"

Please let her be okay.

"She's unconscious but alive."

He grabbed his keys. "Which hospital?"

"Miami-Dade County Memorial."

"Tell him I'm on my way."

Reid sprinted into the hospital emergency department.

"Kenzie Gilmore?" he asked the duty nurse, wiping his sweaty hands on his pants. "She came in twenty minutes ago."

Sebastian had sounded incoherent on the phone. She must not be doing well if he was that freaked out. "She's in Bay 8," the nurse told him, pointing down the corridor. "The doctor is with her now."

Reid strode down the passage, feeling like the walls were closing in on him. Where the hell was Bay 8? Eventually, he found it, but the curtains were drawn. Heart hammering, he pulled them back and poked his head through.

Kenzie lay on a bed looking as pale as the walls around her, eyes shut.

His heart sank. "Kenzie?"

Her eyelids fluttered open. "Reid?"

Thank God. She was alive. He felt weak with relief and clutched the back of the doctor's chair.

"Easy," the doctor said, half-turning in annoyance, but he didn't tell Reid to go. Not that he would have listened, anyway.

"Are you okay?" His voice sounded hoarse to his own ears.

"She's had a shock," the doctor cut in. "But apart from a cracked rib, there's no lasting damage."

Reid exhaled under his breath. It was going to be alright.

"She was lucky."

"Sebastian—" she murmured, fighting to keep her eyes open. It was then he saw her left eye was swollen and puffy.

He moved around the bed. "Jesus, what happened?" Her lip was split, and dried blood covered the right side of her face.

"She was assaulted." The doc's voice was steady, casual even, like he'd seen it a hundred times before.

Reid scowled. "Who did this to you?"

"I don't know," she mumbled. It obviously hurt to speak.

"Shh... it's okay. We'll talk later."

He'd have to wait. Possible assailants flew through his brain. Maria Lopez's goons came first. She was on the run, angry at the leaked story about her illegitimate child. Was this punishment for that? Was she getting back at Kenzie for betraying her secret?

What about the slashed tires, the mysterious break-in? Was it someone trying to warn her off?

He sank down in a vacant chair. If the doctor thought he was leaving, he could think again. He'd let Kenzie down. He'd been so focused on the smugglers and the fire and his own circumstances that he'd taken his foot off the gas on Kenzie's investigation into Maria and the memoirs she was writing so the DEA could uphold their end of the deal.

He clenched his jaw. Dammit. The car tailing her and the break-in should have been enough to warrant his full attention. She'd been on her own, with only a damaged teenage boy to protect her.

"Sebastian fought him off." Her good eye flickered open. "He saved me."

"Where is Sebastian?" Reid asked. He'd thought the boy had come to the hospital with Kenzie.

"He's getting a Coke," she said, with a hint of a smile. She was fond of the boy, he could tell. "It's been a shock for him too, especially after what happened to his mom." Her head fell back, exhausted.

"Can you do this later?" the doctor asked. He was inspecting the cut on her cheek. "I'm going to have to put a stitch in here."

"Sure, I'll be back in a minute." Reid got up. He wanted to speak to Sebastian and find out what on earth had gone down tonight.

The boy was leaning against the soda dispenser, sipping a can of Coke. Long and lanky, he was almost as tall as the machine. He stood up when Reid approached, relief registering on his face.

"Hey, Sebastian." Not for the first time, Reid wished he spoke Spanish. "You okay?"

The boy nodded.

"Can we talk?"

The dark eyes followed him. "Okay."

Reid pointed to a line of plastic seats bolted to the wall. They weren't the most comfortable, but they'd do for a short chat.

"Qué pasó?" he asked. What happened?

Sebastian hesitated. The language barrier was difficult, and he was having trouble forming the words in English. A Hispanic nurse walked past, and Reid reached out and touched her arm. "Excuse me, ma'am. Would you mind translating for us?"

She paused, glanced at Sebastian, then gave a small nod. "Sure, but I can only spare a minute."

"That's all we need." Reid smiled his thanks.

He nodded to Sebastian, who took a deep breath and began to talk. The nurse listened without interrupting until he'd finished.

Reid looked at her expectantly.

"I was inside the apartment when I heard a scream. I looked out of the window and saw a man with a gun. He fired at Kenzie, is it?"

Reid nodded.

"He fired at Kenzie, but it missed. I heard the gun go off twice."

Reid's jaw dropped open. "He had a gun?"

The boy nodded. "Not loud."

"So, it had a silencer on?"

"Sí."

"Where's the gun now?"

"The police took it," the nurse replied.

Okay, that was good. They could get ballistics to look at it.

"What happened next?"

"Kenzie went for him. He dropped the gun, and they fought. She was very brave."

Reid's heart swelled with pride. Atta girl.

"But then the man hit her in the face, and she fell. He was strangling her when I ran out to help." Reid shot Sebastian an impressed look. "I fought him, but he ran away."

"Good kid," Reid mumbled.

The nurse nodded.

"When did you learn how to fight?" He studied the boy's lanky frame. He didn't look much like a fighter.

"Karate," said the boy.

Ah, that made sense. He was into martial arts. Vargas had said something about guns too. The kid obviously knew enough to get the better of a grown man. A dangerous man at that.

"You did well to call the ambulance, too."

He shook his head. "I no call the ambulance."

Reid frowned. "You didn't call 911?"

Another quick shake.

"Then how did they know to go there?"

The nurse repeated the question. Sebastian shrugged.

"Thank you," Reid told the nurse, who flashed a smile and walked off.

He patted Sebastian on the back. The ambulance must have been called by a neighbor or someone who saw what happened. "You did good."

He flushed. "Miss Kenzie is nice lady. I want to help."

"You did more than that," Reid said. "You saved her life."

34

Kenzie sat propped up in the hospital bed. Her face throbbed, and it hurt to breathe, but at least she wasn't dead. For a minute there she'd thought it was game over.

Reid sat on the chair beside the bed, sporting a beard and looking as rough as hell.

"You look like I feel," she told him.

"I had a long night."

"Oh, my God. Gabby. What happened?"

He shook his head.

"We were too late?" she whispered, her eyes filling with tears. She blinked them away. The drama of the last few hours was making her emotional.

"She'd been strangled in her motel room."

Kenzie took a shuddering breath. "That poor girl. Do you know who got to her? Was it Luca?"

"We don't know," he said. "I've got the whole team working on it. We're considering all options."

Standard police speak, for we have no idea who's responsible.

Sebastian shoved his hands into his pockets and slumped against the window. Kenzie's heart went out to him. He'd been so brave, coming to her rescue like that.

"Could you arrange for someone to give Sebastian a lift back to my place?" she asked, changing the subject. "He doesn't need to be here, and he's been through enough."

"Yeah, sure. I've taken his statement." Reid took out his phone and made a call. "An officer is going to meet you downstairs in five minutes," he told the kid, who glanced at Kenzie. She translated, although her Spanish wasn't much better than Reid's.

Sebastian gave a thankful nod.

"I'll see you later." She attempted a smile, but it felt like her face was cracking.

He sent her a tentative one back, then Reid shook his hand and escorted him out. He'd earned Reid's respect, she could see that.

When Reid came back, his face was grim. "Kenzie, we need to talk about what happened. That guy was there to kill you. This was an assassination attempt."

"I know." She shivered despite it being warm in the ward.

"Did you recognize the man who attacked you? Do you have any idea who it might have been?"

"I couldn't see his face," she said. "But if I had to guess, I'd say Maria sent him. She warned me not to publish that article about her love child."

"You think Maria put a hit out on you?" Reid's forehead was furrowed with lines.

"The timing fits. Think about it. She escapes from prison, the article about her love child comes out, then I get attacked. It's got to be her."

Reid balled his hand into a fist. "Maria Fucking Lopez. She's nothing but trouble."

"What are we going to do?" Kenzie fixed her gaze on him. "She's on the loose. What if she tries again?"

"She won't. I'm going to assign you around the clock security."

Kenzie fell back onto her pillow. Right now, that sounded comforting.

"You've got another visitor," sang the nurse, coming into the room.

Kenzie looked up. "Who?"

Nick, the vet, walked in and made a beeline for the bed. He didn't see Reid sitting behind the curtain. "Kenzie! Thank goodness. You scared me half to death."

"Nick!" The memory flooded back. "I'm so sorry. I totally forgot you were on the phone."

He dismissed her apology with a wave of his hand. "That's not important. What's important is that you're okay?"

"I'm fine. Just a few cuts and bruises. Wait, how did you—?"

"I heard you scream and figured something bad had happened, so I called 911. I hope I did the right thing." He came forward and noticed Reid. "Oh, I didn't know you had company."

Reid got to his feet. "Lieutenant Garrett, Sweetwater PD."

"Oh, right. Nicky Murray. I'm a friend of Kenzie's." The two men shook hands.

Reid glanced at Kenzie, but she didn't meet his eye. "I was talking to Nick when it...when he attacked me."

"I see." His face was a mask. "We'll continue this conversation down at the station when you're feeling better."

"Okay." It was down at the station now.

"I'll get a squad car out to your place in the meantime."

"Thank you." It would help to know she had someone watching the apartment in case he came back.

He gave a stiff nod, shot Nick one last glance, and strode from the room.

Nick stood by the bed. "Kenzie, what on earth happened?"

"It's a long story," she said wearily.

He sat down. "I've got time."

She didn't feel like going through it with him. "It's to do with a story I'm working on. Reid, or rather Lieutenant Garrett, is going to provide some police protection until they catch the guy."

"I'm glad to hear it. Is there anything I can do?"

"I'm fine, honestly." She smiled at him. "Thanks for coming to see me. How did you know where I was?"

"I called around."

Of course. Then a thought struck her. If he could find her, so could Maria Lopez. She gulped. The sooner she got out of here the better.

"Actually, there is something you can do," she said, sitting up.

"Sure."

"Give me a lift home?"

"Oh, I'm not sure that's a good idea." The nurse who'd overheard scurried over. "The doctor will want to give you the all-clear first."

"It's only a fractured rib." Kenzie threw back the covers. Christ, it hurt like hell, but she wasn't going to let it show. She gritted her teeth. "The rest is superficial. It'll heal in no time at all." She had three stitches in the cut on her cheekbone, a fat lip and a lovely yellow bruise spreading down to her jawline. Luckily, there was no concussion; her x-rays had been clear. "I'm sure you could use the space."

The nurse couldn't argue with that.

Using Nick's hand to steady herself, she got to her feet. "I need my clothes."

"Here." He handed her the top she'd been wearing along with a pair of jeans. "I'll wait outside."

"Thanks."

Five minutes later, she was walking out, slowly, beside him.

"What time is it?" The sun was already up, spreading its warmth over the parking lot.

"Almost ten o'clock."

She hadn't slept for well over twenty-four hours, not counting the few minutes she was unconscious. A loud yawn escaped her, and she covered her mouth. "Sorry, it's been a long night."

"I'll get you home." Nick took out his keys.

He led her to his Porsche. The doors opened upwards, which was a novel experience. She climbed in and settled back against the cool leather seats.

Nick was true to his word. He drove fast but carefully back to

Bay Harbor Island. As they pulled onto her road, she saw a police vehicle parked outside.

She smiled. Reid had done what he'd promised.

"I really appreciate the lift, Nick," she said, once he'd parked behind the squad car.

"Are you sure you're going to be okay?" His forehead creased in concern.

"Of course. There's a police patrol outside my apartment. I'll be perfectly safe here."

She hoped that was true.

"That's not what I meant. Do you want me to come in for a while?"

"Oh, that's sweet, but no thanks. I'm good."

He hesitated. "Okay, if you're sure. Please call me if you need anything."

"I will. Thanks, Nick." What she needed right now was to sleep.

He popped the door, and it rose beside her.

"Wait there." Nick climbed out, walked around, and helped her out of the car. Kenzie grimaced as she stood up. It felt like a red-hot poker was jabbing her in the side.

"You okay?" he said, concerned. "I can stay, if you like."

A uniformed officer got out of his patrol car and joined them. "Can I be of assistance, Miss Gilmore?"

Kenzie smiled at Nick. "That's okay. I'll be fine. I just need to rest. Thanks for the lift." She took the officer's arm.

"I'll call you later." He hesitated, reluctant to leave. "That is, if you don't mind."

"That would be nice."

Flashing a smile, he got back into the car, performed a U-turn, and took off down the road.

"Lean on me," the officer said. "I'll take you to your door."

"Thank you." His nametag said Hamilton, which rang a bell. "Aren't you from Sweetwater PD?"

"Yes, ma'am." There was pride in his voice. A year ago, it would have been different. Sweetwater had been the laughingstock of the

police force. Dismal arrest rates, shabby leadership, and lazy-ass officers. The backwater police department where you went when
nowhere else would have you.

Not anymore.

Reid had transformed the department into an efficient precinct
that was winning back its reputation. In fact, since he'd taken over as
lieutenant, they'd closed almost every case they'd taken on. It was
early days, but Reid didn't like leaving things undone. Like a bulldog,
he couldn't let go, and it showed in the crime figures. Now his team
was proud to work there. They held their heads high.

Hamilton helped her up the path, but every step was agony. She
leaned on him, gritting her teeth. They passed the spot where she'd
been attacked, and she gave an involuntary shudder. She'd nearly
died there with the grass under her back, having the life squeezed out
of her.

"Is there someone home?" the cop asked.

"Yes, there should be. Didn't you see a young man get dropped
off a short while ago?"

"No, ma'am. I've just been assigned. I arrived just before you did.
Lieutenant Garrett said you'd be coming home soon." He must have
figured she'd leave with Nick.

The cop rang the doorbell, but there was no answer.

"That's strange," Kenzie mused. "Sebastian should be here."

Unless he was sleeping. The poor kid had looked exhausted.

She fished in her purse for her keys.

"Here, let me." The young officer took them from her trembling
hand and unlocked the front door. It was quiet inside.

"Sebastian?" Kenzie walked into the room.

"Wait, let me check it out first." Hamilton stepped past her into
the living room. He looked around, listened, then proceeded into the
apartment. "Hello? Anyone here?" he called in a loud voice.

There was no reply.

He walked into the kitchen and looked around, then shouted,
"The back door's been forced open!"

She stumbled through, clutching her side. "Oh, my God. Someone's broken in."

Not again.

"I'm going to call it in." He hauled out his radio.

"Sebastian, are you here?" She darted into his room, but it was empty.

"Kenzie, wait. Stay behind me." The radio cackled as Hamilton followed her into the spare room.

Kenzie gasped and pointed to the sofa bed. The arm had been knocked off, as if someone had fallen hard against it. Scattered papers lay on the floor, along with a couple of books she'd had on the nightstand. Definite signs of a struggle.

She grabbed Hamilton's arm, her heart pounding.

"They've got him. They've taken Sebastian."

35

REID GLARED at his computer screen.

Who was Nick? A friend, he'd said. Well, he knew most of Kenzie's friends and smooth-dressing, Porsche-driving Nick wasn't one of them.

After he'd left the hospital, he'd taken a call on his cell and seen Kenzie leave with him. Well, Nick, let's find out who you really are.

He ran his plates and got his details from the DVA database. It wasn't strictly police work, but considering what Kenzie had been through, any newcomers in her life ought to be vetted. That's what he told himself, anyway. Nothing flagged on the police national database either. He gave a snort and logged off. The guy was clean. He might have expected it, but part of him was disappointed Kenzie's new friend didn't have a record.

"I think I might have found where our perp bought the camera," Monroe said, stretching. Judging by his bloodshot eyes, he'd been staring at his screen for a while.

"Tell me."

"There's a second-hand dealer in Coral Gables. Camera equipment is expensive, so I thought maybe I'd check out the second-hand stores and bingo. He recognized the guy in your photograph."

"Seriously?" Reid got up and walked over to the detective's desk. "That's great news."

"Except he doesn't have a name," Monroe said. "The dude paid cash."

"Of course he did." Reid's shoulders slumped. "Typical."

"But what the customer didn't know," continued Monroe, a glint breaking through the tiredness, "was that there was a hidden CCTV camera in the store. I've asked for the footage."

"Hell yeah." Reid fist-bumped him. "We might finally get a good look at this guy."

Monroe grinned. "I thought you'd like that."

"Great work," Reid said. At last, something had gone their way. Maybe now they could turn the tide on this gang of traffickers. It was time they had some luck. "Let me know when they send it through."

His desk phone rang, so he walked back to answer it. "Garrett."

"Boss, it's Hamilton."

He'd posted Hamilton outside Kenzie's apartment. "What's wrong?"

"We have a situation," he said.

Reid froze. "What's up? Is Kenzie alright?"

"Yeah, Kenzie's fine, it's the kid."

"Sebastian?"

"He's been taken."

Reid frowned. Did the rookie cop mean what he thought he meant? "What do you mean, taken? As in kidnapped?"

"Yes, sir. The backdoor's been forced, and the kid is gone. There are signs of a struggle in the spare bedroom. Miss Gilmore is very distressed. I think you'd better come over."

Shit.

"Put her on the phone."

Kenzie sounded scared. "Reid, they've taken him. Maria's taken him."

"Maria?"

"It must be. She's getting back at him for coming to my defense yesterday."

"Kenzie, calm down. We don't know it's her yet."

"Who else?"

That was a good question.

"Why kidnap a displaced kid? It doesn't make sense. I can see them coming back for you, but not him."

"Perhaps they came back for me and found him."

"If that's the case, they wouldn't have kidnapped him. They'd have taken him out there and then..."

He heard her sharp intake of breath. "Sorry, but you know it's true."

There was a ragged pause.

"What if the traffickers have found him?" she whispered.

He thought about this. The silence dragged out. "Reid, are you there?"

"Yeah, I'm here. They do have a motive," he admitted. "But how did they find him? You're not in the system yet. Nobody knows where he is, other than me, Vargas, Diaz, and you." It couldn't be one of his team members.

"Could they have seen him at the hospital?" Kenzie suggested.

"Unlikely." If they had, it was one hell of a coincidence, and he didn't believe in those.

"It can't be them then." Kenzie huffed into the phone. "Dammit, I feel so helpless."

He felt the same way. "I'll put out an APB. We'll get everybody available out looking for him."

"I can put an appeal for information in the *Herald*," she offered.

"Yeah, that might work, and I'm sending a CSI unit over to your place to dust for prints."

But she wasn't listening. "He saved my life, Reid. We have to find him."

"I know, and we will." He hoped he could stand by that.

"Please, he's just a boy."

"I'm on it. Listen, I've got to go. I'll talk to you later." He hung up, a heavy sense of foreboding in his chest.

After she'd spoken to Reid, Kenzie pulled herself together and called Keith at the newspaper. He was irate that she hadn't checked in since New York, but then she told him what had happened.

"Jesus, Kenzie. I've never known anyone to attract trouble like you do."

"Thanks, boss." It was a handy trait for a reporter, she thought ironically.

"Stay at home. Don't risk coming in. I'm sending Raoul over. You're going to need him. I want copy and lots of it. Let's tell the world what's been happening."

"That Maria Lopez has put a hit out on me? Are you crazy?"

"What better way to douse the flames than make it common knowledge? She escaped, she's tried to have you assassinated, she's kidnapped the kid."

"We don't know that for sure."

"Who cares? It's newsworthy. If she didn't do it, let her dispute it herself."

How? It's not like she could issue a press release.

A thought popped into her mind. Perhaps she could use this series of articles to send Maria a message? "I'm going to write an appeal for information on Sebastian, too," she told him. "I've cleared it with Detective Garrett."

"Fine," he huffed. "As long as I get the Lopez stuff."

"Deal."

Raoul arrived later that day, laptop under one arm, cables under the other. "I brought a booster in case your WIFI isn't strong enough."

"I'm sure it's adequate," she retorted, nodding to Hamilton to let him in.

Her assistant entered the apartment, looked around, then set up on the dining room table next to her laptop. She couldn't go into Sebastian's room. It was all she could do to keep working. Reid would find him. She clung to that thought. In the meantime, she'd work on drawing out Maria Lopez.

The first article retold the story of Maria's escape. Kenzie called the U.S. Marshals Service and spoke to a polite man who'd been assigned to deal with the press. He gave her the same vague details he gave everybody else.

It was an ambush. Two vehicles cut off the transit van on the freeway outside Atlanta. Four masked men boarded the vehicle and shot the marshals, assaulted the driver, and took Maria. They had no leads, and no idea where she was now. Probably Mexico.

"I'll see what I can find out," Raoul offered.

She shot him a sideways glance. "How?"

He shrugged. "By collating all the information from other news articles and seeing if I can come up with anything different."

"You won't. We've all been fed the same story." She hesitated. "How do you feel about tracking down Maria's baby daddy?"

He raised an eyebrow. "Emmanuelle Lenoir's biological father? That is not going to be easy."

"I know, but let's start with the most obvious, her husband's inner circle, his lieutenants. Back in 1998, he was imprisoned on a drug charge for ten months. Check who visited him while he was inside. Those are the people she'd have the most contact with."

That's what she'd do, anyway.

Raoul gave a quick nod. "I'm on it."

If they could find out who he was, they'd have something to hang over Maria's head. They'd have their own leverage.

At the end of the first piece, Kenzie mentioned the book and that it was still going ahead, despite Maria's disappearance. The publishers wanted to push ahead, and Kenzie felt they had enough material, especially with information that had recently come to light. She omitted to say what that was.

The second article, to be published the day after the first, covered Maria's jaunt in France and the birth of her illegitimate child. Instead of rehashing the one she'd written when the scandal broke, she focused on Federico Lopez, and how he knew nothing about the pregnancy. Who was the father? Why wasn't he in France, too? Didn't Maria want him to know about the child? Had she kept both men in the dark?

Once again, she mentioned Maria's memoirs and the release date for the book. "There are a few surprises," she wrote, hinting at "as yet unknown" material.

The third and final article covered the two break-ins at her place, and the fact a refugee child had been kidnapped.

IS THE MORALES CARTEL HUMAN TRAFFICKING?

Kenzie leaned back and stretched. "That should get Maria Lopez's attention."

Raoul grinned. "She's not going to want to own up to that. You'd better be ready for the onslaught."

"What else can she do?" Kenzie spread her arms. "She's already got a hit out on me. I've got policemen stationed outside my door twenty-four seven. If I'm going to piss her off, it may as well be now."

Then she called Reid and told him what she'd done.

"Are you out of your mind?" he yelled down the phone. "Do you want to make things worse?"

"I'm not sure how they could get any worse," she reasoned. "She's already out to get me."

But she got it, and she'd expected this. As a cop, he was trying to protect her, and here she was causing trouble again. Sometimes they worked at cross purposes, but that was inevitable. He was an officer of the law, and she was a reporter. They both had the same goal, however, and that was to draw Maria out. It was the only way they were going to find out whether she'd kidnapped Sebastian.

"This will make her more determined than ever," he warned. "Christ, Kenzie. Maybe I should put you into protective custody."

"That would defeat the purpose. I need to be where she can contact me."

"I don't like it," he reiterated. "You're purposely provoking a known felon. A dangerous one, at that. You know what Maria Lopez does to people who cross her."

An image of Alberto Torres lying in a pool of blood sprung to mind. Kenzie swallowed. "It might get her to come out of hiding. You know as well as I do the DEA is never going to find her, not unless she wants to be found." There was a pause. The phone felt heavy with tension. "Reid, I don't know what else to do. This could work."

He gave a low growl. "I've got a bad feeling about this, Kenzie."

"If she's got Sebastian, I want to know why." Kenzie walked to the window and looked out onto the street. The squad car was still there, Hamilton in the driver's seat. "You might want to send more men."

"Thanks to your little tactic, I'm going to have to."

"Maybe she took Sebastian to use as leverage," Kenzie said quietly.

Reid was silent.

"Perhaps she wants me to finish the book."

He wasn't happy. When he wasn't happy, he clammed up.

"Do *you* have any news?" she asked, eventually. The forensic experts had been here for hours, fingerprinting the spare room.

"Actually, yeah. The CSI team found some blood in your office that doesn't belong to Sebastian," he said.

"You mean it's the kidnapper's?" She turned away from the window.

"Must be. Who else could it belong to? It's not yours. We ruled you out."

Her pulse quickened. This could be a lead. "That's great, Reid. Let me know the minute you find anything." He couldn't promise that, but she knew he'd inform her if he got a lead on Sebastian.

"Likewise. Call me if Maria makes contact and don't—I repeat, don't—under any circumstances, arrange to meet her alone."

"I won't." Not after yesterday's attack. One thing Kenzie had learned about Maria Lopez is she couldn't be trusted.

The series of articles were sent over to Keith, who was on the blower straight away. "Loving your work, Kenz. Do you know who the father is?"

"Not yet, but Raoul's working on it."

"I didn't know the book was going ahead."

"I may have exaggerated that part," she said. "The book is on hold since Maria disappeared. I don't have enough material to submit a full manuscript."

He chuckled. "You never cease to amaze me. Okay, fine. Let's do it. The media frenzy over her illegitimate daughter is fading out. It didn't have the effect I was hoping for, not after Warner Sullivan and his model girlfriend came clean about Maria."

Kenzie didn't say anything.

Keith would never suspect her. She was a hard-nosed journalist, a seeker of the truth. She'd never sabotage a story like that.

It showed how well he knew her.

Raoul pushed back his chair. "I don't know, Kenzie. I can't find anything that suggests Maria was having an affair with one of her husband's cohorts. There isn't much to go on. It was a long time ago, and the internet didn't exist then."

He was a child of the modern age. They all were.

It looked like the father angle was going to be a dead end.

An engine revved outside, and she went back to the window. A second cop car had arrived, along with an unmarked panel van that parked down the street. She knew it contained at least four officers.

"Pretty obvious," droned Raoul, standing beside her.

"It doesn't matter," she said. "It's a show of force. A warning should anyone decide to come for me." And she shivered.

"It's a brave thing you're doing, Kenzie," Raoul said. "I don't know if I'd have the guts."

She shrugged. "I have to find out whether she's got Sebastian. This is the only way."

He gave a slow nod, then turned away from the window. "What's this?"

"It's my folder. I keep a hardcopy of everything relevant to the case. You know, just in case my laptop gets damaged or stolen."

He sat down. "May I?"

"Sure. There's nothing in there you don't already know."

He began thumbing through it. Notes on her interviews with Maria, the prison warden, Maria's lawyer. Arrest reports, the newspaper articles on Maria's escape, the photograph of Maria at the French hotel.

He stopped and stared at the black-and-white image.

"What is it?" Kenzie asked, coming over.

The guests were standing in a courtyard, surrounded by flowers. The night looked balmy as Maria was wearing an off-the-shoulder dress. Despite her big tummy, she looked exotic and glamorous.

"Who's that?" Raoul pointed to the woman standing next to Maria.

She leaned over the photograph. "I'm not sure. Are they together?"

"Could be," he replied. "It looks like they're both looking in the same direction." He prodded the photograph. "Everybody else is staring straight ahead, but they're looking to the left and laughing, as if sharing a private joke."

Kenzie scrutinized the expressions on their faces. Raoul was right! They were together. "If we find *her*, she'll tell us who the father is."

Raoul grinned. "What's the bet she also stayed at the hotel?"

"Maria wasn't there alone," Kenzie whispered.

The researcher's fingers flew over the keyboard. He brought up the hotel list, and they went through the guests one by one, Googling their names, looking up their nationalities and checking their social media profiles. Only one woman, other than Nora Molina, wasn't European.

"Her Facebook profile says she lives in Tijuana," Raoul said.

Kenzie's eyes gleamed. "We've found her."

Finally, they were getting somewhere. This was the big carrot she was going to dangle in front of Maria—and if the cartel boss knew what was good for her, she'd take a bite. Dialogue would be open, and they'd be one step closer to getting Sebastian back.

36

REID STARED down at Gabby Rosenbaum's dead body. He hated coming to the viewing gallery at the morgue, but waiting for the autopsy report took too long.

She'd been sliced open from her sternum to her navel, the skin peeled back, exposing her chest cavity. He tried not to look at the deep red slash, but focused on the rest of her body, which was pasty white like a wax figure. The medical examiner was reaching inside and taking out her organs to weigh them.

Reid fought back the pastrami sandwich that threatened to rise.

Cause of death was strangulation—no surprises there. So far, all he had from the ME was, "big hands," judging by the bruising around her throat, which meant they were looking for a tall person, a male perp. It fit with what they knew about the gay lover at the motel.

The bouncer, Mr. Piper, had sat with an artist and they'd drawn up an identikit of the killer. Handsome, Hispanic, possibly Cuban, with arching eyebrows and a wide mouth. It was being circulated to the other departments, but Reid knew how these things worked. Without a definitive marking like a scar or a tattoo, there was nothing to differentiate this guy from millions of others. It would be tacked up on the squad room bulletin board and forgotten about.

He thought back to what else they knew. There was no skin or debris under her fingernails, so she hadn't put up a fight. It was most likely he'd come at her from behind, rendering her unconscious in a matter of seconds. Once the blood had stopped flowing to her brain, he could have moved her to the bed and strangled her there.

Her clothing had been sent to the forensic lab for analysis, but Reid didn't hold out much hope. This guy was careful. He didn't leave traces—other than the cigarette butt at the cabin. That had been his one and only mistake, and Reid was betting he'd panicked when he'd seen Diaz filming the onlookers. If he'd stayed put, they'd never have suspected him.

When the ME got to the stomach contents, Reid decided to leave. He couldn't take anymore, and he wanted to stop by Kenzie's on the way home. On the truck radio, he heard an interview with Warner Sullivan. "We had no idea Emmanuelle was related to the notorious crime boss," he told the listeners in his charming baritone. "It came as a complete shock to her. My fiancé was brought up in France. She has no ties to the Morales Cartel whatsoever."

They were doing a lot of damage control, but it was working. America was rooting for the golden couple. The President's son and the beautiful fashion model. Kenzie had been right to warn them. Maria Lopez had caused enough damage.

The stars were twinkling by the time he got to Kenzie's. He had a quick word with the officers on guard, then knocked on the door. She opened it, her phone to her ear, and beckoned for him to come in.

"I need a return ticket," she was saying. "For one person. Tonight."

He raised an eyebrow.

"Tijuana International Airport. I'll pay by card, thanks."

Now he was just plain confused. Why was Kenzie going to Mexico?

"What are you doing?" he hissed. "You can't leave. It's too dangerous." She was going after Maria. He knew it! He shook his head, but she ignored him.

"The passenger's name is Raoul Acosta."

Reid exhaled, feeling a little silly. Kenzie wasn't about to run off to Mexico with a price on her head. She wasn't stupid. Impulsive, maybe, but not stupid.

"You didn't have to check up on me," she said after she hung up.

"I wanted to," he replied. "You've got a bullseye on your back."

Kenzie sighed. "The first article is coming out tomorrow. She's unlikely to contact me tonight."

"Still, I want to check the door and windows, make sure you're secure."

She gestured for him to do so. "Fine, suit yourself."

He walked around the apartment, testing the windows. Everything was locked up, as was the back door. A steel bolt had been added for good measure.

"Why is your research assistant going to Tijuana?" he asked, standing at the kitchen counter.

"Coffee?" she asked, nodding to the pot.

"Yeah, thanks."

She poured them each a cup, then took a seat on the bar stool opposite him. "We've got a lead on the father of Maria's illegitimate daughter, so I'm sending Raoul over to talk to her."

"Her?"

"Yeah, a friend of Maria's from way back. We think she might know who the father is."

He nodded slowly. "Don't you think Maria will have thought of that?"

She raised her head. "All the more reason to get to her quickly."

"Why are you doing this?" he asked after a beat. "You've insinuated you know already. Isn't that enough to get her attention?"

"Not if I want to get Sebastian back. I might need to prove it."

"You think she's going to trust you not to tell the world about her secret lover after you've splashed everything else across the tabloids?"

Kenzie didn't reply.

"I know you're trying to help the kid, but you're putting yourself at risk. She's going to come after you with everything she's got."

"I'm ready for her," Kenzie whispered. "Besides, if she comes anywhere near the apartment, the police outside will catch her. That's what you want, isn't it?"

"Yes, but I didn't mean using you as bait."

"That's my decision."

They glared at each other for a long moment until Reid looked away. He couldn't argue with her. She'd do whatever she wanted, regardless. The most he could hope for was that Maria was foolish enough to attempt to make contact, and that his guys caught her.

Before she got near the apartment.

He got up. Damn, he was tired, and he desperately needed to shave. "I'll be going," he told her, heading for the door. "Make sure you lock this behind me."

"I will."

He was about to leave when his phone buzzed. It was an official number.

"Garrett," he barked, answering it.

"This is Reese Corbin at the CSI lab. I've got the DNA results off the cigarette stub that you wanted."

"Oh, yeah." He paused, his hand on the door handle. Kenzie stood inside, watching him. "What did you find?"

"There is no match with anyone in the database," he said.

Reid sighed. "Couldn't this have waited until morning?" Why call just to tell him that?

"Probably, except there's something else, sir."

"There is?"

"Yeah, it's kinda strange, but the DNA matched with one of the more recent samples, the blood found at Kenzie Gilmore's apartment."

"Excuse me?" He must have misheard. "You're saying the DNA on the cigarette butt belongs to the same person whose blood was found at Kenzie's place, in the room where the refugee kid was kidnapped?"

Kenzie's eyes were huge.

"Yes, sir. That's what I'm telling you."

Reid thanked the lab assistant and hung up.

Kenzie was staring at him. "What does it mean?"

He walked back inside and shut the door, locking it behind him. "It means that the people who took Sebastian are the same people who smuggled Rosa's sister and those refugees into the country."

"I don't understand." She scraped her hand through her hair. "It's not possible. It doesn't make sense." She turned around, her face ashen. "How could they have known he was here?"

"There's only one way." He gave her a grave look. "They saw him when they came to kill you."

Her hand flew to her mouth. "The attack. That was them?"

He nodded.

"Not Maria?"

"No, that's what was bothering me. The whole MO was different. Maria has never tried to harm you before. Warn you off, yes, but not kill you. This was different. This was an organized hit. The killer followed you home, shot at you coming up the path, then tried to strangle you. They wanted to shut you up."

"But why?" She shook her head, confusion clouding her eyes.

"Because you know something, Kenz. Something that could hurt them."

"I don't know anything about the smuggling case." Her voice wobbled. "The only involvement I had was when I went to speak to Gabby at the charity."

"Now Gabby's dead. Strangled, like what they tried to do to you." Kenzie went white.

"You must have seen something, heard something."

"But what? The only other person there was the priest at the front desk." She gasped. "You don't think he's involved?"

He frowned. "I didn't think so, but—?" He shrugged.

Kenzie had a faraway look in her eye. "When I asked Gabby who Luca was, she immediately looked at her boss. I thought it was because she didn't want him to know she was helping smuggle refugees over the border, but it could have been because she was afraid of him. Because he was Luca."

37

"Are you sure it's him?" Reid asked Monroe, dragging him out of bed so he could log on to his laptop at home to check the CCTV footage from the second-hand camera shop.

"Absolutely, boss. I've sent it to Vargas who has just confirmed it's Father Diego."

"I want him picked up," Reid snapped. After a beat. "Yes, now."

He hung up and looked at Kenzie. "Vargas is working on an arrest warrant, but he's having trouble rousing a judge."

"It is the middle of the night."

"I can't believe we didn't consider this sooner." He shook his head. "I wrote him off because he was a Catholic priest, but now that I think about it, he's the right height and size as the guy in the baseball cap. He also looks a little like the picture the sketch artist came up with."

"The guy in the motel room?"

"Yeah. Not a lot, but there is a vague likeness."

"If he is Luca." Kenzie thought out loud. "He set up the charity to help immigrants, but the whole time he was smuggling them into the country, then extorting money from their families."

"Sick, I know," grumbled Reid. "He's a priest, too, but then he did burn down a whole cabin and kill ten innocent people just to cover his tracks."

"He can't be working alone," Kenzie said.

"Nope, and once we bring him in, we'll make him talk. It won't be long before we have the rest of the network in custody."

"What about Sebastian?" Her tired blue eyes filled with worry. "Do you think he's still alive?" Her voice cracked as she said the words.

"I hope so." Although, the more time that went past, the bleaker the prospect. Sebastian had escaped their clutches once before. He could identify them by voice, by their actions. He was a witness to at least one shooting, possibly two.

Now, he was a liability.

Kenzie knew this too, although she gave a brave nod. She wasn't willing to give up hope yet.

"Let me know if there's anything I can do," she said, as he opened the front door. He had to get back to the police station.

"Stay here and remain indoors. You should be safe with the patrolmen outside. Any trouble, call 911."

"Okay, and Reid..."

"Yeah?"

"Be careful."

"Always."

He strode down the path to his car.

"Father Diego, you'd better be home," he muttered to himself as he unlocked it and climbed in. Before he had a chance to start the ignition, his phone rang.

"He's gone," Diaz said. Reid put her on speaker phone. She'd got there ahead of him. "We're at his place now. He's packed up and moved out."

"Shit, he must have got wind of it. What about St. Michaels, the church affiliated with the charity?"

"I've sent a couple of officers over there. He's nowhere to be seen."

"Argh!" He thumped his hand down on the steering wheel.

"Perhaps he left after he murdered Gabby," Diaz suggested. "It was only a matter of time before the cops tracked him down."

"Yeah, probably." He leaned back against the headrest. Now what? "Did he leave anything there?"

"Yeah, lots of stuff. He didn't take much, by the looks of things."

Reid straightened up. "I'm coming over."

He blue-lighted it across town. Maybe, just maybe, there'd be a clue as to where he'd taken Sebastian.

Diego Hernandez lived in a beautiful house in Miami Beach, right on the water. Bought with blood money, Reid thought darkly. His measly priest's salary and what he earned at the Open Arms charity sure as hell wouldn't pay for this.

Reid parked behind the other squad cars and walked through a six-foot wrought iron automatic gate onto the property that was lit up like Disney World. Diaz met him at the door.

"Quite the cover," she said, letting him in. "Human trafficker masquerading as a priest running a refugee charity." He certainly had them fooled.

Reid glanced around at the marble flooring, the extravagant arches, and the terracotta urns out of which tumbled lush house-plants. Hernandez was living the high life, getting rich by extorting money from frightened families eager to see their loved ones again.

"Any idea where he went?"

"We're searching the house," Diaz said. "He left in a hurry, taking most of the artwork with him." Reid noticed the gaps on the walls.

"What about a den or an office?"

"There's one along here. We're going through his stuff now. So far, we haven't found anything incriminating. His laptop's gone, of course, and there are no phones or devices lying around."

"Let's get his phone records," he said, although a man like Hernandez would use a burner. "And his bank details. We might be able to pick up something from his finances."

Diaz gave a curt nod. She was excellent at a crime scene. She had a natural ability to coordinate various groups of cops, forensics, and other law enforcement professionals with minimal fuss.

"And let's bag this stuff up and bring it to the station. I want it gone through with a fine-tooth comb." If there was anything there that could point them in the right direction, they'd find it.

"Yes, boss." She spun on her heel and strode off.

Reid walked out onto the dark terrace. From there, he could see all the way across the bay to the glittering lights of the city. It would be spectacular in the daylight. A five-million-dollar view. He scoffed. Father Diego's hypocrisy knew no bounds. A fluorescent kidney-shaped swimming pool shimmered below and beyond that at the water's edge looked like a boat mooring. The only reason he could make it out was because of a series of solar lights dotted along a paved path towards it. A gingerbread trail.

"Does he own a boat?" Reid called over his shoulder.

Diaz appeared. "I don't know. Good question."

"The bank statements will tell us." Reid turned his back on the view. It wasn't too long ago he'd had a vista like that, over the swamp. It wasn't Biscayne Bay, but it was peaceful, and he missed it.

Fucking Hernandez. He had a lot to answer for.

Buoyed up by more coffee, Reid faced his team. Everyone who was available had been called in. "Thanks for coming in, guys," he told them. "As you've heard, we raided Diego Hernandez's Miami Beach house a short while ago. The contents of his study are in the briefing room. I need volunteers to go through it. We're looking for a missing boy. Sebastian has now been gone for sixteen hours. It's not looking good. Now we know who's got him, and it's imperative we get him back ASAP."

Nods all around.

"I need someone to go through his bank records and phone calls. The warrants have been granted, and we'll get that data as soon as the respective institutions open." He glanced at his phone. "In about two hours."

"I'll go through the bank records," Vargas said.

"I'll take his phone," Diaz chipped in.

He gave them a nod. "The rest of you, let's dig up anything we can find on this guy. I want to know every asset he owns, whether it's a boat, a factory, or a damn restaurant. You got me?"

"Yes, boss," came the unanimous reply.

"I can't stress how urgent this is. A boy's life is at stake. Let's get moving."

They split up and got to work.

"He owns a 32-foot Concept," Lomax, one of the detectives, called out a short while later. "Bought it in 2010."

"Contact the Coast Guard," Reid said. "We need to find that boat. It could be what he's bringing the refugees over in before dropping them off in the Glades."

"It's a fancy boat for people smuggling," Vargas said, looking up.

Reid shrugged. "It would be a good cover if he was ever stopped and questioned. A priest going fishing on a friend's boat."

Diaz didn't have any luck with the phone records. "He must use burners. There's no record of Diego Hernandez ever having a cell phone contract."

"Figures."

"The charity has a toll-free number." Diaz stared at her screen. "It routes to a cell phone, also a burner, but I've got the number."

"Great, see what you can dig up." They could get the call details once they knew the phone number. It probably wasn't in use anymore, but it might offer up something they could use.

"How are we doing on the bank records?" he asked Vargas, who'd been on the phone with the bank since they opened.

"Going through them now."

Reid joined him. It was better than sitting at his desk being drip-fed information.

"Here, you take the last six months." Vargas handed him the printed copies. "I'll do prior to that."

Reid settled down next to him to read. It was the usual stuff. Household maintenance, fishing equipment, groceries, utility bills.

Nothing out of the ordinary. "He must have a separate account for his business transactions," Reid muttered.

"Boss, I've got something." One of the junior detectives who'd volunteered to go through the contents of Hernandez's study rushed in, his face flushed.

"What is it?"

The detective handed him a document listing a Daisy Hernandez as director of a shell corporation called Apostle Holdings. "He can't be married," Reid said. "It must be his sister."

"Yup. Daisy Thornton, nee Hernandez," read Diaz, after tapping away at her computer. "Born 1981, here in Miami."

"I'll get the bank statements for Apostle Holdings," Vargas said, reaching for the phone.

"This is more like it," Reid announced, scanning the new lot of bank transactions. "He bought the Concept through the company, along with a warehouse in South Florida." He slapped his hand on the desk. "We need the address. Now."

Twenty minutes later, they were racing south, sirens blaring. Vargas was driving, as Reid didn't trust his judgment after thirty-two hours without sleep. Two more patrol cars followed in case they needed backup.

The warehouse was a six thousand square foot commercial property that looked like a giant blue matchbox with a lid on it. "He bought it two years ago," Reid said, as they parked out of sight. "And according to the real estate agent, it's been recently renovated with upgraded electrics and air-conditioning."

Drawing their weapons, they approached the warehouse. They moved cautiously, alert for any sound or movement, but there was nothing.

"I'm going to take a look around the back," Vargas said.

Reid nodded and crouched down outside one of the front windows. He craned his neck to see in, but there was only darkness. Next to him was a large overhead multiuse door, but it was locked.

"It looks like this is the office and reception area, with a factory behind it," Vargas said, coming back. "How'd you want to do this?"

"It appears to be deserted, so let's go in the front." Reid assessed the risk level as low. "But get the others to watch the back in case he is there and tries to run for it."

"Gotcha." Vargas relayed the information to the backup team, who spread out around the building. They crept up to the front door. Reid rang the buzzer as a matter of protocol. There was no reply. He nodded to one of the backup crew members who was waiting with the battering ram. Crude, but effective.

The door flew open.

"Police," called Reid, ducking in first. Vargas was close on his heels. The reception room was empty, as was the adjoining office.

"Clear," yelled Vargas.

They proceeded into the dark warehouse through a connecting door. It was noticeably colder here and smelled musty and damp. They switched on their flashlights.

"Hello? Anybody here?" Reid shouted into the darkness.

A faint scuffle made him freeze.

"Vargas, wait."

They stood still, listening.

Another scuffle, louder this time.

"It's coming from over there." Reid took off, moving as fast as he dared in the beam of his flashlight. The warehouse extended quite a way back. He wondered what Hernandez used it for.

"Hello? Is anyone there?"

He hoped it wasn't going to be a giant rat or something.

"Sebastian, is that you?" A muffled moan floated out of the corner. Reid pointed his light in that direction and gasped. "Jesus Christ!"

The teenage boy lay in the fetal position, a gag over his mouth, his hands tied behind his back.

"Get some light in here!" Reid yelled, darting forward. He bent down to inspect Sebastian. He was alive, but in some discomfort. He'd been badly beaten and was desperately in need of water. There didn't seem to be any around. That bastard Hernandez was going to let him die here.

Vargas found a light switch, and the warehouse lit up as a series of fluorescent bulbs flicked on. Sebastian squeezed his eyes shut, unused to the brightness, and whimpered.

"It's okay," Reid told him, holstering his gun. "You're safe now."

He gently pulled the gag off the boy's mouth and cut through the plastic ties that bound his wrists and ankles. Angry purple welts cut into his skin. It was clear Sebastian had tried to free himself but lacked the strength. Not surprising given the state he was in.

With Vargas's help, they lifted the boy to his feet. His legs were wobbly, but he managed to walk, supported by the two detectives. Very slowly, they made their way out of the warehouse and into the sunlight.

38

KENZIE SCREAMED when she got Reid's message. They'd found Sebastian, and he was alive!

Thank you, God!

She was at home, under police watch, bored as hell. Keith didn't mind her working from home, especially since they were following up on a lead on Maria's secret baby daddy.

"Have you heard from Raoul?" he barked into the phone, when she called to give him the good news about Sebastian. She had to tell someone.

"He texted me this morning when he arrived in Tijuana," she said, crushed he wasn't as happy as she was that Sebastian was safe. "He's on his way to meet Anna."

"Let me know when you have something," he snapped. "I can't talk, Raymond's traipsed off to the Keys, and Lucian's come in hammered from a boozy lunch with the editor of the Yachting Times, and I'm waiting for his piece on the American Open."

Clearly, Keith was in a foul mood, but it sounded like business as usual at the newspaper.

"Will do." She hung up, feeling deflated.

"I'm glad your little friend has been found," said a voice behind her.

Kenzie froze. She knew that voice. It was unmistakable.

Maria Lopez.

Slowly, she turned around, her heart hammering. To her surprise, Maria stood in her kitchen as if she were here for a social visit, elegant as always in a white, two-piece suit with silver heels. Kenzie glanced behind her, expecting to see a hit squad with semi-automatic rifles aimed at her.

"They're outside," she confirmed. "I wouldn't come alone."

No, of course not.

"How—?" Kenzie started to say before she was cut off.

"How did I get past the guards?" She laughed, a throaty sound that set Kenzie's teeth on edge. "Easy when you know how."

Kenzie glanced at the window.

"Don't worry, they're not harmed. They're just under armed guard for the time being. If they give us any trouble, however, things might not turn out as well."

Kenzie hoped it wouldn't come to that.

"What do you want?" she hissed.

"I want to talk. So do you, judging by that article you published in the *Herald* today."

It had worked. She'd drawn Maria out, but contrary to what she'd expected, the cartel boss didn't have anything to do with Sebastian's disappearance.

"I want to finish the book," Kenzie lied. It was a way to start negotiations.

"I want that too," Maria said. "Which is why I came to see you." There was a pause as Maria gazed around the room. Eventually, she said, "Let's make a deal, Kenzie."

"You didn't keep your end of the deal," Kenzie pointed out.

Maria smiled. "You didn't honestly think I was going to give up the Californian side of my organization, did you? Not after the Miami branch has been torn apart?"

"No, I suppose not." She'd been naive. Maria Lopez had no plans to slide into obscurity. She wasn't ready to give up the organization she'd been running for the last two years. Perhaps she had visions of rebuilding it, running it with her son, Matteo. She scratched her head. "But I thought that's why you were getting death threats, because you were going to betray them."

Maria threw back her long, black hair and laughed. "Betray my own son? Please. There were no death threats. I planted those there myself."

Kenzie shook her head. They'd been so blind.

"You planted those masks in your own cell, so that when the transfer order came through, there was a legitimate reason for moving you."

The cartel boss inclined her head. "You're beginning to catch on, Kenzie. I like that about you. You're a fast learner." She frowned. "Too fast sometimes."

"You're referring to Emmanuelle."

A wistful look passed over the crime boss's face. "Emmanuelle, yes. All these years, I've been watching her career from afar, her relationship with Warner Sullivan. Do you know how hard it's been to stay away?"

For a moment Kenzie thought Maria's eyes filled with tears, but it was so fleeting, she must have been mistaken. She wasn't human enough to cry. "I can imagine."

"Can you? I don't think so. Perhaps one day, when you have children of your own, you'll understand."

"Why *did* you stay away?" Kenzie asked.

Maria scoffed. "I chose this life because I had no other option. She does."

Kenzie got it. She didn't want to pollute what Emmanuelle had built for herself, yet it had happened anyway.

"It wasn't my choice to reveal her identity." For some bizarre reason, Kenzie felt like she owed Maria an explanation. "I tried to keep it under wraps, but once my researcher found out, he told the Editor, and then it was out of my control."

Maria studied her under her dark eyelashes.

"That's why I flew to New York, to warn her. It was the least I could do. I thought if they released it themselves, it wouldn't be so damaging."

"To whom? Emmanuelle or the President."

"Both." Kenzie looked her in the eye. "I didn't want to cause a political scandal, and Emmanuelle doesn't deserve to have her life ripped to shreds."

The dark eyes narrowed.

"If it was anyone else, I wouldn't believe them," she said. "But I like your integrity, Kenzie. I always have, which is why we work so well together."

Is that what they were doing?

"Do you want to continue with the interviews?" Kenzie asked, sticking to her theme.

"I said I would, didn't I?"

Kenzie thought back to the last time she'd spoken to Maria face to face.

Don't worry so much, Kenzie. You still get to finish the book. I will make sure of it.

Back then she hadn't understood, but it made sense now.

"How?"

"I'll contact you. We can conduct the interviews via Zoom. It's the modern era. We don't have to risk our lives to meet in person."

This was true.

"You realize half the country is looking for you," Kenzie said. "If they knew I was meeting regularly with you, albeit via Zoom, I'd have them swarming all over me."

She laughed. "That's why you won't tell them." Her voice dropped to a conspiratorial whisper. "This is just between you and me."

"I'm not sure I can do that."

The smile vanished. "If you want to finish the book, you'll keep our little secret. Think of the scoop, Kenzie. Secret meetings with the notorious Morales cartel boss. It gives the book something extra, don't you think?" Kenzie couldn't fault her there.

"There's one condition," Maria said.

"Another one?" Kenzie raised an eyebrow.

"You don't reveal who Emmanuelle's biological father is." Kenzie thought of Raoul on his way to Maria's friend's house at this exact moment. "That is non-negotiable."

The woman's petite frame stiffened as she waited for Kenzie's reply. She was scared. Now that was interesting. What did she have to fear from the father of her illegitimate child?

She thought of Maria's son, Matteo, working in California with Romeo Herrera, being groomed to take over the family business.

Of course! That's what this was all about.

"He doesn't know, does he?" Kenzie's eyes were glued on Maria's face.

"Of course he knows," she hissed.

"I wasn't talking about your lover. I was talking about your son."

Her face darkened. Her hand slipped behind her back, and Kenzie found herself looking down the barrel of a slim, single stack pistol. "I'm not going to have to silence you, am I, Kenzie? Because it would be a real shame. We have an opportunity to do something great together. The book will raise both our profiles, give us fame and fortune."

Like Reid had said, she was a narcissistic maniac.

"No." Kenzie swallowed. It was time to be diplomatic. "I know how hard you've worked to get where you are. I know what it's like to get ahead in a man's world. I wouldn't ruin that for you. For us."

Maria had said something similar when they'd first met. Kenzie knew her words would hit home.

And they did. Maria relaxed, and the hand holding the gun dropped to her side. Kenzie breathed a silent sigh of relief.

"I knew you'd see reason."

"We both want something here," Kenzie continued. "You want the book published, and I want the recognition. Sabotaging everything for a flash-in-the-pan scandal would be stupid."

Maria was much calmer now. "I'm glad we see eye to eye."

Kenzie's phone rang in her pocket.

"Don't get that," Maria snapped.

"I wasn't going to." Kenzie kept her hands where Maria could see them.

The cartel boss began backing out of the kitchen. The back door was ajar. Somehow, her men had managed to open it without a sound.

"I'll be in touch," Maria said, and then she was gone.

39

Kenzie rushed to the window and looked out onto the street. The two squad cars were still there, so was the van across the road.

Huh?

Fearing the worst, she pulled open the door and ran down the path. Immediately, all four officers leaped out of their vehicles. Thank goodness they looked unharmed.

"What's wrong?" a tall cop from the first car asked.

She came to a halt, willing her pulse to stop racing. Maria had said they'd been held at gunpoint, but she'd lied. Somehow, she'd managed to get into the apartment via the backdoor without the cops seeing her. "Oh, um... nothing. I thought I heard something out back, that's all."

"We'll take a look for you. Go back inside and lock the door."

Kenzie did as she was told while the officers checked out the perimeter. "All clear," he told her afterwards. "There's nobody here."

"Thanks." She gave a sheepish smile. "My nerves are on edge."

"That's okay. That's what we're here for. Give us a shout anytime you feel worried."

"I will. Thank you." He had no idea how close he'd come to being shot.

Maria was full of surprises. The cops were guarding the only access road into the complex. To bypass them, Maria must have come by boat, climbed over the wall, and walked up the back garden into the condo.

Kenzie went back into her apartment and collapsed on the couch. She was still processing what had happened. Had she made a deal with the devil?

Reid would kill her.

No, she couldn't tell Reid. No one must know.

"Raoul!"

She whipped out her phone. She had to call him off, now. If he found out the truth, she'd never be able to keep it quiet.

To her dismay, she saw the missed call had been from him. She tried to call him back, but it went to voicemail. Dammit.

Her head was spinning. At least she knew Maria hadn't kidnapped Sebastian, not that she could tell Reid that either. God, what a mess.

Another text from Reid. Sebastian had been taken to the hospital. He was fine, but severely dehydrated and needed treatment.

Can I see him? she replied.

Yeah. Get one of the officers to give you a lift. It's not safe to drive alone.

On my way.

The two cops dropped her at the front entrance to the hospital, and she ran in, past the reception desk and straight to the elevators. Reid had told her Sebastian was in Ward 9 North. She got to the ninth floor only to find she'd missed another call from Raoul.

Crap! She paused in the hallway and called him back.

He answered after the first ring. "Kenzie, can you hear me?"

The connection was bad, but she could hear him well enough. "Yes, it's me. Did you find her?"

She cringed, waiting for his response.

"Yeah, but it's not good news."

"Why's that?"

"Because she's dead." Static crunched down the line.

"Did you say dead?" Kenzie exhaled slowly. Maybe it would be okay, she'd be able to keep Maria's secret.

"Yeah, she died in a car wreck a week ago."

"A week ago?" A chill swept over her. That was when Kenzie had first hinted to Maria that she knew what had happened in France. "Are you sure?"

"Yeah, I'm sure. I've just spoken to her neighbor. Hell of a coincidence, don't you think?"

Kenzie thought back to Maria's visit, how her eyes had hardened as she'd pulled out the gun.

I'm not going to have to silence you, am I, Kenzie?

Had Maria killed her old friend to silence her?

Whoever her lover had been, it was too big a secret. Maria wasn't going to risk it coming out.

"Too much of a coincidence."

Maria assumed she knew as well. That made her a liability, too. Was she biding her time before she took Kenzie out? Was she waiting until the book was published?

Suddenly, Kenzie wished she'd never said anything in those articles about Emmanuelle's father. Even if she confessed to Maria that she didn't know who he was, she'd never believe her.

Well done, Kenzie. You've really done it now.

"What should I do, Kenzie?" Raoul was still on the line.

"Come home," she said. "There's nothing more we can do. It's a dead end."

Kenzie put a hand on the wall. If the last few weeks had proven anything, it was that she couldn't trust Maria Lopez. Book or no book, her days were numbered.

How on earth was she going to get out of this one?

She'd have to tell Reid and the DEA. She might even have to go into protective custody or witness protection like Torres. God, she didn't want to think about that.

"Get a grip," she muttered, sucking in a deep breath. Maria wouldn't do anything until the book was written. There was time.

Right now, Sebastian needed her. She could think about Maria later. Trying to hide her trembling, she opened the door to the ward.

Sebastian was in a room with two other patients, each within their own curtained cubical. He looked up when he saw her and his face broke into a smile, or what she thought was a smile.

God, he looked awful. She ran over to him.

"Are you alright?" she asked, in Spanish.

He shrugged. "It's not so bad."

He was a brave kid. She told him so, and his eyes lit up.

"I'm glad you're okay." She took his hand. "I was worried."

The curtain scraped back, and Reid walked in. Kenzie threw her arms around his neck and hugged him. "Thank you. You found him."

Reid gently disentangled himself and stepped back. "In the nick of time, too. Any later and he'd have died from dehydration. Hernandez left him with no water. I don't think he planned to go back to that place."

Kenzie shook her head. That man was responsible for so many deaths.

"Are you any closer to finding him?" she asked.

"Actually, I just got off the phone with the Coast Guard. They've spotted his boat southeast of Florida, heading towards the Bahamas. They're going to pick him up."

"Really? That's great news!" The sooner that man was behind bars, the better.

She told Sebastian, who gave a heart-felt nod. He was glad Hernandez had been caught, but it wouldn't bring back his mother or make up for everything he'd been through.

Reid patted the boy on the shoulder. "I'm glad you're feeling better." Then he turned to Kenzie. "I've got to go." He had that impatient look on his face.

"Why? I thought the Coast Guard was bringing in Hernandez."

"They are, but there's something else I have to do, something back at the station."

She gazed at him, trying to work out what it was. "Sure, if you have to go."

"Will you stay with Sebastian?" he asked.

"I was going to."

"Good. I'll be in touch."

Strange, but she had Sebastian back, and that's all she cared about right now.

———

Reid drove back to the station as fast as he dared. On the way, he called DEA Agent Wilson and filled him in on what he was going to do.

"Are you sure it'll work?" Wilson asked, skeptical as ever.

"No, but it's worth a shot," Reid replied.

"It's a lot of resources for someone who's not sure," he pointed out.

"Do you want her or not?" Reid retaliated.

"Yeah, okay Garrett. I'll give you this one, but if it doesn't work out, it's on you."

"Deal."

Reid got back to the station to find Vargas waiting for him. "How is he?" his sergeant asked.

"He's doing okay. He's a tough kid."

Vargas nodded. "He sure is."

"Update on Hernandez?"

"The Coast Guard is closing in. They're going to let us know when they have him in custody."

"Excellent." At least that was one bad guy who was going to get what was coming to him. "I need to speak to you in private."

"Sure." Vargas followed him into the briefing room and closed the door. "What's up?"

"We have a situation. There's a leak at the DEA Miami office, and we suspect one of Wilson's men is feeding information to Maria

Lopez on Torres's whereabouts. We think that's how she knew he was still alive."

"Holy crap." He frowned. "Has Torres been warned?"

"Not yet. Wilson was going to send a couple of agents over to take him to a safe house, but he's worried about the leak, so I suggested we'd do it."

Vargas's eyes widened. "You know where Torres is?"

"Yeah, but I can't get away right now. Hernandez is going to need processing, and I want to see that son of a bitch behind bars. I need you to do it."

He stood up straighter. "Sure thing, boss."

"I'll send you the details." He lowered his voice. "It goes without saying that this is highly sensitive information, and nobody else must find out about it."

"Obviously." Vargas took his job incredibly seriously. Out of all his detectives, Vargas was the one he trusted the most to get the job done.

"Thank you, sergeant."

Reid watched Vargas walk from the room, then he pulled out his phone and called Wilson. "He's in play. Now we wait."

40

REID SAT HUNCHED in a nondescript white van parked opposite Alberto Torres's house in North Carolina, along with Agent Wilson and two other DEA agents. The sun was beginning to take the edge off the darkness, bathing the street in an orange glow, ironing out the shadows. They'd been here since three o'clock this morning, and it was smelling a little musty.

The tinted back window allowed them to survey the house without being seen. Torres, the undercover agent who'd infiltrated the Morales cartel, was inside.

This was his new life. He worked part-time at a hardware store, but his shift didn't start until later.

"Are you sure this is going to work?" Agent Wilson asked again.

"Give it time," Reid snapped, his patience wearing thin. Wilson was beginning to annoy him. The DEA agent liked to do things by the book, and Reid had thrown it out the window on this one. He was relying on a hunch that may or may not pay off, but he was betting on the former.

Vargas had taken an early morning flight to Charlotte Douglas International Airport, and to avoid suspicion, would hire a rental car and drive the twenty miles to Torres's house. He'd pretend to be his out-of-town cousin, come to pay a visit.

Reid checked his phone. The flight had landed twenty minutes ago, which meant Vargas would be on his way. He shifted position, easing the tension in his back. These surveillance vans weren't made for comfort, neither were the bullet-proof tactical vests they wore. Adrenaline coursed through his veins, adding to his impatience.

A camera positioned at the back of the vehicle was recording everything, even though nothing had happened. Yet. It would, though. Reid could feel it.

He was also betting that Maria would come in person to take out her former disciple. She'd been fond of Torres, trusted him. She'd taken his betrayal personally. So much so, she'd gunned him down in a South Beach hotel in front of a room full of witnesses. Except she'd failed that time. Torres had survived and been placed in witness protection.

She wouldn't fail again.

"Anything?" Wilson barked into a two-way radio.

"Nothing yet, boss," came the grainy reply. He had an agent cycling around the block feigning a newspaper route.

"Come on," murmured Reid. Vargas would be here soon.

"Perhaps she's waiting to see where he's taken?" Wilson piped up. "Or she's going to stage another ambush and intercept your man with Torres in transit."

"Maybe," Reid acknowledged. Everyone was on edge. Anticipation hung heavy in the air. "But that adds an extra layer of security. I think she'll strike now, before he leaves."

"She's running out of time," he growled.

Reid ignored him.

Time ticked on. It was going to be close.

"Where are you?" he muttered. Vargas would be here soon.

"She's not coming," Wilson groaned. "She—"

"Shh... what's that?" hissed Reid, staring down the street. A gray Mercedes was approaching. They all held their breath, but it turned off the block before Torres's house and disappeared up the road.

"False alarm," one of the agents muttered.

Reid frowned. The Merc was out of place in this working-class neighborhood. And it had been driving slowly, cautiously. "Tell your guy to do another round."

Wilson did as he requested. "Yeah, now," he told his mobile agent.

A few moments later:

"The Merc has pulled over two streets away," the agent reported. *"A man and a woman are getting out."*

Reid glanced at Wilson. Could it be her?

"They're armed. I repeat, they're armed. The woman is Maria Lopez."

"Get out of there!" Wilson yelled.

Reid picked up the radio. "We have visual confirmation," he said to the SWAT team, waiting out of sight around the corner. "Stand by."

They'd taken shelter in a nearby resident's double garage, which would now be opening. The assault vehicle ready to spring into action.

"Awaiting your go-ahead," came the leader's curt reply.

They watched, but no one approached the house.

"She's going in the back way," Reid hissed. "Let's go."

All four of them slipped out of the van, weapons drawn. "You take the back," Wilson said. "We'll cover the front."

They moved into position. The plan was to wait until Maria was in the house, then send in the SWAT team. They were just there for backup. The timing was tight. If they went in too early, she would be forewarned, but if they left it too late, she'd realize it was a set-up.

"There they are," whispered Reid.

They crouched down behind a large dumpster. Maria's hench-man, a burly guy with an automatic rifle, kicked in the door.

"Go!" Reid hissed into the radio.

He heard a roar and a screech of tires as the assault vehicle skidded to a halt outside the house, blocking the drive. The SWAT team piled out. Men dressed in full assault gear, holding Heckler &

Koch MP5 submachine guns. He knew they had backup semi-automatic pistols, flash bangs and tasers, should they need them. The well-trained team broke into two groups, one heading around the back, the other running up to the front door.

Chaos ensued as they joined the fray.

Reid heard shouting, and multiple shots were fired.

Maria's men were shooting back. He didn't expect them to go down without a fight. A windowpane broke and shards flew out onto the porch. A bullet pinged off the mailbox, ricocheting to who-knows-where. He crouched down beside Wilson and waited for it to die down.

Suddenly, three more men ran up the drive, rifles drawn. Maria had backup too. They'd enter behind the SWAT team and take them by surprise.

"Police, put down your weapons," yelled Wilson, jumping out from behind the dumpster. Instead of complying, the three thugs opened fire.

Wilson dove for cover, but Reid was ready. He fired back, hitting one guy in the shoulder. He went down, clutching his wound. Wilson, who'd scrambled back to safety, took out another, but the third made it to the back door and disappeared inside.

"Shit!" Reid raced after him.

The interior of the house smelled like a gunpowder factory. Reid peered through the haze, trying to make sense of what was going on. The third man had taken out one of the SWAT team members, but it wasn't fatal. The officer was bleeding from a thigh wound, but it didn't look like the bullet had hit a main artery.

Reid stepped over him and into the hallway. Once the immediate threat was over, he'd go back and see to the injured man. There was a warning shout, and a bullet flew past his head, burying itself in the wall behind him.

Fuck, that was close.

He fired back and heard a yell. The third man was holding his groin and rolling around in agony. Served him right for taking out the SWAT officer. Reid kicked his rifle out of the way and cuffed him.

The gunfire had subsided. He wondered where Maria and her henchmen were.

"Clear!" he shouted from the living room.

"Clear!" came a responding yell down the hallway.

Reid proceeded with caution. Most of the SWAT team were in the main bedroom where Maria lay on the carpet, a dark stain seeping out beneath her. She held a Glock 9mm in her hand, the gun she'd planned to shoot Torres with. Her torso was riddled with bullets.

"It's over," the SWAT team leader said, looking down at the notorious crime boss. "We got her."

41

"What do you mean he wasn't on the boat?" Reid had just returned to the station after a two-hour flight during which he slept the entire way. He was groggy and in desperate need of a shower, but the news that had greeted him meant that would have to wait.

Monroe shrugged. "The Coast Guard boarded the vessel, but he wasn't on it. It was his brother-in-law, who'd taken it out for a spin."

"To the Bahamas?"

"That's what he said."

"Shit."

"Yeah." Monroe looked at him. "What do we do now, boss?"

"We can't let him get away," he fumed.

Vargas, who also looked worse for wear, and was still irritated because he hadn't been let in on the Maria sting, nodded in agreement. "There must be some way of tracking him down. What about the bullet casings found at Kenzie's place?"

"Ballistics have confirmed they're the same as the ones used to shoot the victims in the Glades. It was him alright. No doubt about it."

"But nothing on the gun?"

"No, it wasn't in the system."

"We've got a team sweeping the warehouse," Diaz informed them. "Not that it makes a difference. We know it was him."

"Has Sebastian remembered anything?" he asked.

"No, he's still in the hospital. I believe Kenzie's been there the whole time."

"That's good."

Perhaps he'd swing by the hospital later on his way home and check on them. Not because he wanted to see Kenzie, but in case the boy had remembered anything that could help them.

"You look like shit, boss," said Diaz, after he'd sat down at his desk. "Why don't you go home and get some sleep?"

"Don't have a home," he grunted.

She cringed. "Sorry, I meant the motel. You haven't slept for nearly two days."

It was more like three.

Perhaps she was right. Sleep deprivation was making him irrational, and he needed a clear head if he was going to catch this bastard.

"Okay, I hear you. I'm going, but I'll be back later. In the meantime..."

"We know what to do," she cut in. "And if anything breaks, you'll be the first to know."

He gave a curt nod.

Vargas also looked bushed. "I'm going home to get some sleep," Reid told him. "I suggest you do the same. We can pick this up tomorrow."

His sergeant nodded. As they walked out together, Reid said, "I'm sorry I didn't tell you about the sting op. I had to know if the leak was coming from this department."

"It was," he said dismally. "It came from me."

"No, it came from me," Reid said. "I sent you those details and somebody hacked my email to you. I've got IT looking into it, and hopefully we'll know who it was soon."

"Do you think it's internal?" His eyes were as bloodshot as Reid's.

"I don't want to, but that is the most likely scenario."

Vargas shook his head. "I can't imagine any of the team selling us out to Maria Lopez. How would they even know how to contact her?"

"I don't know," he said wearily. "Let's see what IT comes up with. Right now, I can't think straight."

Vargas yawned. "I'm with you there."

Kenzie called on his way to the motel.

"Is it true? Is Maria Lopez dead?"

He shook his head. She was incredible. "How did you find out?"

"Diaz told me."

He grunted. "She shouldn't have done that."

"Don't be cross with her. When I heard you'd gone to North Carolina I figured out what you were doing. Why else would you go there, if not to see Torres?"

"I never said he was in North Carolina."

"No, but with you and Agent Wilson both out of town at the same time, it was easy enough to figure out."

Kenzie was a good investigator. She didn't really need him, other than when she got into trouble. "So, are you going to fill me in?" He sighed. "You know I can't talk about this."

"Bullshit. She's dead. It's going to come out sooner or later, it may as well be via me."

He was too tired to argue. "I'll call you later and fill you in," he said. "I'm on my way to the motel to sleep. It's been a rough few days."

"Did you get Father Diego?" she asked.

"No, he wasn't on the damn boat."

There was a pause. "Should I be worried?"

"You're still at the hospital, right? With Sebastian?"

"Yeah, and those guys you posted at the door are still there, too."

"Good, stay put. You're safe there."

"You don't think he'll come for us, do you?"

"Not now, no," Reid said. "He needed to shut you up before, but now his identity is blown. He's on the run. I can't see him coming back for you or Sebastian. But just in case, I'll keep the guards on the door until we have him in custody."

"Okay." She hesitated. "Will you be stopping by?"

He hesitated. "I don't think so. I need to get some shut-eye, and then I've got a bad guy to catch."

"I see." Her voice was quiet. "Reid...?"

"Yeah?"

"Never mind."

He pulled into the parking lot in front of the Gator Inn and cut the engine. Damn, he was tired. Opening the door took more effort than he had, and he stumbled out.

He hadn't even closed the truck door when he felt the air move behind him. He turned around just in time to see Father Diego standing there, his gun above his head. Then the butt came down hard, and everything went black.

A loud rattling sound brought him to his senses. He tried to open his eyes, but the world was blurry. He shut them and tried again. Better.

He tried to move, but discovered his wrists and ankles were bound.

Hernandez.

The bastard had been lying in wait.

He smelled diesel fuel and something else. Leather? Canvas? Then it came to him. He was in the back of his own truck, under the truck bed cover. Hernandez was driving after having thrown him in the back.

He couldn't kill him in the parking lot, that would be too obvious, so he was taking him somewhere isolated, where no one would find him for days. If ever.

He struggled, but the bindings held fast.

Shit, now what?

He shifted his position to check if his cell phone was still in his pocket, but it wasn't. Hernandez was too smart for that. The device was probably at the bottom of the canal by now.

Anger fueled him, and he grunted as he strained against the ties. They wouldn't give. This must have been how Sebastian had felt when he'd been tied up and left at the warehouse. The only consolation was that Hernandez didn't know he was awake. If he could just get out of these ties, he'd have the element of surprise.

He felt around the bed of the truck with his legs, looking for anything sharp or protruding with which to break the ties. On one side, he found a handle. There might be just enough leverage if he got the plastic tie around it. He positioned his legs on either side and pulled, but it was too round, and he couldn't get a firm enough grip.

Cursing, he felt around the top half of the truck bed with his arms. It was completely smooth, but the bulkhead had a hook sticking out. It wasn't sharp, but it would do. He raised his hands and wiggled them until the tie was on the other side of the hook, then he pulled hard. It snapped under the stress.

Bingo.

Reid bent over, careful not to raise the canvas, and grabbed the pry bar. Splaying his knees, he put the bar between his ankles, twisted it. He grimaced as the plastic cut into his skin, but then it snapped, and he was free.

Hernandez didn't know what was about to hit him. The moment the truck stopped, Reid would spring from under the canvas and beat the shit out of him.

He couldn't wait.

42

THE TRUCK GROUND to a halt on the dusty road. Reid heard the door open and heavy footsteps as Hernandez walked around to the back.

He fought to stay still. Any minute now.

There was a shuffle as the priest unhooked the canvas cover, and then it was time.

Reid sprang from the truck bed like a phoenix rising from the ashes and launched himself at Hernandez. The people smuggler went flying backwards, landing on the ground with Reid on top of him.

He yelled in surprise, but Reid didn't let him take a breath before he yanked him up by the collar and punched down hard. Hernandez's head snapped back.

"That's for Sebastian," he growled, as he drew his fist back to hit him again.

The next punch broke Hernandez's nose. Blood spurted onto the gravelly ground.

"That's for Daniela and the others." Reid got to his feet.

Hernandez rolled onto his side and groaned.

"And this is for burning down my house." Another kick in the ribs. There was a satisfying snap.

Through the red haze, the voice in his head was screaming enough.

He's had enough.

Reigning himself in, Reid stared down at the bloodied killer. "Fucking hypocrite."

He yanked Hernandez to his feet, but there was nothing to tie him up with. The priest reached behind his back for his gun.

"Oh no, you don't." Grabbing his arm, Reid twisted it until his captive screamed. The gun dropped to the ground. Kicking it away, he growled, "Nice try."

But Hernandez wasn't done yet. Wrestling free, he attempted to dive after the weapon, but Reid stomped on his hand. A howl of agony. Picking up the weapon, Reid thumped the priest on the head with the butt. He sank to the ground.

"And that's for Kenzie."

He was sick of the guy's antics. It was time he was put away.

Wiping his hands on his trousers, Reid patted the pastor down until he found the burner phone. It was in the thigh pocket of his combat pants.

Locked. But thanks to modern technology, not a problem. Using the unconscious man's thumb, he unlocked the phone and dialed 911.

Kenzie hovered outside Reid's motel room. Vargas had called her and told her it was safe to go home; Hernandez had been apprehended. When she'd asked how, she'd got a convoluted story about how he'd kidnapped Reid, taken him to some place in the middle of the Glades to kill him, but Reid had escaped and beaten him to a pulp.

Reid must have lost it to do that; he wasn't a violent man by nature. She hoped he was alright. He wasn't answering any of her calls or returning her text messages.

It was now or never.

She took a deep breath and knocked on the door.

"Yeah?" came a muffled voice.

"It's Kenzie."

Silence, and then the sound of feet walking across the room. The door opened.

Reid gazed at her. "Hi."

"Hi."

"What are you doing here?"

"I came to see you. You're not returning any of my calls."

"There's a reason for that," he murmured.

"Oh, yeah? Want to enlighten me?"

He held the door open. "You'd better come in."

Nodding her thanks, she walked past him into the room. It was a standard double, with a bed, an adjoining bathroom and a coffee maker on a dresser.

"Can I get you anything?" He gestured towards it.

"No, thanks." She took a seat on the bed. There was nowhere else.

He inhaled. "Listen, Kenzie, I think it's probably a good idea to put some distance between us. I'm not very good at playing games. I like to know where I stand and right now, I have no idea what's happening between us."

That was the most revealing thing he'd ever said about their relationship. He'd obviously been giving this speech a lot of thought.

"I'm sorry," she said. "That's my fault. I shouldn't have said that the other night, and to be honest, I don't know why I did." She dropped her gaze. "I think I was lonely."

Scared. Vulnerable. In need of his reassuring presence.

He studied her for a long moment. "That's not a good enough reason for me to stay over."

"I know," she whispered. "It won't happen again."

He ran a hand through his hair, still damp from the shower. She noticed his knuckles were bruised and battered on top of the burn marks that hadn't healed yet.

"Is that from Hernandez?" she asked quietly.

He glanced at them. "Yeah. Bastard knocked me out and hijacked my truck."

"I heard." She hesitated. "I also heard you beat the crap out of him."

"He was asking for it."

She couldn't argue with that. He'd tried to kill her outside her own home.

"I understand you want to be friends, but I don't know if I can."

"Why not?"

He didn't reply.

"We make a great team," she said, rushing over her words. "It would be a shame to lose what we have."

"You're a great investigator," he said, voicing what he'd thought earlier. "You don't need me. After this business with Maria, you'll be a reporting superstar."

Kenzie gnawed on her lower lip. "There's something I have to tell you."

He frowned. "Kenzie..."

"I know, but I need to tell you what happened."

He sat down on the bed next to her. "What happened?"

"Maria came to see me."

His head snapped up. "When?"

She couldn't meet his gaze. "The night before she died. She came to my apartment to talk. I turned around, and there she was, standing in my kitchen."

He stared at her. "And you didn't think to mention this?"

"Wait." She held up her hand. "Let me finish."

He shook his head. "What did she say?"

"She wanted to talk about the book."

"She wanted it to go ahead?"

Kenzie nodded. "We were going to have Zoom interviews. It sounds ludicrous now, but at the time, I was seriously considering it."

"She was a wanted felon," he whispered.

"I know, and I'm a reporter. Can you imagine the scoop?"

Reid inhaled sharply.

The lines were becoming very blurred, but they always were in this job. That was something Reid had never understood. "On condition that I never mention who the father of her illegitimate child was."

"But you don't know."

"She didn't know that."

Reid stared at her, his expression unreadable.

"I was convinced she'd taken Sebastian," she said. "As it turns out, she hadn't. Still, it worked to our advantage. She pretty much admitted who the father was."

Reid cocked an eyebrow. "Yeah?"

"When I mentioned her son, she flipped, pulled a gun on me."

"Jesus, Kenzie!"

"It was a gut reaction. You said Matteo Lopez was making waves in California, and that unless we got the list of names, he'd be running the cartel before long."

"Yeah, that's what Agent Wilson told me."

"Well, what if Maria had slept with her husband's second-in-command, Romeo Herrera, the man he trusted more than anyone else, other than his wife?"

Reid blinked at her. She could see him trying to connect the dots. "Why would you think that?"

"Because he runs the Californian branch of the operation and Matteo is working with him. From what I can understand, he's training Matteo to take over."

Reid got it. "And if he found out he was working with the man who slept with his mother when his father was in prison..."

"Shit would hit the fan," Kenzie finished. "Not only that, I think he may have been the one to put Federico there."

"You mean he ratted him out?"

She raised a meaningful eyebrow. "The Mexican federales were operating on a tip-off by a local informant. Nobody ever found out who."

Reid blew out his cheeks. "He must have known Maria was pregnant."

Kenzie nodded. "He was buying her time to get away and have the baby. Being Catholic, she wouldn't have wanted an abortion, or he wouldn't have let her."

"And Emmanuelle was the result."

Kenzie nodded.

"Also, what if it was Romeo Herrera who slashed my tires outside the penitentiary that day? He'd have reason to want me to back off. The last thing he'd want is for the book to come out, in case it hinted at his affair with Maria."

"That does make sense," Reid admitted, scratching his smooth chin. Being freshly shaved made him look younger. "It could have been Herrera who broke into your place and wrote that warning on the wall."

"Exactly what I was thinking," Kenzie replied. "That's why the apartment was such a mess. He was looking for a rough draft, or proof of what was in the memoirs."

"Okay." Reid was nodding slowly. "Even if that's all true, you have no real proof."

"No, it's all supposition at this point," she said, a smile playing on her lips. "But there is a way to check."

He frowned. "How?"

"According to forensics, the blood found in the van transporting Maria Lopez upstate belonged to Roman Herrera. That he was shot when he helped Maria get away."

Reid watched her warily. "How do you know that?"

"Vargas told me."

Reid sighed. It was clear he knew what was coming.

"If we can get the blood from the transit van and compare it to Emmanuelle Lenoir's, we can see if they're a match."

The muscles in Reid's jaw tensed. "Is that why you came here?" he asked, getting up. "To ask me a favor?"

"No. I told you, I came to see if you were alright. I heard about Hernandez and tried to call, but you were avoiding me."

He gave her a hard look. "I'm tired, Kenzie. Let's take this up tomorrow."

"It's not why I came," she insisted, pushing herself off the bed.

He opened the door. "Okay, I'll think about it. Goodbye Kenzie."

She had no choice but to leave, but a big part of her didn't want to.

The story continues in *Deep Heat*, the next Kenzie Gilmore Crime Thriller. Head to the next page for a sneak peak or order today by clicking the link or scanning the QR code below!

www.amazon.com/B09WZ8CXDN

Stay up to date with Biba Pearce's new releases:

https://liquidmind.media/biba-pearce-sign-up-1/

You'll receive a **free** copy of *Hard Line: A Kenzie Gilmore Prequel.*

**Did you enjoy *Burnout*? Leave a review to let us know
your thoughts!**
www.amazon.com/B09WZ8CXDN

DEEP HEAT: CHAPTER 1

It was the height of the summer solstice, the longest day of the year. But here, in the makeshift temple in the backroom of a dingy store in Little Haiti, Miami, it was dark as night. The only light came from aromatic candles positioned around the room, casting flickering shadows on the skulls, potions, and other voodoo paraphernalia in the shop.

The Voodoo priest, a man called Emmanuel Utanga, danced around the room, seemingly in a trance. The rhythmic drumming, at first low and pulsing built to a pounding crescendo. A female voice – a recording as there was no woman present – joined in, rising above the music, her angelic tones conjuring the spirits.

The priest's chanting got louder and louder until it became a mournful cry. He rubbed his hands on his white tunic, smearing crimson across the front. A headless chicken lay on the altar in front of him. A sacrifice to the ancestors. They were here, he could feel them. They were listening.

The priest evoked their power and told them what he wanted. A curse. A non-believer had disobeyed the spirits and must be punished.

The ancestors answered.

The priest's eyes rolled back, he grasped the air, clawing at an invisible entity. His shoulders shook, he quivered from head to foot like a puppet on a string. Just when it couldn't get any more frenetic, he collapsed forward, onto the altar, breathing heavily.

The music stopped. A pungent fragrance enveloped the shack, making it hard to breathe. Incense, perhaps. The priest lay still, only his chest rising and falling as he gulped in the cloying air. Slowly, he rose, his eyes glittering in the candlelight with some unearthly quality. He lifted his face to the spirits and muttered something in a different language. Haitian, most likely.

His voice was different. Deeper, creepier. Unlike his normal voice. Was he possessed? Were the spirits talking through him?

He chanted some more, then closed his eyes. Nothing happened. For a brief moment, time seemed to stand still. Hollowed eyes stared down from the shelves above, bared teeth grimaced. The beaded curtain hanging from the door frame tremored, even though there was no breeze.

The customer waited.

Eventually, the Voodoo priest opened his eyes and relaxed his body. His breathing returned to normal. The spirits had left him.

His face broke into a wide grin. "It is done."

***

Reid Garrett turned his face to the sun. Christ, it was humid. The air felt hot and heavy, pushing down on him like a damp cloak. The pressure had been rising throughout the day. They'd be in for a hell of a storm later.

Sweat glistened on his bare torso as he lifted planks of timber from the truck to the ground next to what remained of his cabin, which wasn't much.

The wildfire earlier in the year had wiped out half of the Everglades National Park and along with it, his three-roomed wooden cabin, his pickup truck and all his belongings. He didn't even have a damn coffee cup left.

Thank goodness the insurance company had finally come round to his way of thinking. Act of God, seriously? The perpetrator was now serving multiple back-to-back life sentences at the Jefferson Correctional Institution, and even that was too good for the lowlife human trafficking scumbag.

The rebuild was underway but in the meantime, Reid was living at the Gator Inn, a two-bit motel deep in the South Florida Glades. At least he could drown his sorrows at Smiley's, the next-door dive bar within stumbling distance of the motel.

Reid bent down and picked up a twisted plastic object that may have, at one point, been part of his stereo system, but he couldn't be sure. The cleanup job had taken months, and only now had the construction begun. His wasn't the only residence to have been leveled by the inferno. Several Glade communities had lost their houses and were in the long process of rebuilding, relocating, or moving out of the area altogether.

He'd considered that, but after two years in the Glades, he'd realized with some surprise that he didn't want to leave. Despite moving out here as a way of escaping his life, of running away from his problems, the deep murky waters of the swamp had seeped into his soul, and healed it. Now he felt restless without it. The thought of living in an urban area turned him cold.

There was nothing like looking out over the sea of grass, feeling the warm breeze against his skin, and smelling the pungent odor of the swamp. The chirping cicadas sent him to sleep at night, and he awoke to the fluttering of birds squawking overhead. And he sure as hell did not miss the constant hum of traffic, blaring sirens, or noisy neighbors. Out here, the only neighbors he had were the four-legged kind.

"Over here," called the foreman of the construction crew that was building his new property. Even now, the foundations were in place and the stilts had been secured into the swampy ground. Reid picked up the planks and moved them, the sun burning his back and shoulders.

Weeks pouring over plans with an architect had not only cost a bundle but had filled him with a desperate need to see the structure come to life. Gone were the three dilapidated adjacent buildings, and instead, they were building one long wood structure on chunky stilts with a deck that extended over the water, along with a wide launching jetty for his airboat and a garage at the back for his new pickup.

It would be incredible once it was finished. A phoenix rising from the ashes. To save costs, he was helping out on weekends. The manual labor took his mind off his cases and prevented him from thinking (too much) about Kenzie. Self-analysis had never been his strong point, and because of this he'd become adept at blocking things out. There were a lot of unopened boxes in his past, and he doubted if he'd ever properly mentally sift through them. Kenzie was just another one.

His phone vibrated in his pocket. Detective Vargas, his colleague, was calling from the station landline.

"Vargas," Reid said, straightening up. "What's up?"

The young detective rarely called him on the weekend unless it was an emergency. Reid steeled himself for what he knew was coming.

"Hey boss, sorry to interrupt you." Everyone knew he was working on the building site "But I thought you'd want to be informed. We've got a male DB near an alligator farm down Homestead way. He was found by some bird watchers."

"Yeah? Was he attacked?"

"No, that's the strange thing. The first responder on the scene says he can't figure out how the guy died."

"It could be natural causes." Reid relaxed. There was no point driving all the way down south for a heart attack. "How old is he?"

"Mid-thirties. Unlikely to be a heart attack or anything like that. There are no obvious signs of an attack, no puncture wounds, no stab wounds, no bullet holes. I'm going to go down and check it out."

"Okay, keep me posted." There must be something. People didn't just drop dead for no apparent reason.

"Will do. Oh, the other thing is the expression on his face. The officer at the scene said it looks like the victim's seen a ghost."

"The death grimace," Reid pointed out. "We often see that post-mortem."

"It's worse than that." Vargas wasn't one for hyperbole.

Reid frowned. "Got a pic?"

"Yeah, sending it through now."

Reid's phone buzzed. Holding it away from his ear, he checked the photograph that had just come through. The man did indeed look terrified. His body was rigid with shock, not helped by the rigor that had set in and the eyes that bulged almost out of their sockets.

Something stirred in Reid's gut. This didn't feel right. He couldn't explain it, but the man's expression was disturbing. Not like anything he'd seen before.

"If I didn't know better," Vargas was saying. "I'd say he died of fright."

Reid wiped the sweat from his forehead. Fright, nah. But something had happened before he'd died to put that expression on his face.

He ran a hand through his hair. It came away wet. It was time for a break anyway.

"Send me the location. I'll meet you there."

DEEP HEAT: CHAPTER 2

Kenzie was about to sit down with a much-needed coffee when the doorbell rang. Darn, who was that? She wiped the errant tendril from her face, stood up, and opened the door.

"Nick, hi." Her cheeks burned as she shot him a sheepish grin. Last time they'd talked, she'd stood him up. Not something she was proud of, especially since Nick was such a nice guy. He had a great job, he loved animals, he drove a Porsche. On paper, he was perfect.

But he wasn't Reid.

That realization had pole-axed her on the way to the restaurant. So much so, it had taken her breath away. She was over Reid. It had been her who'd called it off, after all. Not him. She'd looked him straight in the eye and said, let's be friends.

Then she'd asked him to stay over. Kenzie squeezed her eyes shut at the cringy memory. To be fair, his house had just burned down, not that he was a charity case or anything. He'd said no, of course. But not after staring at her with those unfathomable eyes. The kind that either burned with an intensity that shook her to the core or were so guarded she had no idea what he was thinking.

"Hi, Kenzie," Nick said.

Halfway to the restaurant where they were having their date, she'd pulled over, unable to go any further. Taking out her phone, she'd made some dumb excuse like she'd been held up at work. It didn't really matter what she'd said, Nick had been sitting at the restaurant waiting for her.

Of course, he'd been chivalrous about it. Don't worry. It doesn't matter. They'd take a raincheck. But they both knew it was a lie.

Now here he was, standing outside her door in the pouring rain. A crack of lightning exploded overhead, making her jump. "You'd better come inside."

He traipsed in, leaving a puddle on the floor. "I'm sorry to surprise you like this," he began, smoothing his hair back. "But I needed to talk to you."

Her heart sank. The last thing she felt like was talking about their relationship, or lack thereof. To be honest, she didn't know why she'd pulled out at the last minute. It wasn't as if she had any future with Reid. He'd made that clear after their last case together. That was it. She couldn't have it both ways. He'd practically shown her the door.

Sighing, she said, "Look, now isn't a good time, Nick. I'm sorry. I've just got in and it's been a long day."

"This isn't about us." He waved a hand dismissively in the air.

"It isn't?" Now she just felt stupid. What was he doing here then?

"No. I need your help."

"I don't understand."

"It's my brother-in-law. He's gone missing. He hasn't been home for three days."

Kenzie stared at him. That was not what she'd been expecting. "Okay, why don't you come and sit down. Can I get you some coffee?"

The guy was soaked through. The storm had broken late afternoon, as was the pattern in Miami. The humidity built throughout the day, only to dissipate in a sticky, drenching washout just before sunset. Most locals knew to expect it. The pressure built and built until the sky was charged with static, and then bam! ... The lightning would erupt accompanied by a deep rumble and the heavens would open. Kenzie could almost sense the moment it was going to happen, but even so, she'd been caught running to her car.

The same must have happened to Nick. He nodded distractedly as she led him to the living room and gestured for him to take a seat. A moment later, she was back with another cup of coffee.

"Have you reported his disappearance to the police?" she asked, handing it to him.

"No, my sister thought he'd come back home, but—." He shook his head.

Kenzie sat down opposite him. "What happened? Did they have a fight?"

"No, nothing like that. As far as I know, they're happily married. Jacob left one morning last week and hasn't been seen since. Lesley called me when she couldn't get hold of him, but I couldn't do much. I've been driving around all day looking for him. He's not at his usual haunts."

That would explain Nick's disheveled state.

"My advice is to go to the police," she said. "They can file a missing persons report and get officers out looking for him."

Nick nodded. "Yeah, I know you're right. My sister still thinks he's holed up somewhere. Apparently, he was acting weird."

Kenzie frowned. "Weird? In what way?"

"Erratic. Nervous. Like he was scared of something, or someone."

"Did he say what?"

"Not that she told me. Kenzie, I need your help to find him. You've got contacts, you're good at finding people."

Kenzie scratched her head. "I'm a reporter, Nick. My contacts are for work purposes, besides, I have no way of tracing a missing person. You really need to go to the cops for that. They might be able to track his phone or his movements."

"His phone is switched off," Nick replied. "Les has tried repeatedly to call him, as have I. It goes straight to voicemail." He paused, gnawing on his lower lip. Finally, he sighed, "What if Jacob's got himself into some sort of trouble and is in hiding. I don't want to waste the police's time. Please can't you see what you can do? If we don't come up with anything in a day or two, I promise, I'll go to the Miami PD and file a missing persons claim."

Kenzie pursed her lips, then sighed, "Okay, I'll see what I can do. But only for a few days. After that, you must let the police know. Your brother-in-law may be in danger."

Or worse.

But she didn't say that. If the guy had been acting scared, he'd probably gone into hiding like Nick had said, or was laying low at a friend's house or a motel somewhere.

"Did he owe money?" That was usually the cause of this type of behavior.

"I don't know. Lesley didn't say."

"Okay, well the first thing we have to do is talk with your sister."

Nick gave a weary nod.

When she raised her eyebrows, he straightened up. "Oh, you mean now?"

"Yeah, now. No time like the present, right?" Besides, she still had work to do. This little investigation was going to put out her schedule. Keith, her dictatorial editor, was expecting 500 words on Congressman Leonard's new proposals for greener energy in the city by 8am tomorrow morning. To be fair, it wasn't something she was looking forward to writing. Everything seemed to be an anticlimax after cartel boss Maria Lopez's death and the subsequent media frenzy over that.

Reporters all over Florida had dined off her dramatic demise for months, rehashing her life story, her secret takeover of the Morales cartel, and her rise to fame—but the momentum had finally stalled, and Maria had become old news.

Kenzie got to her feet. Nick downed his coffee and did the same. "We can take my car," he said, fishing in his pocket for his keys. "Lesley lives on the other side of the bay."

"Okay, let's go. You can tell me all about your sister and her husband on the way."

He hesitated. "Thanks, Kenzie. I mean it." There was an

awkward moment where he gazed at her. Unlike Reid, she could guess what he was thinking.

She shrugged. "I haven't done anything yet."

"Still, I know it's an imposition."

"Don't worry about it. Come on, let's go before it gets any later." And she grabbed her purse and walked out of the house.

Loving *Deep Heat*? Scan the QR code below to order today!

ALSO BY BIBA PEARCE

The Kenzie Gilmore Series

Afterburn

Dead Heat

Heatwave

Burnout

Deep Heat

Fever Pitch

Storm Surge (Coming Soon)

Dalton Savage Mystery Series

Savage Grounds

Scorched Earth

Cold Sky

Detective Rob Miller Mysteries

The Thames Path Killer

The West London Murders

The Bisley Wood Murders

The Box Hill Killer

Follow the link for your free **copy of** *Hard Line: A Kenzie Gilmore Prequel.*

https://liquidmind.media/biba-pearce-sign-up-1/

ALSO BY WITHOUT WARRANT

More Thriller Series from Without Warrant Authors

Dana Gray Mysteries by C.J. Cross

Girl Left Behind

Girl on the Hill

Girl in the Grave

The Kenzie Gilmore Series by Biba Pearce

Afterburn

Dead Heat

Heatwave

Burnout

Deep Heat

Fever Pitch

Storm Surge (Coming Soon)

Willow Grace FBI Thrillers by Anya Mora

Shadow of Grace

Condition of Grace

Hunt for Grace

Time for Grace (Coming Soon)

Gia Santella Crime Thriller Series

by Kristi Belcamino

Vendetta

Vigilante

Vengeance

Black Widow

Day of the Dead

Border Line

Night Fall

Stone Cold

Cold as Death

Cold Blooded

Dark Shadows

Dark Vengeance

Dark Justice

Deadly Justice

Deadly Lies

ABOUT THE AUTHOR

 Biba Pearce is a British crime writer and author of the Kenzie Gilmore series and the DCI Rob Miller series.

Biba grew up in post-apartheid Southern Africa. As a child, she lived on the wild eastern coast and explored the sub-tropical forests and surfed in shark-infested waters.

Now a full-time writer, Biba lives in leafy Surrey and when she isn't writing, can be found walking through the countryside or kayaking on the river Thames.

Visit her at bibapearce.com and join her mailing list at https://liquidmind.media/biba-pearce-sign-up-1/ to be notified about new releases, updates and special subscriber-only deals.

Made in the USA
Las Vegas, NV
12 July 2024

92227425R00164